The Night Wandering

Matthew Sitler

The Night Wandering
Editor: Susan McLeod
Cover: 'Saara In The Moonlit Garden' - Oil painting by Matthew Sitler

ISBN-13: 978-1-7753607-0-4

To the ones who pray

MATTHEW SITLER

Chapter One

For most of that year he'd been in two worlds.

Mid-October and only now was he noticing how fall had basically closed up the town for winter. The late afternoon sun dipped low and the streets were quiet as he strolled from Fern Avenue to Crescent Chase, the silent red sentinel casting vibrant hues into the shadows of Bracebridge's back laneways.

Earlier Ethan Charlish had stopped by the river to light a cigarette and had caught his own tired reflection in a nearby phone booth. Unshaven and tattily dressed, albeit in a favorite worn tweed sports coat, his arranged meeting with the Police Inspector loomed.

It wasn't like the recent sleepless nights had been noticed by anyone or pried him entirely from the professional world in which he still had a footing.

Sitting by the water contemplating this and what he'd be telling the cops, he watched sail boats coast lazily out to the lake. Rustling through his pockets, he couldn't find a lighter.

Sigh. Some people on one of the boats waved.

Later at the station he'd provided the requested testimony about what he'd learned from his own sources.

On August 27th, Aleksi Heikkinen's younger brother Elias had been with his brother at the site where the bodies were discovered. They'd both returned to their jobs the following day, each covered in hundreds of black fly bites.

He told Inspector Dax Hallett he thought this latter point indicated a lengthy stay at the location. He'd also been told Aleksi had prior arrests for cutting up animals.

The Inspector seemed to bristle at that, but it was all in the dossiers Ethan had been granted via access to information.

Aware he was being watched and probably filmed by other cops through a cheap two-way mirror, he didn't push the issue. The Inspector just kept jotting things in his notepad and the mood remained cordial.

He didn't mind telling them the obvious - it kept relations up and made them think he was working with them. Besides, it bought more time to look into the other tips he hadn't mentioned. By 7pm he'd been thanked and was on his way.

It was starting to get dark. The activity in the pubs and restaurants that were still open was beginning to ramp up. *Check out the Winged Dragon,* he thought, making his way up Chancery Lane.

"And what will it be tonight?" asked a server once he was settled. A pretty young brunette named Lisa balanced a plate of fries and draughts.

"Whiskey - on the rocks."

The place was still far from full. In the corner some lawyers from Klein-Wetherby discussed the latest courts gossip. He listened to this for awhile before starting some small talk with the bartender, a leggy redhead, about who'd be playing that Friday night. Three drinks later he left.

The thoughts came to him as he ambled beneath the large elms on Water Street. It was around 8:45pm and in his hand he held a white crumpled piece of paper containing a new cell number and a single name. Saara.

The murders had been particularly gruesome. Carrie Watkinson's body had been found cut into small pieces which had been left in rotting cardboard boxes. A chemical had been added to the mix, leaving a mainly gelatinous mass that was only identifiable through dental records. Chloe Germaine's body was discovered out in the open in the same grassy area at the same Deer Lake property. There was a cottage there, but no one had used it in years. It was last owned by a man named Ian Wagner who lived in Toronto, but any connection with him had been ruled out. The bank had foreclosed on the property five years prior.

Chloe's body appeared to have been cut in half by an electrical saw near the beach. Most of the corpse had been chewed by predators during its time at the property where it had been left laying beneath washed up tree trunks.

Both girls had been in their teens - Chloe was 18, Carrie 19.

Police believed they'd both been beaten by at least two perpetrators the night they were killed and had told media they were looking for three males - two white and one middle eastern. How this had been determined hadn't been revealed, forensics, maybe.

Besides the extreme violence, the location was nothing out of the ordinary. Beneath Chloe's breasts investigators had discovered a recent tattoo. Written in Sanskrit, it translated to the English word 'Orange'.

Nobody knew what it meant - friends, boyfriends and family had all been canvassed, but no one had a guess. Tips that came into the news room had provided nothing further either.

There were rope burns on the girls wrists from where they'd been bound with a type of heavy twine. The times of death were placed at about a week prior to their discovery, putting it around the last week of August. The bodies were found naked.

He'd taken to walking during the evening hours after he'd left his job at the paper that September. It helped him think. He'd quit to write a book about the murders and in the months since his departure had made great headway. Sources were proving valuable, money wasn't a question and the solitude at his large estate home just outside of town was invaluable. Owls hooting - he was enjoying that.

But the angle the police were taking bothered him.

The Heikkinen brothers were common goons and depraved as they could be in that sometimes druggy, white trash way, many locals thought they couldn't possibly have been responsible for the killings.

There'd been rumours Carrie Watkinson had been a prostitute working out on the Bohemian Island trail. Multiple sources told him she'd taken frequent trips to the island by ferry on nights throughout June, July and August of that summer.

She'd been seen having breakfast at a local joint on the mainland too on several mornings during the same timeframe - always with different men. 'Wealthy tourists' was one description.

Despite this, the pair of construction workers had been implicated, at least tentatively, because a wooden shill found at the crime scene had Aleksi's prints on it.

He'd vigorously denied knowing anything, but the pair were still under surveillance. They'd told coworkers they'd been building part of a dock crib at the site, using it as a staging area just down the road from where it was to go in.

Prostitutes were nothing new in cottage country. Checks with taxis and ferry captains confirmed that on any given summer evening, escorts were regularly taken out to the inns and resorts on many of the area lakes. This was the angle he was massaging.

He drew a deep breath and put away the files.

Now 3am, the Friday morning moon lit Saara's light brown silky-smooth skin as she rustled in the sheets.

He rose from his armchair and gazed out over the dark lake.

"A boat ride when we wake up?" came her soft, half asleep voice in the darkness.

"Sure," he replied.

Chapter Two

Never focus too much on one thing less it keep you blinded.

In his years as a journalist and then as an editor, he'd developed a unique relationship with information. 'Pure Information' was how he put it.

37 year old Saara Khan loved hearing his theories.

She'd been the editor at a competing paper for five years before he'd quit. Now they were starting to relax the secrecy of their relationship, loosening up a bit, being seen around town.

She looked fabulous and they made a dashing couple, her wispy air complimenting his rakish, slightly rough-round-the-edges persona.

On this particular morning she listened as he expounded on how cops mainly follow basic logic, but that this kind of thinking often isn't enough. It was a little much before breakfast.

"I need coffeeee," she yawned, wiping at some sleep while almost lunging for the Lavazza.

She liked it strong - it was in her Arabic background to like strong things. Tousling her long dark hair to the side, she stirred the cup in firm, steady strokes, adding a touch of cream, swirling it all to perfection.

Watching as he made his way out the back door, she saw him stop to tie a shoelace on one of his new runners. Then he was off across the back lawn and over the cobblestone wall to the dirt path that connected to the road.

The sprawling nine-acre estate complex Ethan lived on was about 25 minutes from town. A long driveway meandered from the main road up through thick stands of pines and Canadian Shield lending the property a mysterious old-world privacy.

A set of rustic, but deteriorating iron gates where the road met the driveway creaked whenever vehicles approached and whenever wind rattled their hinges. This morning it was the wind. On warmer days she'd sit outside on the main building's patio and listen to the swaying tree branches and the soft lush whisper of the courtyard's fountain dazzling in the sun.

It was where she'd be until he returned from his jog.

The closest occupied land near Charlish Manor was the Morton Lodge property next door.

Like Ethan's estate, the Lodge had a rich 250'ish year history. Mainly active between Spring and late Fall, it catered to guests from around the globe who visited annually to summer in 'the Muskokas'.

Then, after the boats were all in, the lodge would fill up again come late October, mainly with vagrants who'd stay on through the winter doing odd jobs like hauling timber across the lakes for contractors.

Ethan was back within 20 minutes and she could tell he'd become bored with jogging already.

He'd only taken it up to lose the few pounds he'd earned over the stressful final years at the copy desk. Wiping sweat from his forehead, he leaned in for a kiss as she poured him a cup.

"Knew you'd need one," she smiled, watching his first slow sips. "You've been burning the midnight oil."

"Isn't that the truth," he replied, squinting over the rim through the early-morning haze. "What time was it when you came and got me?"

"Two thirty - you looked like you were about to fall off the couch. I put the manuscript on the side table. You have to watch those candles. I blew them all out."

Lighting a joint, she broached the next subject with a slight air of trepidation.

"You're not going to like this," she said, after a sharp, brief, inhale, "but I think you should leave the case behind this weekend and just have some fun."

A cool, perfect O came his way as if to send the message home.

Clearing the air, he nodded and beckoned for her to pass it.

"For at least *half* the weekend," he agreed, taking a toke.

"But don't forget," he continued, releasing a long white plume, "we have to meet or call William Sunday night."

For the better part of 10 years, William Aisler had been a friend of the newsrooms.

None of the other reporters knew it, but he'd helped the papers break many stories with the tips he'd provided Ethan.

Their clandestine arrangement had germinated during a police corruption case back in 2001 and when Ethan had proved trustworthy, the relationship developed when it could. Aisler was now a Senior Detective Constable and his help continued with the current case.

With cops, every town has one and there were times Ethan knew he was being used. All relationships are at least a two-way street and in the information biz, it was always give and take.

Standing over the washing machine an hour later, Saara rolled her eyes as Ethan scurried past with his heavy black leather briefcase. Eyes still red, the sheepish glance they threw only compounded her annoyance as he hurriedly set up his laptop in the living room.

"*About that boat ride?*" she asked, half sarcastically.

"How about in another 20 minutes?"

"I'm holding you to it."

A Friday morning in Bracebridge - chores done, fridge stocked and nothing to do but get out on the water for one of the last tours of the season. If only it was so easy, she thought, watching the clock wind towards noon.

But there he was, still typing away, raising his hand as if to banish time itself beneath the weight of her continuous stares.

There were things she still didn't know about the case that he did, and he knew she knew it.

Tap, tap, tap. Another final note finished.

In faux earnestness, he slammed the laptop shut, beaming up angelically as she brought out some lunch.

"Did I do good?" he asked, peering at the clock.

"That depends. Can I see?"

She said it so coyishly, but he pulled the computer away quickly, yanking its cord from the wall.

"When everything's ready," he replied, sizing her up suspiciously.

"Oh but c'monnnnn," she cried, adopting her famous mock child voice.

With eyes crossed and mouth wide like a porcelain doll, it was quite the act to behold.

"I slave all day making these delicious meals and rolling these pinners and all I want is to seeee..." she cried, eyes darting between his and the computer.

It was a grabbing game and he took both her wrists, wrestling her down onto him over the couch until they were nose-to-nose.

"See this," he said, dropping his hands to her waist.

"Mmmm, that's good, but are we still going for a boat ride?"

His attention enslaved, her left hand slipped away, grabbing a piece of paper he'd mistakenly left on the couch.

It was too late. Arched back on her ass, she was reading its contents to the air:

"'The Scene,'" she announced emphatically, dodging his attempts at grabbing it back. "'Testimony from the boy:'"
"A black Porsche pulls up, out steps this woman, tall with dark red hair."
What happens next?
"I'm not done telling about her - she had pale skin, wore a short black leather jacket with a wolf hair collar. Tells the driver and two others to get the girls out of the car."
Go on.
"They get the girls out - they're wearing blindfolds. One of the men pushes them to get moving. They head away to the ferry dock and the driver takes off in the other direction. It's about 9."
Did you see more?
"I heard one of the girls beg for her life, but then nothing. They got in some kind of large boat that was waiting. Voices got muffled once they got inside."
Would you be able to identify them if you were shown pictures? Would you be able to identify the woman?
"The woman, yes. The one man, yes - he was taller."

Jumping back to her feet, she nearly tripped over the coffee table and gasped, a look of shocked disbelief spread over her face.
Standing, he quickly snatched the sheet back and crammed it deep inside the briefcase.
"And *that's* why I didn't want you coming with me Wednesday night," he snapped.
"*Oh no, no, no, no,*" she stammered, blocking his attempted exit.
"That is.... that is... unbelievable," she sputtered. "That'll get us arrested. That is...really.....*something.*"
"Yes, it is and because it's extremely delicate you'll understand it was best handled the way I handled it. Now, if you'll excuse me, I have a boat to start and *clean up* before it goes anywhere."
The living room seemed greyer as he bolted, laptop and briefcase very much in hand.
Charlish Estate backed onto the Black River which connected with Lake Muskoka six km downstream, which surprisingly, was still extremely busy at that time of year.

Outside, the leaves were nearing the height of their annual turn and the cool air was refreshing. He'd turned 40 two months prior and had been feeling it, but on crisp fall days, this was easily forgotten.

Luckily, he'd kept himself in shape, coming out of the wilderness of his 30's with nothing but a wonky right knee. He should have kept working on the notes, he thought, with a feeling of slight annoyance.

Despite his having left the paper for good, texts had kept coming in from various media cops about all the mundane crimes. This day was no different.

Leaning on the bow of his sandy-beige 1956 Cliff Richardson, he read the latest one:

'Ethan: FYI - homeowner returned to her residence in Gravenhurst Tues n to find a woman inside, confronted her and she left. Noticed jewelry missing. Suspect fled - on foot, 20-30 years old, 5'3", black pants, black tank top, some kind of pink scarf on head, slim build, round face.'

Watching Saara arrive, he put it away and helped her in. He'd reply out on the lake.

It was one of the last days of the year actually suitable for boating and soon they were crashing over waves through bursts of warm, foggy, Indian summer.

In the back, Saara lounged in grey slacks and a light blue sweater on a bright red beach towel which protected her from the chilly vinyl seating.

She stared distantly as the boat rocked, skipping whitecaps at an all conquering speed.

Saara was a hell of a reporter - one of the best. Together they'd gleaned several elements of the case completely on their own - the orange aspect and the exact location and state of the bodies.

But the cops had the lid clamped tightly now so nothing was coming from them proper - just William and his info, which, as of late, was down to a trickle.

The tips about break-ins and mischiefs had ramped up though, almost as an unspoken courtesy.

Saara was one of the few who actually understood reporting - many amongst her younger peers were little more than PR people in training, happier to friend a mayor than to hold them to account.

The whole mid-market media world was headed that way and the rising tide of untalented, flashy sycophants made them both sick.

But this was only partly why they clicked. The book they were writing and their growing romantic bond - it was all in defiance of a world that kept coming up short.

Easing back on the throttle, Ethan veered towards the channel's mouth, and, coming to an idle, texted the cop.

'Thanks - will forward to the right people.'"

There was a quick response:

"Great - one more thing. Suspect had tattoo half showing above tank top. Some kind of Indian writing."

"*What are you doing?*" called Saara, sounding a tad peeved as she stared at him staring at his phone.

"You'll want to see this," he said, passing it back.

"Wow. We'll have to get on this," she replied, taking his side at the wheel.

"I know. Cop on weekend duty is obviously a rookie, thank Christ. I'll do them a favor and wait to talk with the Inspector before I pass this on to the office. He'll appreciate it and then you know what the fucking response will be. He'll be pissed we know anything about tattoos, and this one could be nothing, but if it is, there'll be no official release if they catch her. We'll have to use William. You contact him and let him know it could be coming and that if they find her, we'll need to know her identity."

Grey clouds loomed overhead and the waves were getting choppier. A first splash hit the bow and he turned the boat around, raising the roof awning.

"Fuck," he muttered. "So much for a nice clear day."

Saara had returned to her calm, pensive stare, this time at his side with one hand at her lips, looking like a living question mark.

At the dock they ran to the main house as the winds picked up, hurtling small branches, dirt and leaves all around them.

Fix some food, he thought, *at least try to unwind*.

Following showers, it was about an hour before they regrouped.

"William, we will need to keep in *daily* contact on this ok," he heard her saying in the hall outside the kitchen.

"*I know this will be tricky William,*" she continued. "Position yourself in a manner so that others are there when you first hear it, so it can't be traced back just to you. Regardless, we won't be talking, but we'll be learning as much as we can without crossing any lines. This could be the break that blows everything wide."

In the kitchen Ethan reached for a clanging shutter just as she entered - the wind had been playing the hanging pots like a maniacal xylophonist.

"What'd he say?"

Her look was grim.

"He said 'he'd do what he can'. Could be they may time the arrest for when no media officer is on duty - get her on another charge, maybe drugs - whatever they can muster. Then the tattoo detail could conveniently disappear, along with her connection to the theft."

Hearing this, he brought a boiling pot to simmer, adding some plain white rice for their General Tao chicken.

"We'll get it," he assured her. "We have to. Our nice weekend's fucked though. We'll have to check in with the usual."

The 'usual' was a mixed bag of losers - mainly grungy downtown loiterers and area drug addicts.

In the district's smaller communities he often played an existential game of charades with them - check in with a source looking for information, while avoiding their narc 'friends'.

Sipping some freshly opened red wine, Saara sat at the island, playing with her hair.

"If we could find out which home it was and the identity of the owner we might be able to learn more and narrow it down and find her ourselves," she said.

The lights flickered and a downpour came hard on the estate's clay tile roofing.

"Maybe we can check it out this weekend?"

"We'll have to," he sighed.

Chapter Three

An unusually balmy Saturday night, it was around 7pm when he pulled his black BMW M4 into Gravenhurst Muskoka Wharf, alone.

Along Main the tourists were out eating ice cream and browsing the shops, while some teens bantered outside a pot paraphernalia & tattoo shop.

The scene at the wharf was much the same. Couples strolled by the steamships and milled along the boardwalk. He parked and lowered his window.

In a few minutes a young brunette appeared, opened the passenger door and stepped inside, all in one graceful, smooth move.

"Hey handsome," she said smiling. "I brought you something."

Passing him a small package, he held up $200 in return, waving it slowly in front of her eyes.

"I need to ask you a favor," he said.

A blur of smoke shot out her half-opened window and she turned, staring up at him like a little lost lamb.

"For you babe, anything," she said, her blue emerald eyes glowing in the parking lot light.

God, he was entranced by those big wondrous things.

He met Rachel Fortune at a party a few years back and they immediately hit it off. At 22 she was a gorgeous little package, with short auburn hair and a tight, busty figure - but oh lord, filled with the typical small town trouble.

She couldn't shake her vices, which in a good year included a nasty coke habit, lust for whiskey and petty larceny. Besides her tips and the weed now in his hand, he'd tried to keep her at arm's length.

She knew this, but he treated her like a lady, so they stayed friendly and until recently even more.

"I need you to keep your ears open for anything on a recent home robbery here in town," he said. "See if you can find out who did it or who got robbed."

"Gotcha," she replied, after another long exhale. "Haven't heard anything yet, but I've been out of town with my mom in Barrie. She's dying of cancer."

"I'm sorry to hear that. Where does she live?"

"Bracebridge. She's only got two months to live, but I don't wanna talk about it. Hey, can you drive me uptown if we're done? If I hear anything I'll let you know."

Tucking the weed between his legs he checked the rear view.

On the lake, the Segwun steamship was just departing for its last trip of the day, the three hour evening cruise.

"Hey - I'm just going to see some people who might know," she said. "Do you want to meet later?"

"Sure," he replied, eyes still on the boat.

She let out another puff and smiled as he turned the ignition.

More and more, life was becoming a series of these disparate moments, he thought, throwing the stick into reverse with a glance to the left. And the more of these side trips he took, the harder it was to reconcile any of it with a normal life. Each day was more like a fragment of life. *That's what we do*, he thought, *disintegrate*.

"Meet you in front of the Opera House around 9:30?" he asked.

A nod. She took out a stick of gum and kneaded it slowly in her fingers.

A few minutes later he watched her disappear on Main behind some old crumbling buildings.

Then, about three blocks away, he turned onto a side street and parked just down from a non-descript green/white bungalow.

The sweet aroma of a nearby bakery scented the air and the sun finally headed down. The sky filled with aching reds. He loved this time of night. Made him feel alive.

He checked his watch, it was now 7:30pm. He knocked on the bungalow's half open wooden door and waited.

In seconds he heard shuffling and a sloppy, overweight man with thick black glasses and dark greasy hair appeared.

"And to what do I owe the pleasure this time?" the man asked, pushing the door ajar further.

"Looking for tips. Need to know if you heard anything this week about a break-in here in town."

Phil Wesserman was a local police radio scanner nut who helped him when the cops were withholding details.

Beaming, Phil folded his arms proudly, exposing the fat of his pits through his sweat stained wife beater.

"You know they let her get away that night," he said.

"What do you mean?"

"The woman who broke in - they let her skee-daddle. Heard it all on the scanner. Called it a Code 2. Means they're waiting to get her on something else or are hoping she'll graduate to something bigger. Last I heard they were following her. Up on Minerva. She went to the big building there. Has an apartment."

"They say why?"

"No, but it came down from the Inspector. I hear a lady's voice every time it comes from him. I just laugh. The criminal justice system."

Licking his lips, greasy Phil watched as Ethan rifled his half empty wallet.

Beyond the door, the place was a pigsty full of broken electronics and mouldy furniture. By the looks of his shirt, he'd probably caught him mid-dinner.

Handing him a fifty, the standard fee, his informant's smile widened "Easy money," he laughed. "Just the way I like it."

On the way to Minerva Ethan squeezed the weed bag like a tension ball. Then, thinking better of it, shoved it deep inside the centre console and closed the lid.

It was only 7:40 so he headed to a nearby park where he could sit and watch the building.

A large rooming house with a storied Gravenhurst history, 325 Minerva stretched back decades as the local junkie haven. Everybody in South Muskoka knew where to go for their meth and cheap sex. 325 Minerva.

So far he'd been extremely careful while investigating the case. The cops were probably already staking the building and would be pissed to see him there. The local force was small, so around-the-clock surveillance meant rookies would be taking shifts. This had obvious benefits for he and Saara, but they still couldn't afford to be seen.

The dusky streets were mostly quiet now. A few people walked dogs and a couple skateboarders were out. Gentle, ambient sounds lilted through the park - playground shouts and bursts from a distant raging backyard BBQ. Swarms of bugs danced high in the sodiums over the tennis courts and he heard the Segwun's final foghorn of the evening.

His own existence was a kind of dance, he thought, sitting on a bench in the park's east end. Where would he be if he allowed life to just carry him away? His thoughts turned to his Chief Dark Horse motorcycle which waited patiently back in the Estate garage. He could just quit all this and head out on the road if he wanted, leaving the job, his home, the whole damn thing.

There's beauty in that word, he thought. *Leaving.*

Through the trees at the fence line the dark building had become a series of tiny yellow rectangular lights and in those lights, he could see people watching tinier, square white ones. Some came and went to the corner store. Nobody ever left 325 Minerva for long.

Later, in front of the Opera House she stood in the darkness, new cigarette dangling in her fingers.

At her place they stared out across the bay. The waves sparkled far below in the brilliant moonlight. Then, drinks in hand, they wandered out closer to the cliff's edge.

Each time they kissed it was delicious poison and tonight she was on him fast, but he pulled away, unsure about a lot of things, but not Saara.

"So this is how it is if I don't have info?" she asked.

"No," he replied absently.

Later, when he got home, he made himself another drink but didn't drink it.

It was just after 1am and he sat at the end of his large bed, alone in the empty moon rays.

In the wardrobe he could see one of his former wife's slips sticking out from the suits and belts and remembered the last time he saw her wearing it - it must have been 10 years ago.

Well, it had to have happened. 19 years of marriage is never what it seems. Now its precarious position, still on a random hanger seemed fitting testimony to everything that had occurred.

Another symbol of a life he couldn't understand, only feel. More memories flooded back. The battles over money and alcohol. All the failings. Perversely, he'd dreamt of nights like this when he was young. Of just surviving through the thick of things, of anything that life threw in one's way.

It would be a kind of battle weary success, he'd imagined - pure, stark survival.

As long as things keep moving, he still told himself, as long as nothing stalled. Stalling means death.

In the morning he awoke around 10 to the sound of his cell buzzing. Saara would be over to plan things out at noon. God, he'd have to shut Rachel out for good soon, he thought, rubbing his head. It wasn't fair to any of them and she wouldn't really care - who was he kidding?

It had rained through the night and was supposed to start getting dark again around 6pm. The plan was to get into 325 Minerva to photograph the tenant list that evening.

There was one in the entranceway. He remembered it from years ago when one of his friends stayed there.

To help them they'd bring in Emma G, a mid-20's contact Saara had cultivated.

At 9:30pm they met her on Becker Street as planned.

"When you go in, just make it look like you're buzzing a number, talking on your phone at the same time," Saara cautioned.

True to his suspicions, a pair of cops were holed up in one of the houses listed for sale across the street.

But this would work. It had to.

At the manifest the girl pretended to say goodbye and ended her call. Back to the door, she pushed a buzzer and looked down at her cell as if a new call was coming in.

Click. click.

Later at the Estate they looked at the photo and could see there were 29 names in total.

In about 10 minutes they'd found their suspect.

On her Facebook page, Corrina Anna Racquell, who lived in apartment 602, appeared to be in her late 20's.

A tall skinny caucasian with jet black hair, she stared out of her main profile pic with a mysterious half smile. In others, chincey angel imagery and vapid inspirational sayings fought for the attention.

In most of her pictures, she didn't have the tattoo, just the main profile one which had been uploaded about a week prior.

In it, she stood next to an older, middle eastern looking bald man who had a salt and pepper beard.

They were in some sort of harbor - maybe Orillia - with sailboats and yachts moored behind them along spindly rows of finger docks.

He looked refined and well-off and wasn't likely her father. Wrong skin color.

Standing about 5 ft, 4" her wavy hair and green eyes exuded a casual, don't give a fuck coolness. Weathered now, she was likely beautiful once.

He, on the other hand, looked dead serious. One arm hung over her shoulder, fingers lingering just above the tat which was done in that font which was so popular with people in the 90's.

Saara would follow up with background checks on the woman's family. Most everything was on the net if you knew how to search.

It was just after midnight when Saara left. Nestled in his warm bed, he dreamt of being followed by a young girl through a moonlit canyon.

Down through crevices and paths, whenever he'd stop to look back, she was there watching from the shadows, which twisted like tentacles, somehow more alive than both of them in the weird dream twilight. It grew windy and the canyon sang with low whispers of which no sense could be made, save for them carrying fragments of names he knew.

Dressed in a white robe the girl tread barefoot and he heard the crunch of sand as she descended behind him in the passes. The whispers grew louder as they drew closer to a strange centre.

Down, down, they travelled and far below he could see a solitary campfire, otherwise empty at a barren dusty base. There was strange music there too, pumping to a low but surf pounding, orgiastic beat.

At the campfire's edge the music grew louder and the girl could be seen clearer. Her masculine, foreign looking face shot through with dark inset piercing eyes.

Soaked in sweat, he awoke, perched up on one elbow, gasping as his heart raced furiously.

Outside, the winds were shaking the crab apple trees wildly, causing their branches to cast jittering shadows throughout the room.

After a time he fell asleep and dreamed again.

This time he was in a snowy, dark landscape devoid of life. As he stood in complete darkness, his knees quaked beneath the full crush of an unbearable gravity as a shrill, high pitched noise sounded, seemingly from one fixed point which was everywhere at the same time.

It was the voices again from the previous dream, now at hysterical high pitches with flashes of the same mysterious woman/girl. Attempting to move, he crawled on all fours, though there was really no ground, sky or purpose.

The shrill grew louder and he pulled at imaginary earth and air to maintain focus. A morning bird cried out in the black and the void began shifting through hard to grasp landscapes.

Bewildered, he pressed on, plunging deeper into the darkness.

It was 4:35am when he awoke again covered in sweat.

Chapter Four

The District had endured a drier than normal summer that year, resulting in a general restlessness for many.

Dogs had seemed edgier and there'd been more of them in the streets it seemed. A ban on sprinklers had been in effect, with many area lawns scorched brown with parched yellow patches.

Now well into autumn, the nights were cool with winds coming up off the bay making it sweater weather for those who lived in the cliffs.

On some of these chilly nights Ethan still sat outside, watching over the estate's garden with a warm coat and coffee as the shadows fell in empty, desolate angles.

The garden was large with vertical posts and overhangs, which, during summer, had been covered in climbing vines. Numerous trellises dotted its courtyard during growing season, twisting with hostas, orchids and hyacinths. The gardening was done on contract with Morton Lodge and if he was lucky, the same workers familiar with its layout returned annually.

It was a big part of the charm of the place. A stone path led through the garden from a gated entrance at the side of the main estate building, stopping just short of its front porch.

About mid-way along the path was a large fountain which was stocked with koi each spring.

Often as the light fell on summer evenings, he'd doze, read a book or listen to podcasts by lamplight on the porch. Science topics were a recent favorite.

Between July and August he'd found that the lamp and moonlight worked to bring the garden alive in a powerful way and he'd wondered whether it had been designed with the darkness in mind.

It was now Sunday at 7pm. Lighting a joint, he recalled how when he'd first considered buying the place, it was the peculiar cast of evening shadows and twisting vines that had helped convince him to purchase. He'd thought more about the garden prior to his decision than he had the estate's home and was glad he had.

'Eternal' is a largely forgotten concept, he thought, but here it sprang to mind effortlessly.

It had even been named 'Noctivagus' - Latin for 'Night Wandering' - a bit of info which was included in some notes from the Real Estate firm. The section on the garden had been fascinating.

In the late 19th century a treaty had been signed between the British and local Ojibway tribes where the garden now stood. In exchange for a repatriation of the land, the Ojibway offered the British passage during a critical time when a section of railway was being built.

The land had been a burial ground sacred to tribes of the distant past. On his own he'd learnt they would never disturb their ground permanently in the belief spirits inhabited the soil itself. In advance of the treaty ceremony, which also stood to ensure preservation of the burial sites, tribal elders had conducted a rite in an antechamber amongst the temporary shanties erected there at the time. Its location had been the garden's courtyard.

Crushing the roach, he left to pick up Saara. She had to be involved with *everything* from here on out - she'd told him.

By 9pm they were back at the park bench near Minerva.

The building's entire parking lot in clear view, they waited, but by 10:15 there'd still been no sign of Racquell.

Nearing 10:30 he suggested one of them go for coffee. Saara was quick to offer her services.

Several families had rented the park for a function and to the south, outdoor fire pits sizzled while clumps of people roamed near the entrance. A band was just wrapping up their set with a stunning rendition of 'Good Golly Miss Molly' as Saara set off for drinks.

Moments later a black van pulled slowly into the lot, creeping to an idle near the rear entrance where the driver flashed the headlights twice.

High above, in one of the yellow rectangles on the sixth floor there was movement. Racquell was on her way.

Quickly he texted Saara who was just entering the lineup at a nearby Tim Hortons.

"She's moving. I'm going to follow."

Exiting from a side door, the woman sprinted towards the van, shooting a familiar wave at its bald driver.

If the cops were awake, they might tail her too, he thought, fumbling for his keys.

In seconds he was behind the wheel, heading west on a laneway bordering the park. At the closest intersection, he knew if the van wasn't already there, he'd have to take a nearby roundabout on Hodgins. There were only two exits off Minerva and the red light always took forever. When they didn't materialize, he turned left and drove to First and Queen.

Sure enough, it was there - stretching onto Queen with a possible undercover in tow a ways behind.

Maintaining distance, he followed as the van increased speed through the still wet residential streets out towards Highway 11.

Saara's texts buzzed in his pocket, but he couldn't reply. They were heading north.

Twenty minutes later he was parked discreetly down the road from where they'd pulled in at the Baysville docks.

The village of Baysville, northeast of Gravenhurst, had an arena, a few shops and some homes all nestled between Lake of Bays and the Muskoka River.

From where he sat, he could see Racquell and two other men at the end of a long dock. Staring out on the dark lake, they were searching the water for something. In the distance a murky light approached through the thick mist.

For now, no one else was around and there'd been no tail.

At 11:10, a sleek, dark grey speedboat pulled into the bay, docked and the trio boarded.

Quickly, it accelerated to full throttle heading west. He knew where it was headed - Bohemian Island.

Using his laptop back at the estate, he was able to match the van's license with its owners.

Ontario plates, the vehicle was registered to the Siren Shipping Company, a multinational conglomerate based out of Vancouver - an import business in a modest sized market, mainly fine antiques and shipping for hire.

Finding the owners wasn't a problem, but what was their connection with Lake of Bays and Bohemian?

According to a mid-90's news article, the company had been fined $156,000 following a 1987 workplace harassment suit alleging sexual interference. It had happened on one of their three flagship vessels, the Condora, and had involved a deckhand and female ship captain named Angelicka Freedmore.

Other than that, things looked clean.

It was 1am and his cell now flashed with four missed messages: Two from Saara, the others from William, who'd apparently just hung up.

"Where the fuck did you go? Worried." said one of Saara's. "Call me," read the other.

Outside on the porch, the wind was hurtling an old thunder drum against the wall in explosive loud crashes.

Taking it down, he went back inside, grabbed his laptop from the couch and headed to bed.

Chapter Five

Monday he awoke early to the sounds of birds and the soft patter of
rain.

If he had to say, the birds were louder, but sound waves are just
information and there was no louder to it, just the capacity to make it
seem so.

That's how his mind worked and, at times, like at 6am, it drove him
crazy.

Pondering this, he lay in bed lost in the sounds before he shuffled
downstairs to the kitchen for some food.

Fixing some toast and the first of the day's coffees, he went outside
and reattached the drum.

A pair of ruby throated hummingbirds, the last birds to leave
Muskoka before winter, darted amidst the dying vegetation, pecking at
spilled seed.

It's too easy to classify things in levels, he thought, sparking a joint,
that's only really our end of the perception deal.

Insect kingdoms bled into vertebrate worlds, weather systems into
space. Only a perceiver deconstructs it all, framing things as separate
worlds with localized attributes. In the final analysis, it all resolved into
one - first down to atoms, then to quarks, then.... presumably nothing.

The smoke was hitting him hard.

The flimsy artificial controls man had in place to separate and govern
'worlds', he laughed. It was so obvious.

There was no real control in the world. Where were the courts of
law, for example, for birds - the killers of worms? There could only be
the concept of law for creatures who understood it, carved out of
chaos to create 'order' if they had the ability, while really, existence
continued unabated, just signals and their home, noise.

William, he had to phone William. Maybe later - after 9?

The rain came harder now hammering the small pools that had
gathered on the porch transforming the reflections on their surfaces
into waves of concentric circles.

A heavy storm threatened, and the wires hummed, their static tension coursing through him too like pure mystery.

Mondays were work days and not even amazing stoned reveries could shake the old ethic out of him. Inside, he settled in the Estate's library with a cheese omelet and his laptop hoping the already flickering lights wouldn't bite the bullet.

Easing into a worn Victorian chair in the centre of the circular room, he brought up some photographs he and Saara had taken at the Deer Lake site.

The library comprised the bottom of the estate's 'tower', which was basically the library at ground level, then a spiral staircase beginning at the 2nd floor which climbed to a third and then the attic.

Outside, the now roaring winds served to heighten the cozy silence of the book lined space.

An old oil lamps' quiet yellow flames acted as backup, as if to challenge the hot white flashes shooting outside. This cast a mysterious battle across the bookshelves, which were in fact the library's circular walls.

At the room's one side, a large Tibetan mirror rested atop a cream mantle. The drifting marijuana haze, a greenish-yellow in the library light, circled upwards and in the mirror he could see his own fiery pupils, red like Chinese tigers, staring back at him like weary, long lost explorers.

Fuck. He couldn't get into it.

The work. The murders. It was too bloody early.

Soon the lonely coasts of unfulfilled motorcycle trips filled his thoughts - he'd steal some moments for himself instead, there was nothing wrong with that.

A pair of moths fluttered at the lampshade beside the chair and he brushed them away, watching as they rose majestically to the wall above the door.

The room seemed darker now and..... chillier too.

Pulling an old afghan around his shoulders, he opened a book he'd just bought about recent experiments in psychokinesis.

Then it happened, fast without any warning:

Directly in front of him, a dark mist had somehow formed, no, somehow *burst* into being, accompanied by a strange feeling of being slightly overtaken.

Almost instantly all sense of self dissolved, his once sharp attention now fused with the weird writhing mass, which hovered quivering in the air like a mad, life size shadow puppet.

In shock he stared at its dark twists and vague shapes, triangles at first then strange turrets manifesting and morphing into each other. The air had turned from chilly to ice cold too and he gasped, watching his breath merge with the smoky entity as it jittered in shuddering, dark flashes.

A profound presence took hold as the thing hovered. It was speaking now too, or at least it seemed to be - inside his head, but not in any language he knew. His animal self shook in ecstasy as sinewy black tendrils reached out from its icy centre like cascading hydra.

Growing in size rapidly, the maw swirled now in a more defined shape - so much so that the little light the table lamp had provided was completely blotted out.

Then images came, flashing in a successive inner maelstrom of rapid scenes. Some seemed like distant memories culled from his own past, while of others he knew nothing.

Clutching his temples, his pulse raced like a train.

With only one eye ajar, he reeled as a figure took form by the mantle.

The thing was tall, lean and dark. What the fuck was in this shit?, he wondered - was it laced?

Eyes now firmly shut, he listened as calm, even steps creaked across the mahogany floor, causing the pressure in his veins to drop from low to nonexistent as the thing moved towards the chair.

Squinting, he could make out a pair of shoes as they clacked across the hardwood - worn, but well polished brown leather brogues.

The thing also wore grey gentleman's trousers, and at the waistline, a cherry leather belt and neat, tucked in white dress shirt inside a tweed smoking jacket.

It stopped just short of his chair, Ethan's half open eyes rose to see a blue-red pinstripe tie below a strong masculine jaw line.

The figure's lips, full and red, parted as if it were about to address him.

It was a man, perhaps middle aged, with a brown moustache and piercing, silver blue eyes.

Raising its right hand, its fingers toyed with the ends of its dark brown locks, casting an indifferent stare through him to the door and back.

"I'm dreaming," Ethan screeched, not daring to meet the stranger's stare again. "I... I must be dreaming."

The black mass from which the man had sprung was gone and it was now as if he'd always been there - with him in the library - at least since from when he'd come in.

Outside, the storm sleet slashed at the windows as the sky, pitch black in angry, violent squalls, spat shocking white lightning until a final wave of penultimate crashes reset the equilibrium to zero.

And once again he was sitting alone.

Still in the library, but alone. With barely a recollection of what had just occurred. Shocked. Upright. Confused.

Leaping from his seat, he rushed to the window and clawed at the drapes, pulling them back as far as he could to allow what little light there was outside to flood in like a saviour. It was clear again out there - daylight, with simple white clouds - some still flashing, but drifting calmly, *normally*, out over the lake.

It was then he saw, just beyond the hedge at the main gate and a ways through the forest, car lights.

Gawd, he muttered, peering at his own pale reflection in the drizzle covered panes, sweat beads dripping from his forehead. Above, the moths had stopped dancing and were now looking down at him from the storm hatches like eyes.

What the fuck was going on? The stress of the case had been eating him and he knew he needed some rest. What he really needed now was a hot shower and stiff drink - *was he losing it?*

Tapping the window, he was relieved to find it and the room still solid. Outside seemed real enough too. On Mondays, farmers would walk cows along the back roads around the estate to and from market. The estate's full civic address was 1029 Vankoughnet Road and often vehicles would miss the market's entrance four farms over, finding their way to his property through the usually open gates expecting to see stalls, country crafts and wares.

It was one of these he hoped to see when he opened the front door. Either that or someone who'd done something understandable, like hit a cow.

But there she stood, outside her cruiser in the sparkling, steaming driveway staring up at him when he opened the door: Inspector Hallett's no nonsense second in command, Constable Shelley Svestik.

A 12 year veteran of the force, the tall Norwegian was all business all the time. Towering close to 6ft two inches, the hawkish blonde's cold reputation was always in step with her demeanor. Not altogether unattractive, Svestik was a tough mix of austere female qualities with a blockish face that sought instant submission.

"Good morning," she half barked, kicking some dirt from her boot.

"Morning," he answered. "What brings you here so early?"

"We have to.... talk about the case," she replied, her eyes not flinching.

"Oh, about what?"

"Look," she said, rolling up a sleeve, as though preparing for a brawl right then and there. "We both know what's going on here and I need to know you know where I, *We*, stand. People talk and they're saying you and Ms. Khan are working with us and since that's not true, we'd like it if you'd please stop the overt inquiries as it hampers our efforts. I'm sure you understand."

"We're doing nothing overt," he responded. "I can assure you of that."

"Oh, c'mon," she growled, voice growing scratchier. "You've been following vehicles that are part of our case and we just can't have it. In order to bring this to conclusion the investigation must be focused, and it can't be with half the town gossiping and not seeing police as leaders. As you *also* know, we're dealing with dangerous people, whom frankly, you should be wondering if you'll need protection from."

The part about everyone gossiping probably amounted to two cops, but she'd betrayed no hint about William, which was the only thing that worried him.

"You have my word we aren't meddling... in your case," he said, hesitating like a child trying to evade discipline.

"I'd better," she answered.

A half sarcastic offer of coffee fell flat and she waved him off.

"I was only up here because there was a disturbance down near the Hampton farm," she said, already backing towards her cruiser. "Pigs escaped a broken fence in the storm and had the lane blocked. It's why I'm covered in mud. Stopped by as I'd been asked to."

Throwing up more mud as she left, he watched her disappear back through the woods out to the main road. They would have to be more discrete.

After nine, a call to William determined police were now following up the prostitute angle after a local auctioneer's daughter had been viciously attacked while returning home from a party one morning that week.

Worried, William said even he was on a need to know basis now. The only reason he'd heard about it was because he was friends with the auctioneer's wife.

The girl's story was that two men had ambushed her close to the family farm at 2:30am Wednesday but that she'd escaped through a field.

But according to her mother, police suspected the girl knew her attackers. They weren't buying her story and William suggested she could be another target as she'd been picked up for soliciting in the city a few years back and was known to have hung with the Watkinson girl.

Hanging up, he immediately thought of the library and froze.

Should he get checked out?

Squeezing the bag in his pocket, he had another idea.

"Time to lay off this shit."

Chapter Six

For as long as anyone in Bracebridge could remember, Maurice Dupluis had been the auctioneer.

He and his family lived on a large farm to the north of town. The gothic property was known for its huge weather-beaten barn where auctions were held each Tuesday over the course of both summer and fall. People would travel from across the province to the affairs, such was the reputation of his authentic old-time auctions.

The family originally hailed from northern Quebec. Dupluis lived on the farm with his wife Emilie and their two daughters Charlotte, 23 and Suzanne, 21.

It was Charlotte who'd seen the trouble the other morning.

Saara's description was of a beautiful, if not shy girl, with short pixie-cut brown hair and an autumn complexion with pouty nose and lips. The family were well off, but, as is the case with farm families, didn't display it in their sense of dress or humble rural airs.

Charlotte would wear cut off jean shorts in summer with halter tops. Stereotypically, she lived an existence of immediate gratifications - farm boys, drugs, short term goals. Cocaine, she'd heard. Not unlike other teens.

Her family's farm could be seen across the valley from Ethan's estate and he stared out across the muddy fields and hills considering the new information.

The description of the men was suspect too, according to William, and police instead thought she'd been with them that night when something had gone wrong.

It was the mother who'd made the call to police, not the girl.

William said some farmhands told officers they'd seen a struggle between she and the men on the road that morning - they'd still been up watching stars.

In their version, they'd thought she'd opened the door of a slow moving white or silver SUV and jumped out as it was travelling the laneway near her home. But witnesses were often wrong.

Since Ethan had left the paper his razor-sharp clarity had slowly been returning after falling a little rusty in his final years.

The frenetic, fast paced modern workday, coupled with advancing age erodes it - 'the stuff', leaving many with little more than stumps for heads.

Tomorrow there'd be an auction - might be worth checking out, he thought.

There were still pockets of small town society he'd not become intimately acquainted with and the world of auctions was one of them. In the news world there'd never been enough time to get involved in anything outside work. Its pace was hard to unwind from and was still stealing his private time even now, though he'd quit over four weeks earlier. But the war for leisure was improving. Instead of all out assaults, there were now only minor skirmishes.

As of today it would be up to Saara to relay any news tips to editors and just after 1pm, when she arrived with a lunch of fish and chips, he told her this.

Between grabs of greasy thick battered cod and newspaper-wrapped steaming hot fries, they forked together a plan.

The following day they'd attend the afternoon auction to see if they could learn anything.

The rain had again returned with a noisy vengeance, but he didn't dare relay his experience in the library, nervously scoffing when she suggested he quit reading books on weird topics.

With that uncomfortable way she had of staring after her sentences ended, she'd also called him a dreamer - the stare lingering about a half second too long for his liking this time.

She was right of course. She knew him.

"There - you are doing it again right now," she laughed. "Lost in your own little world."

"I'm just getting ready to do the dishes."

"Bullshit. I can tell when you're 'thinking'," she laughed, grabbing her keys and one of his books from the marble counter.

"You better snap out of it. I'm taking all these books and having a bonfire."

Saara hugged him, said she was on her way back to work, and, with a peck on the cheek, told him she looked forward to going antique hunting. On her way out, she bumped into a table in the hall, knocking an old picture onto the floor. Picking it up, she held it for a moment, seemingly puzzled and eyeing it closely.

"Who is this - here at the far end?" she asked, a forefinger tracing the outlines of a face in the aged black and white. "I recognize Robert and your parents, but not her. Is she a cousin?"

It was Darby. God, he hadn't thought about her in years.

"It's our...sister," he answered, his hands falling limp in the warm soapy water.

"You never told me you had *a sister*," she said, peering closer. "She looks a lot younger than you and your brother. Did I meet her at the corn roast and it just not register?"

"No, you didn't meet her," he said, wiping the countertop aimlessly. "She disappeared while we were still young and we don't talk about her much now."

"*Oh my god*. I'm so sorry. Do you feel like saying more? I understand if you don't. That's so sad - what happened?"

For a moment it all came flooding back. The warm summer breeze in the truck stop field where they'd had a picnic. July 23rd, 1981. He'd only been six, but he still remembered it clearly. His mother's forlorn sobbing in his father's arms and the flashing lights from the police cars. His father seemed so helpless that day. He hated seeing and feeling that.

No, daddy, I didn't see her go there. I was near the tree.

Darby had been all of five when it happened. A simple picnic, suggested his mother: *Why don't we stop up near old Anderson's on 45? They have a nice space there with trees. We can let the dog have a run. I packed sandwiches...*

Darby had wandered off after the dog, a collie named Piper, into some bushes at the edge of the woods.

"Are you...ok?" It was Saara touching his shoulder.

"Yes, just, y'know, remembering..."

"I'm so sorry I brought this up."

"It's ok," he said, stirring the dishes at the bottom of the sink. "Like I said, it happened so long ago. I'd forgot that picture even existed, even though I walk by it every day."

"We can talk more about it when I get back if you want," she said, gently letting him go. "Ok?"

"Ok."

When she'd gone, he held the picture in his hands, staring down at the missing one's tiny, sun dappled face.

Police had suspected a trucker had snatched her and an all points bulletin for a large white rig was put out along with roadblocks in both directions. But there was never any trace. The dog came back within 20 minutes of her disappearance, panting like it had just run a marathon.

They scoured the fields for a week, but there was no sign. It was like the earth swallowed her whole.

Years later, in 1992, the family was contacted when police discovered her blanket which she had always carried with her. It was sheer luck they'd noticed it in the attic of a local drug dealer's home after a raid in Ottawa. It was definitely hers. Her name was sewed in its side in red thread.

She'd had it at the time of her disappearance too and thankfully, an old detective who'd worked on her case had double checked while collecting evidence.

The home it was found in had had three owners since the time she'd gone missing and each were interviewed intensely. All had had multiple renters through the years, many of whom there were no real records for.

The names they did come up with all checked out and were dismissed as suspects for various reasons - lack of evidence mainly. In the end, there was no real way of knowing how that blanket came to be in that attic. Could have been bought at a second hand or Goodwill.

It had killed his parents - the not knowing.

For years his father drifted from job to meaningless job as depression sunk its talons into he and his mother. Parents don't recover from things like that. Takes the heart right out of them. He and his brother were young enough that eventually she had become just another old memory, one defined by their parents' grief. She'd just started at a new kind of special kindergarten too - he remembered that much because it'd been his job to help get her dressed each morning before breakfast.

He'd finish the dishes and get back to work, he sighed, but a coldness filled his mind at the thought of doing anything.

From the warm, cozy kitchen the library seemed a world away, but it was just down the hall.

What if that morning had really happened?

Supposed portals and apports filled the literature, he remembered, fighting off a sharp pang of panic. Why they manifest, if they even really did, remained a mystery.

Some authors posited they were triggered by subconscious calls - either a thought or configuration of thoughts or other, seemingly innocuous psycho-physical acts. Or a combination of both. The unconscious was weird. Such events may be a type of puzzle piece, thought some authors, 'fitting' into an unknown reality information system.

That they appeared random may just be our ignorance, he remembered one saying, what with our limited knowledge about the true nature of consciousness.

These dishes aren't getting done, he thought, trying to bring his attention back to the task at hand.

But in the science journals top down causality suggests systems at higher conscious levels orchestrate events in the mundane, and, theoretically, if some part of a higher system or 'program' should change, a chair in the here and now could disappear - or specters could manifest.

He watched a housefly land in the dish water and drown, wings fluttering rapidly in final, spastic twitches.

It had flown in to a part of reality completely hostile to its existence. The same often happened with people. Carrie and Chloe had found theirs, and....so had Darby.

Finished with dishes, he decided to just walk by the open library door and peer quickly inside. He was alone - it wouldn't look foolish.

Approaching though, he paused.

Somehow, he could still feel it, or at least *he thought* he could.

He walked past to the living room and lay down on the couch.

Ethan stared at the ceiling watching the light from outside dance across the crown moulding.

His thoughts returned to the plan. They'd pose as auction goers, gain access to the farm and learn more.

His cell buzzed in his pocket. It was Saara, who left a message:

"I'm really sorry I brought that up - I can tell it really affected you - it was an accident. Anyways, hope you're feeling better. I'll be over in the morning."

He must have drifted off, because when he awoke an hour had passed and he'd received a text from Rachel.

"Was wondering if you could drive me up to see my mom. My ride fell through. Let me know ASAP. Supposed to be there by four."

It was now 2pm and the thought of getting out of the gloomy estate pleased him.

"Sure. Be there in half an hour."

For an ordinary day of the week, the hospital in Bracebridge was a shit show.

Rachel's mother Carla was going downhill fast, but it still took her over an hour to see a specialist - an hour later than her prearranged appointment in the building's east wing.

In the ER, things were crazy. On their way in, a woman burst past to let doctors know four people with life threatening injuries were being admitted. Then the place erupted, swarming with cops and paramedics escorting the injured on stretchers and wheelchairs.

He couldn't quite make out what was happening, but the look of horror on their faces, the way they cried and hugged each other intimated something serious - even extraordinary.

The second patient to arrive - an older woman with white hair was being fed oxygen. She'd suffered massive trauma and her sheets were blood soaked around her chest, the thin blankets dripping all over the floor as she was rushed in for surgery.

Rachel had missed this part, having stepped into an office to speak with admissions, but on the way back to Gravenhurst later, commented on what she'd seen in Oncology.

"It was like the doctors didn't know what to do," she said. "A bunch of them were just standing there, fighting over what was happening downstairs. One of them - a nurse I think - ran out of the room crying. Air ambulance was called in."

"I'll check with Saara, but there weren't any sirens either, which was weird," he said.

The next morning, he retrieved the paper, but there was nothing, just a story about an arrest made overnight, when police had been called out to a home in Bala where a man had barricaded himself, claiming harassment by undercovers.

After some time, he was taken into custody by force, suffering a shotgun wound to the leg and the Province's Special Investigations Unit had to be called.

One witness, who spoke anonymously, said he'd seen unmarked police vehicles near the man's home on several occasions throughout the summer.

He was reportedly in stable condition now at the hospital in Bracebridge, but there was no mention of the prior day's excitement in the ER.

Checking his messages, he saw William had called again.

"I'm sure you'll find this interesting," said the officer. "The man involved in this morning's takedown is connected with the case. Don't know how, but there was a big meeting between the Inspector and the other investigators just before a few of us were sent out there. The man's name is John Gretchen - It's all I know."

The message was left at 2am. According to the paper, police took the man into custody around 1:30.

A quick search on the internet came up with a John Gretchen owning an antiques business near Bala. 'Gretchen's Antiques' was located on Highway 169 just outside Torrance.

At noon Saara arrived, looking tired.

"I've been thinking about where I know this Gretchen from," she said, grabbing a seat. "It was back in 96 when we were cub reporters working the Cranberry Festival. He had a booth there. Bought one of his butter churners. Seemed like a nice enough guy. Folksy."

He offered her some French toast which she accepted with glee.

"There are all sorts of reasons why someone would have issues with the cops," he said. "Usually starts with neighbour disputes. Cops take one side and it goes downhill from there. William says it's tied to the case though. Obviously, any connection between this guy and the auctioneer's daughter or the murders should be found. We're still on for this afternoon. Starts at 1pm."

Shifting on her stool, something had her preoccupied.

Setting her mug down matter-of-factly she shot him a serious look.

"I think the auctioneer's daughter is one of them - a hooker," she said. "One of the things I learned yesterday was that she was seen with the two girls on several occasions at Bohemian. I got that from the head of real estate at Booker/Reison. He was there on a golf weekend and said she was definitely there partying with the other two girls, I showed him her picture."

"He said to be careful because from what he knew, these people do not fuck around," she added. "Most are from Toronto."

"So we know it's a ring servicing rich tourists," he said. "We know where they're based and who some of the girls are. We have to nail down the Gretchen angle though. We need to get on that island soon."

She didn't reply.

"Hey - what should I wear to this thing?" he exclaimed, changing the subject, holding up an old farmer's hat he sported when he gardened. "Casual country gentlemen suit me?"

"That'd be lovely," she giggled. "But don't go too far - I have a reputation to uphold."

"I'll be 'the antiques collector'. Got to look the part."

If nothing else, it'd be a fun way to spend an afternoon.

Chapter Seven

Cyclists and joggers dotted the landscape as they passed through the outskirts of several villages on their way towards Castle Hill.

Soon the grey barn emerged on the horizon and upon arrival, it still looked far off when they had to park in a sea of vehicles that had materialized in a muddy side field.

From there they trudged up the hill. At the top, they separated, each taking their own places in the growing lines of deal hunters.

It was a classic chill autumn afternoon and the buoyant masses busied themselves in pockets checking out the different booths. Children ran through these crowds as farmers moved livestock around behind the barn. Tuesday was the outdoor market day too.

The first auction was scheduled to start at 1pm. Passing through the main ticket gate, Saara took off in the direction of the back horse stalls, while he remained by the entrance. It was nearing start time and the crowds were surging, many still awaiting their turn to be stamped for entry.

Inside, Ethan found the dark interior drafty with random sunbeams illuminating dry, dusty air.

Lit mainly with old fashioned oil lamps hung along massive walls and post beams, he marveled at how many items had been packed into the old building - some were huge, taking up whole sections of stage areas, while others remained draped at the sides on a multitude of tables.

The old were seated along benches lining the walls and many appeared to know each other. Others stared furiously at their programmes, calculating what they could afford to bid.

At 1:15, the auctioneer made his first appearance, rising to the main stage in slow methodical steps aided by a cane up a side wooden staircase. The crowd's murmurs sharpened to a hush, which was quickly swallowed by the rustling of programmes as all eyes trained on the front.

Through the towering open barn doors beyond the stage, Ethan could see men in beige coveralls leading horses and cows to and from pasture. He didn't see anyone familiar in the sea of faces.

Re-calibrating to the auctioneer who was about to start bids, he watched ushers unveil an 1850's Quebec armoire with recessed panels and its original feet.

In a few seconds it was gone for $3,500 to a pot bellied grey haired man who beamed with excitement

Saara was nowhere to be seen in the bobbing heads and raised hands and the auctioneer spoke again in a staccato gibberish as the next items were unveiled.

Making his way to the right wall, Ethan climbed the side staircase to the upper deck for a better view.

Shoulder-to-shoulder with others there (for a second he feared the floor would collapse from so many people) he watched intently from above.

"$7,500," shouted the auctioneer, aiming his cane at a 19th century inlaid wood daybed with a marquetry sleigh design and scrolling head and footboards. "Going once, going twice..."

Leaning in, his eyes darted to and from each face, but still no Gretchens booth, Charlotte, or identifiable cops.

Mainly rich tourist types, the crowd seemed a mix of professional deal hunters and the relaxed wealthy just out for a leisurely experience. As the afternoon wore on, winning bidders shuffled off to arrange for deliveries as more and more items got hauled up to the stage.

The registry desk at the rear was presided over by an older, severe looking black haired woman who was busy stamping forms amidst stacks of fluttering paper and thick leather bound books. This was the auctioneer's wife, Emilie.

At her desk, successful bidders presented items they could carry. One man, dressed in a light green suit, looked pleased with a small antique rocking cradle snuggled in his arms, as he made his way from the desk back towards the entrance.

As he left, two Eastern European looking men dressed in black suits entered and made their way through the crowd up to the front.

Definitely not police, he thought - too obvious.

One wandered off to the side looking like he was expecting to meet somebody. Under a huge support beam, he pulled a cell out and started texting, looking up from time to time for whoever he was expecting.

In a few minutes the cell flashed and he nodded. Putting it away, he sauntered back to the other man and after speaking briefly, made his way around the stage, exiting through the huge doors.

Without thinking, Ethan followed.

Outside the suit was already back on his cell, facing a field beyond one of the corrals, seemingly straining to see in the distance.

Placing the phone on a post, the man reached into a pack sack, retrieving a small pair of binoculars, which he used to again scan the hillsides.

In the distance there was mostly dense forest, a few cliffs and the odd stone outcropping. With the naked eye, cottages could also be made out deep amongst the trees, which were now close to their height of crimson fall hues.

The man nodded, listening to whoever was on the phone's speaker. It was all just semi-curious, until Ethan noticed the holster.

Yes, it was there - a small black pistol in a tight leather shoulder strap. But this wasn't a cop, at least not your average local one. And what was he looking for?

His hair and dress manner, while conservative, hinted at a complex social makeup not easily pinned down - there was almost an air of worldliness about him, but this could have been due to his eastern European complexion.

Whoever he was, he was staring off into those hills again. His partner had just joined him and they moved off towards the barn, walking past Ethan approaching the muddy field and its glinting sea of chrome.

They were too interesting to lose so he followed. He sent a text to Saara and let her know what was happening.

They walked to a dark hummer parked close to the front gate. It was a struggle finding his BMW in the maze of vehicles and he became a little stressed when the hummer started up and made its way to the entrance where it turned right, quickly disappearing over a hill heading east.

Eventually he found the BMW. Saara'll be alright, he thought, pulling out after them.

In a few minutes he'd caught sight of them again, maintaining a discrete separation behind three other vehicles.

For a good 10 minutes he tailed them through rolling, sun kissed farmland. Two of the cars turned off at a lane near a sign that announced they'd just entered Muskoka Lakes.

Three stop signs later and the Hummer made a right.

Pulling off to the side, he let they and the last car between them go until they were barely dots on the horizon. As he again increased speed, he noticed the landscape had become more hilly and dense. They were still there though, reappearing whenever he hit clearings.

After 20 minutes, they eventually turned onto a side road leading up through more hills towards an old farmhouse. This building, located at the end of a large stone outcropping was flanked by a wooded valley on both sides. Seeing no road beyond it, he pulled over along a river far below, parked and stepped out.

It was now mid afternoon and the sun glared down, illuminating the location in hazy, kaleidoscopic shades.

The property appeared to only contain the one main house and a mid-sized barn. A clump of rocks lay just west of the buildings, but it was too far to make out details. Only the one hummer was parked there.

Snapping a few pictures, he returned to the car and jotted down the name of the road, 'Speicher's Lane' for future reference.

Speeding back to the auction, a text arrived from Saara:

'Still here. By the front'

At the barn entrance he could see her up by the stage, looking a little lost.

"Anything worth staying for?" he asked, once he'd reached her.

"Yup," she replied, nodding for him to look to his far left.

In a corner, close to the back, a large brute of a man in orange overalls was speaking heatedly with the auctioneer's wife.

"Came in just after you left," she said. "Went straight up to her looking angry. Might be of interest."

The man stood a good six and a half feet and was annoyed about something, but it soon became obvious it was just an argument about damaged goods. A bit bothered Saara hadn't discerned this herself, Ethan suggested they get some fresh air.

Outside she did have something of interest to offer:

"While you were out watching your guy, his friend was talking to a man just behind the barn," she said. "He seemed to be asking him questions and writing things down. Your guy had a gun? This one seemed peaceful, just interested in what this man was saying."

"It was weird though," she continued. "The man kept pointing out towards the centre of the field. He was already here when they got here. I saw him helping move some of the big items. Think he's an employee."

A puzzled frown formed across Ethan's face.

"Doesn't seem like cops," he said. "These guys are something else. This employee - where is he now?"

"Back inside, I presume," she answered. "It's odd, because a woman walking by stopped and said hello to the employee and he touched her arm and seemed to be reminding her about something. Then she got excited and pointed to the sky over by those hills too. The suit guy wrote everything down - what she was saying too."

"Something's going on," Ethan answered, eyeing the fields. "It might be related with the case and it might not."

It was 3pm and the barn was starting to clear out. Emilie and the tall man were now speaking quietly outside, the dilemma apparently resolved.

"Not much more we can do here today," Ethan said, as workers hauled yet another grand piano across the stage. "Let's head."

Chapter Eight

Fidgeting at the table, Saara barely touched her cordon bleu. He could tell she was frustrated.

"Don't worry, there's always a break in every case," he reassured her, not believing a word of it. "Besides, we have the other two leads - the island and the shipping company."

Instead of agreeing, she cracked a beer cap with a twist of finality.

"I suppose I could infiltrate the island as a divorcee," she mumbled, staring up at the track lighting.

Now she was talking. And unless they were wrong, the island wasn't likely to be swarming with cops just yet.

Bohemian was one of the premier Muskoka destinations for the jet set the world over, hence its being a magnet for high class rough trade. He suspected the ownership turned a blind eye to it. Hosts and parasites. Bees to pollen.

The more he thought about it, the more a single debutante playing her cards right sounded like the perfect cover.

"Ok, but let's look at timelines," he said, psychically attempting to lower her eyes from the ceiling. "Could you go in next week? Time's ticking - the season will be ending soon."

"I need a holiday," she admitted, forcing a half smile.

In truth, she could already see herself in that red sundress she'd just bought.

"I could watch for Charlotte and any others there," she continued. "Track their movements and the people they visit. Might learn a lot."

He nodded approvingly. It would buy him some time to visit that farmhouse too, which he hadn't mentioned, after telling her he'd lost them near Muskoka Lakes.

"How long would you stay?"

"A week. That's all we'd need I think. If it warranted more I guess I could stay longer, but I don't think it'd be necessary. It's the end of the season - we have that working for us. It's probably the best timing possible."

One of the hummingbirds whirred outside the window around the empty feeder.

Clearing some beer bottles from the table, Ethan returned clutching two more.

At midnight they were in each other's arms in the old hammock chair in the basement den. He'd almost brought up the situation in the library, but had thought better of it.

Outside, down the road, others were still up too.

Through the window, a TV could be heard at Morton Lodge broadcasting some hockey game or other, its sounds mixing with the shrill of tree frogs and the lonesome horn of a passing freighter.

Somewhere in the alcoholic blur of the night he'd seen a social media post trumpeting a new discovery about dark matter.

That's what they were doing too, he thought - getting closer to an answer.

Leaning forward to blow out the votives she'd lit, her body shifted in his arms and she mumbled something into his shoulder.

"Time for sleep," he whispered, gently removing their blankets.

On the main floor he watched as she climbed to the first threshold and turned towards their room.

Out on the front porch he saw the Dupluis farm the valley over, its tall silo glowing brilliantly like some fabled minaret. Swirling mists were steaming up too from the valley, creeping through the expansive, ragged black country. Further to the east lay more farm lights appearing as fireflies in the rolling swirls.

They slept deeply and by the time she awoke the next day, he'd already chopped wood, fetched the paper and prepared breakfast.

"Can't stop smoking I see," she announced wryly, as she entered the kitchen, sniffing the air.

"Nothing but the very best attention for my omelettes," he laughed.

Placing a hot plate piled high with his concoction before her, she brought a fork load to her mouth, as he rattled off its ingredients:

"Two eggs, dash of Worcestershire sauce, cumin, red pepper, mini Bella's, onion and some cayenne pepper - the Charlish omelet."

"It is creative," she laughed. "I'll have to let you know how it stacks up against island food."

"Look at it as an adventure," he said. "Document everything, but enjoy yourself too. Remember, I'm only a 10-minute boat ride from there and I expect to be here the whole week. You'll have to keep messages limited to cell. No guessing how secure email will be out there."

He'd didn't inform her he'd already triangulated the farm property on Speicher's Lane on a map. They agreed to split costs and as breakfast wrapped up, he bid her well.

"Sorry I have to leave so early, but you know the last day before vacation," she said from the car in the driveway. "So what'll you do while I'm all on my own out there?"

"Oh, get some of the usual work done around here - close up for winter. I'll be talking with William more about things too. I will keep you informed."

She didn't believe him and was kind of miffed she'd been sucked into making the trip. It wasn't exactly how she'd wanted to use her fall time off, but it wasn't like she wouldn't have an opportunity to relax. She'd treat it as a working holiday. She'd always wanted to see the resort.

She'd book it to start that weekend if she could.

Ronnie

In a dilapidated musty old warehouse Ronnie Watson waited for his adversary to come down the stairs from the second level before he opened fire.

He didn't have to. The other guy was running on empty and he could have just drilled him through the hole in the floor, but he knew he'd either come down the stairs or jump through the hole in order to attempt taking him down with his bare hands and he wanted to humiliate him for even thinking about trying. So, in a grotesque display of torn limbs and blood splatter, he took him out with his backpack howitzer the moment he started to come down and the crowd in the theatre exploded in roars of laughter.

Ronnie had won the title, which meant he was taking the $20,000 home, plus the new Concore gaming system along with its complete lineup of exciting new games. There were high fives all around as he walked down the aisle to the stage through the pimply faced fans and gamers.

Taking the trophy in his hands he raised it high above his head just like the winners do after NASCAR races. The only thing missing was the champagne being sprayed all over him. He'd have to wait until later for that. With the theatre's bright floodlights in his eyes, he couldn't see much, given the rest of the place's darkness, but knew they were all still out there. He could just make out the envious jeers of those who he'd defeated and that was enough.

It was a glorious day for Ronnie, who was now the all time Barrie champion gamer in the age 25-45 category, having just defeated Ozlo Norwick, who had come all the way from Vaughn, which was the cut off area for this year's competition.
Norwick had been so sure of himself early in the SS Werewolf death match that he'd catcalled Ronnie under his breath for the first 30 minutes of game play, mocking his subtle lisp and awkward shy gait.

So it was with great pleasure when he, the 30 year old champion with the squinting eyes and bright red hair, was able to look Norwick straight in the face in the hallway on the way out, slowly mouthing the words: Fuck. You.

He'd had to deal with Norwick types all his life and reflected upon this as he drove his 1987 Silver Camaro towards AA's strip joint later that afternoon. The look on Norwick's greasy olive visage when he saw Ronnie's cock stiff middle finger waving triumphantly had been priceless.

AA's was in Barrie's west end in a non-descript strip mall that didn't have much else going for it.

There was a fish and chips shop, nail salon and a company that did people's taxes. Other than that, there was a big empty place where a grocery store had once sat. The whole mall needed some sprucing up and the absentee landlord's answer to the one time a vagrant had been run down by a car leaving AA's at 3am back in the 90's had been to place no less than five speed bumps throughout the parking lot's main laneways.

It was Wednesday at 4 o'clock and Jordanna would soon be finishing her shift.

He backed the Camaro into a parking space so it faced the front door, lit a bent cigarette and waited. He couldn't wait to show her the trophy.

At 4:15 the front door swung open, and, after giving the muscle-bound bouncer a peck on the cheek, his girlfriend came bounding out to the car.

"OMG," she cried as he held up the trophy, knocking the rear-view mirror out of place at the same time.

"You did it, you really did it baby I'm so proud of you!" she screeched, giving him the biggest hug imaginable. At 23 years old Jordanna King was a four-year veteran of AA's, having stripped before that in Orillia and Bracebridge. He'd met the buxom brown-haired chain smoker at a gaming expo in Toronto three summers ago. Their eyes had locked across a Super Mario exhibit that his seven-year old nephew was fascinated with at the time.

She'd been good to him, as far as he knew, and three years later her enthusiasm for his achievements weren't waning. He'd just picked up some beer to celebrate with later. For now they were off to their regular Tuesday night bowling league down on Dumont Street.

He told her how he'd flipped off Norwick and how easy it was to win this time round.

"You know me and SS Werewolf," he said, grinning from ear to ear as he drove.

"Awe baby, I was thinking about you all day, it was driving me crazy," she said, throwing her arm around him again giving him a big wet kiss on the cheek which only broadened his satisfied smile.

At the Rotator Bowling Alleys, they met up with their partners Mike and Sue, who were busy polishing their balls as they arrived. Mike was wearing his lucky black Anthrax shirt, sipping on a large draught of Old Milwaukee as they came in and he greeted them with a sudden excited look and a thumbs-up as he saw Ronnie, trophy in tow.

"Heard about your win - everybody's talking about it," he said, standing up to give Ronnie a congratulatory backslap.

These were his kind of people, thought Ronnie, setting the trophy down on one of the seats.

They'd started bowling two years earlier and together with Mike and Sue were now in the league's Top 10 standings, vying for the Terminator Cup.

They played three games before the first break. Ronnie recorded a strike in the tenth frame of the second game, meaning he bowled two more balls to win that game. The luck was with him. He could see the others saw it too, as he causally threw on his jacket and strutted towards the door draught of Old Milwaukee in hand to go out back for a smoke.

The back lane smelt like it always did - of rotting, uneaten food from the Rotator's kitchen, thrown out at the end of each day into two large brown dumpsters.

No one was back there with him and he was glad he'd put on his jacket - it was getting chilly.

Just down the lane behind a Chinese food joint, he could see two kids playing pig against the back crumbling-brick wall. When the tennis ball bounced towards him, out of reach of the kids he went and picked it up, tossing it back with a smile and a flick of his smoke.

A jeep was coming up the alley behind him, so he stepped aside and backed up against the wall to let it pass.

The red Cherokee stopped behind the restaurant and an elderly bald white man stepped out the driver's door and walked around to greet another older man who came out the restaurant's back kitchen door to meet him.

There was something about the way the Cherokee driver walked that drew Ronnie's attention as he stood smoking in the shadows.

He could barely walk, but that wasn't it. Something about the stride length of his legs and the permanent seeming steps of his feet. Yes, he knew him from somewhere - somewhere a long time ago.

The two men shook hands and the one from the restaurant handed him a large package of food. It was just a pickup, but the identity of the driver continued to gnaw at him.

Walking back slowly with the food, the man placed it on the ground as he opened the driver door, then picked it up, placing it on the passenger side seat before stepping in again slowly and driving off.

Behind him, Ronnie Watson heard the bowling alley door open and Jordanna's voice call out to him saying they were getting ready to start.

But he was in no shape to play another game.

His heart was beating too fast and he was gasping for breath as he watched the Cherokee's lights fading in the distance.

He'd remembered how he knew the man.

Chapter 10

Ethan woke with a start, knocking his book from his chest to the floor.

Squinting at the clock, he righted himself in the chair and listened. It was 1am and he heard it again. Another muffled crash on the main floor by the kitchen.

He tip toed to the door and leaned his head out in the hall. Voices wafted along the corridor, their words he could not discern. Save for the moonlight, the estate was completely dark. Whatever was happening, it was in the hall near the library, but there were no footsteps and there should have been as the entire main floor always creaked like a bastard when anyone came in.

The voices sounded again. Whoever it was wasn't worried about making noise. Moving down the stairs he made the threshold. Through the spindles he could now see long shadows moving across the wall in a flickering, ephemeral light.

Shaking, he unconsciously took a fire iron from the landing hearth, which provided him some confidence as he again descended, more slowly this time, towards the first floor.

Reaching bottom, he could see there were at least two apparitions moving in a translucent mist at the end of the hall just outside the kitchen. The tallest, no more than a shadow, was moving back and forth in place, almost as if frozen in one spot. The shorter one made the same idiotic passes.

They were like holograms, and now, just feet from them, he had the curious impression they couldn't sense he was there.

Hands gripped on the iron, he moved forward, his back hugging the wall. The light was now pulsating and in the flashes the two figures appeared to be fading in and out of view, like glitches in space time.

The photo of his family and Darby had been knocked off the shelf again. This time its glass cover was broke and spread out across the hall's floor.

Intimately close now, the scene crackled with a strange electricity and with his eyes half shut, he reached out and gasped.

Nothing. His hand went right through the tall one.

What is this, he wondered, drawing it back quickly, not pushing his luck.

The one in the library had seemed real - but these were different. Kind of half real - if that made any sense. And now, like the other one, they were fading away.

In seconds he was alone again and knelt where they'd just stood, running his hands across the shards.

Curiously, Darby's face was the only spot in the photo scratched during the fall. Her tiny eyes gazing up at him almost pleadingly. *Why didn't you watch me? Why did you let me go?*

A shudder coursed through him and he quickly turned it over, placing it back on the floor.

Those things - they'd been like thought forms. The photo was really smashed though. Maybe he was still asleep? No, he was there alright, standing in the hall holding a fire iron.

A noise caught his attention and peering back, he could see the front entrance foyer by the stairs bathed in moonlight. But there was something else too, something moving outside on the lawn.

In amazement he could see the grounds were lit up in a brilliant white light - more than any moon could provide. Rushing to the windows, he pressed both hands against the glass and gasped. There were figures, hundreds of them, walking amongst the grounds.

Racing to the side door, he stepped out onto the stone path which led to the lawn, then made his way towards it, slowly at first, out amongst the strange crowds.

It was some sort of outdoor ball. The guests were dressed glamorously, the men in suits, the women in gowns - it looked like it was in the mid-1920s, but it was hard to say.

It was a strange thought, but there was nothing he could do about his own attire. He'd fallen asleep in black slacks and a grey v neck.

At the back of the lawn where his boat should have been, a makeshift bar had been set up.

Lifting a Bee's Knees from an abandoned bar tray he listened as the laughter and chatter centered around a row of tables where a long food spread was laid out.

Groups were gathered in four main areas across the property - the food tables in the centre, the bar at the back, a front area where a stage was lit up and the main side gate by a pool where bathers frolicked and splashed.

Several people nodded his way as he passed, each with courteous, welcoming smiles.

The drink was well made. The sting of the whiskey and seltzer was real enough. Hell, it was a better goddamn Bee's than they made at the Winged Dragon. Just as he thought this, he was cut off by a group of four distinguished looking men who were making their way towards the stage, where a man was preparing a microphone.

Surely he'd awaken at any moment, he thought.

Quiet descended as the men took the stage. Then a woman with long red hair, dressed in a gold metallic lace evening dress and Parisian headband greeted them. Nodding graciously at the woman, the tallest member of the group spoke:

"We are so pleased you all could make it once again to our yearly gathering," he began, a wide grin complimenting his twinkling eyes. Dressed in a dark suit, he tipped his half-filled highball towards the crowd in appreciation. "This all could not have happened if it weren't for the impeccable help my wonderful wife Angelicka has provided us once again this year."

Claps and cheers erupted. The woman half-bowed, gracious and smiling, touching her husband's side as he continued:

"We have a wonderful evening lined up for you, but before we get there I have some important folks I must introduce."

Turning to his left, he acknowledged his stage guests with a snappy regal bow.

"You might know Frankie Jones, leader of the Hub of the Lakes Jazz Quintet," he said, arms sweeping to acknowledge a gaggle of musicians waiting patiently at the curtains.

"I'd also be entirely remiss if I didn't introduce the man behind all the recent changes in these parts, our MP Alexander Cockburn," he said. The crowd erupted in wild applause.

"I'd like to personally thank Alex," he continued. "Because although he's Conservative, we really appreciated the locks being opened in Port Carling and the main road being opened through to Vankoughnet for our, er, rum running."

More applause sounded and nodding to his wife, he handed the mic to Frankie and the curtains rose.

As the band launched into their first number, Ethan continued watching as the couple spoke privately on a small platform above the lawn.

It seemed serious, both his hands gripping her bare shoulders like he was impressing something of great import. Planting a kiss on her right cheek, he then took the stairs to the lawn where Cockburn and two other men dressed in smoking jackets, waited.

Lingering momentarily, the woman stared off into the crowd. Already, heavy banks of smoke hung like phantoms over the lawn. The band were just kicking into their second number as a dance area was cleared. One by one, couples took to the section, gaily moving to an upswing jazz.

Pulling out her own pack of cigarettes, she lit one, then moved down, greeting friends and engaging guests.

Shifting from beneath an old Oak, Ethan moved past the stage following the men who were tracing the western flank of the property. Outside the large house, *his house*, they stopped in its shadows.

Above, endless brilliant stars shone in the primordial darkness, making him and the scene feel almost insignificant. A pair of headlights approached and the man who'd been speaking motioned for it to stop.

A driver stepped out of a chocolate brown Rolls Royce, and opened the right passenger door, allowing a tall man with grey wavy hair and thick glasses to step out. Chin up, his eyes met the others in cold, steely resolve. He moved in curt steps, shaking hands with the entourage. The driver bowed, got back inside the car and drove off.

From his spot in the trees Ethan watched as they entered the building, disappearing behind a set of heavy iron doors into a warm amber hallway.

Moving quickly past a line of vehicles, Ethan paused for a moment before reaching the door. Looking both ways, he quickly turned the brass handle and slipped inside.

A gold and green carpeted hallway stretched into the building before meeting up with another hall that veered left. It was like his estate, but things were different and he marveled at this opportunity to see its earlier incarnation.

Walls were adorned in sconces, old pictures and oil lamps, their main brocades being faint floral patterned scenes. He barely had time to take any of this in before he heard a door slam down the second hall. Following slowly, he passed an entrance with a sign above it that read 'kitchen'.

This passage gave way to marble flooring in an open circular rotunda. Moving to its centre, he tried to figure out the direction the four men had taken. During the day this space would have been lit from above through large skylight windows which hung low in a sunken ceiling. This was now his main living room - he'd just had the same windows replaced and reframed that past summer. But here the room had large stone columns and gold leaf figurines, unlike the cream IKEA wainscoting of his own abode.

Trying a new hall, he ducked into a service area when a door opened suddenly at its far end. The speaker was moving objects from a storage room into another and when he was finished, went inside, while one of the other men, who now looked like a butler, remained in the hall.

When the man turned away, Ethan took his chance, dashing into a pantry the next room over from the one the men were in.

A roll up window at its south end opened into the bigger room, which was a great hall, and he could see them seated on chairs in a semi-circle. Creeping on all fours to cupboard space below the window, he tucked himself in behind a large meat slicer and watched through a slight crack in the divide.

The speaker was holding up a globe, which he motioned to as he talked:

"And so, we can manifest anywhere and at any time while the doorways remain open," he said. "The trick is remembering. We don't 'visit' a place, per se, but manifest within it - as part of its very fabric."

The cold grey haired visitor interjected. "Jack, you needn't explain all this. We are well versed. Did you prepare for the next ceremony? Where will it be performed? And on what date? Charles, you leave on November 23rd, is that right? We need to execute it before then."

Jack, he thought. He seemed almost familiar.

Walking to the wall behind him, 'Jack' drew back a large wooden panel revealing a chalkboard with some writing.

Pointing to its first lines, he said that a ceremony was planned for Halloween.

"It will be conducted on the property in one of our barns," he stated. "It will be two days after the departure of our guests and hired help, providing the prerequisite privacy and adequate space to deal with any.... mistakes."

"We can't let what happened last time happen again," intoned a short fat man. "We must have more patience, allow it to flow smoother."

"Yes," replied Jack. "We were not prepared last time. This time we will be."

"What happened to the boy?" asked the politician, Cockburn. "Did he heal?"

"He's at the infirmary recovering slowly," replied Jack. "It's masking itself as mental illness. The main thing is she has time to recover."

The politician's chair shifted in a series of spastic scrapes backwards and he let out a half cough.

"This time we'll aim for no repercussions," he said firmly.

The short man again spoke up, asking if there would be a reconnaissance beforehand.

"If there isn't one planned, the people I represent are requesting one," he stated.

Jack nodded.

"But only one of us will be making the trip," he told him.

"*But two are needed to verify,*" grunted the short man, a sneer widening across his face.

"Jack's right," interjected the politician. "We all know the rules, but if we are to understand the landscape as soon as possible, we can only send one - the Russian - is that right?"

"Yes"

"You'll pay dearly for another mistake," hissed the short man. "It will only further unnerve our people. They will soon stop trying with her, she's growing old. We have to get her here in order for the rite to work."

"Shall I show you now to the barn?" Jack asked, his gaze shifting to the eyes of the others.

"Yes, by all means," said the visitor, motioning to Cockburn and the rest. "We shouldn't take too long as we have much to discuss even after we return to our guests. Following my speech, I would also like to see the object that has been chosen."

The short meeting over, he watched as they left the room, disappearing into the bowels of the building.

He wouldn't be following them. Something about it had taken a turn for the weird. What were they all talking about? Ceremony? Whatever this was, it felt spooky.

Moments later, he brushed a chamber maid who seemed the first that morning to actually be surprised to see him. Reaching the side entrance, the growing sense of dread crystallized and he wondered if he'd ever truly return home.

On the lawns the crowds were still in full swing dancing and swarming the tables around the bar.

Beyond the makeshift watering hole, a set of stone gates opened onto a small bluffs overlooking the river.

Merging with revelers he was almost through them when he suddenly felt ill.

In seconds, he was back, staring blankly at empty lawns from his cold, leaf strewn porch.

The clock in the living room read 4:23am.

Chapter 11

I

For a long time Ethan stood in silence, trying to figure out what had nudged him towards this second unsettling experience. Was he drugged? No, drugs don't wear off instantaneously. Hallucinations don't either, at least he didn't think they did. And they don't damage the only remaining picture of your adopted missing sister.

Was he losing his mind? During that arduous past year at the paper he'd been under added pressure to perform, but it was nothing he couldn't handle. Could he be sick? A brain tumor maybe? No, brain tumors show other symptoms and otherwise he felt well - more alive than he had in a very long time, in fact.

Another one for the psychological detachment file, he thought, and it was getting full.

It had been like watching an old film, but *he had been there* - hadn't he?

If he were to take it at face value, what would be lost as part of the bargain? The much-hallowed objectivity? Perhaps there were different orders of experience. *He could* simply trust and go with it. But he wasn't there yet. Part of him was sure it was a real time he'd seen and that this character Jack may really once have owned the estate, but the part standing there right now couldn't reconcile.

Wait, he had records. Pulse quickening, he remembered a set of historical documents the estate's previous owner had provided him with when he'd purchased the property in 1998. They were in a chest up in the attic.

Jaunting up the stairs, he grabbed a flashlight from the second-floor landing table drawer. On the third, there was a pull-down ladder. There was electricity up there, at least there was last time he'd checked.

He yanked the cord. The ladder crashed down, missing his skull in the darkness. Stepping nimbly, he climbed into the opening, reaching for the light switch on the nearby joist beam. A dusty bulb surged to life, humming like it was mildly annoyed at being woken.

As his eyes accustomed, he scanned the space, pouring over a scatter of boxes which lay across the floor. The flashlight was dim, but the chest he'd placed the documents in 15 years earlier was still where he remembered.

Climbing all the way in, he crawled over to it and opened the latch. Ethan reached in and retrieved a brown leather satchel.

Taking the deeds in his hands, he aimed them towards the faint light to make out the writing. There were 10 of them with some dated back to the early 1800's. The one he was looking for would be around 1920, or so he reckoned, if their clothing was anything to go by.

One was dated June 12th 1918 and was signed by a Jack Hansen! He'd bought the property from a Shirley L. Graham and attached was a map of the land with deed lines and some information about distances to local water bodies. The document had an attachment of its own - a brown sheet of worn parchment. It was another agreement of some sort, written in a different handwriting than the main document which had been done up properly by lawyers.

Unfolding it, its contents were strange.

Both Hansen and Graham had signed it - an order stipulating Hansen must never disturb the ground in one specific area of the property near the southeast gate. No reason was provided, but a public notary had lent his authorizing stamp. The spot was near where a small vacant guest house currently sat, which had only been used on occasion during his own term of ownership.

Some owner, perhaps Hansen himself, hadn't honored Graham's wishes.

Taking the documents with him, he went to bed.

II

Dust drifted from the roadway later that morning as he put his old blue ford pickup into high gear. It was around 11am Thursday and he was back along the winding roads speeding through the crimson hills towards the farmhouse on Speicher.

There was little traffic - the odd taxi and a few natural gas delivery trucks. As he turned onto the final road before the intersection, he slowed.

He could already see it, way atop its stone outcrop surrounded by lush green fields. Mist was still rising from the river which snaked near him hundreds of feet below and the hummer was still parked out front. Things looked quiet.

The outcrop was surrounded by several cliffs, save for its west end, where the road led in. Stopping his truck close to where he had the previous day, he parked and got out.

Across the road were two fly fishermen and some kids tubing at a small falls. He pulled out the binoculars and adjusted his view.

Besides the hummer, he could now see another vehicle parked behind it. A tarp was drawn over it, but he could still see its front grill - it was another hummer and this one was white.

Out back of the main house the upstairs window seemed to have a large black pole protruding from it, like one of those long, thick microphones they use when shooting movies, but much bigger.

The thing was aimed out over the valley between there and the auctioneer's barn in the distance. It looked like a monitoring device, but for what?

Hearing a splash, he watched as the anglers gently tugged at their lines, sunlight dancing in the cobalt flows. On the opposite shore, a trail led up the cliffs providing a steep climb for whoever dared.

He'd spent most of the previous evening getting ready for his real return, which he planned for that night.

At the local hardware store he'd bought night vision goggles, boots and a handheld GPS. After dinner, he switched into all black clothes and packed his hip waders, in the hopes of crossing the river and taking the trail to the plateau.

From there he'd position himself perfectly and spy on the home with a modicum of good site lines.

It was almost 9:30pm when he drove out again, parking as had become his custom down on the road by the river.

On the opposite shore, he removed the waders, concealed them beneath some brush, found the trail and started his climb. A fairly even slope, it wasn't as tough as he'd imagined. Nobody was around, which was the main thing.

Halfway up he stopped and stared into the limitless night, its dark depths teeming with primordial mystery. As a teen he'd scaled cliffs like this after beach parties along the Scarborough Bluffs. He'd loved those years, back when things were simpler. The family had moved there after their time in Montreal. Right after Darby's disappearance in fact.

He maneuvered through a tangle of dense underbrush, an especially difficult patch of terrain, pulling at tree roots and trunks, using them to yank himself up over the ledges until he could reach higher.

On the plateau, the open grassy space shone like silver, with clumps growing wet from an early dew.

Sitting on a stump, he trained the binoculars on the building.

Some of the windows didn't have blinds and Ethan could see several moving figures.

Scanning the back wall, he saw the top right window with the microphone thing stuck out.

In the next room over, a tall dark haired white woman was speaking with a man.

She was gesturing at some chart, a map of some type with black dots, some with red circles around them.

On the lower floor - in what looked like a living room - an older man leaned forward in a leather armchair pouring over papers he had spread out across a footstool.

Outside on the back deck, a blue tarp covered something big and box shaped. It's edges appeared to have protrusions though, which stretched the tarp outwards in sections.

His binoculars wandered back upstairs. The man and woman's attention were still on the chart and its dots. If they were one of the acronym agencies, they were probably looking into drug shipments, he thought. The District was long known to be a halfway point for dealers looking to get their products north. It might be bigger than that though - possibly terrorism, but both possibilities seemed remote.

To be sure, the device's purpose was for monitoring, gathering or relaying some kind of information. But with today's technology, there was no ordinary data that couldn't be sent from a simple phone, unless it was being used to monitor weather, but then why the gun and the interviewing people?

The pair were now talking animatedly, peering into a screen at the end of a long bank of tables. Nodding, the woman chewed on a pencil when another man, different from the one downstairs, entered the room and handed her a cell. That was four people in the home and none were the two he'd seen at the antiques barn.

The night vision binoculars could take pictures, but he'd have to get closer to achieve anything near clarity.

He wanted to read that chart and the screen. Walking down and back up the other side of the valley wasn't possible. Heading back the way he came and driving closer posed other risks.

Just after midnight, things began to shut down. The main room where the microphone was remained lit and he could see they were taking shifts staying up with it as it monitored whatever it was tracking.

Was it detecting airplanes? That must be it. Air traffic. But then, why not work with the local airport and its radar?

A stir in the loose sand near the cliff he'd just climbed sounded and he froze. There it was again - more falling pebbles and rocks.

The bright full moon had bathed the whole plateau brilliantly and while the edge was further along he could just make out two figures climbing up onto the solid ground between the trees and boulders.

They didn't have flashlights, but he was directly in their trajectory.

Slowly they wound their way along the rim to where he'd come up on the trail. Jumping behind a large boulder, his binoculars fell from the stump in the process and he watched as they revealed themselves to be two males, perhaps both in their early twenties.

One was tall and lanky, the other of middle height. Each carried backpacks and were dressed in dark clothing. They were close enough now that he could just make out their whispers:

"I don't know, I think this is it," said one. "Yes, it's here, this is where we were last night."

The tall one pulled out binoculars, and confirmed to the other there were still people in the farmhouse.

"That means they haven't found anything yet - or not enough," whispered the shorter one. "So last night when you and Mike were here, where did you say it was?"

"It was right there," said the other, pointing almost directly above them.

"Wow. You must have shit your pants."

"Mike has footage," he replied. "We're sitting on it, like the rest. They are getting pretty sneaky though. Threatened his father with litigation, but they have nothing. That was just from Mike's emailing me about it today. I'm living at Jenna's until I find a place, so it's hard for them to find me. Not answering phone calls. Destroyed our cells today."

"When do you think it'll die down?" asked the shorter one.

"When it does - maybe it won't" replied his friend. "If it happens tonight, you'll see what I mean."

Returning to their watch, the pair passed a thermos between them. The shorter one started eating a sandwich.

It was still hard to hear them. What could happen again? His heart was beating louder now, drowning out his own thoughts as he fought to maintain silence behind the large rock.

Then the short one got up, walked a few feet in his direction and bent forward reaching into the tall grass.

"Shit, look at this," he said, holding up the discarded night visions. "Do you think they're fucking with us?"

Without thinking, Ethan stepped out from behind a boulder and spoke: "Guys, I'm right here. I'm not one of them, don't be scared. I'm here following up on something, I don't know what is happening."

They stood frozen, staring at Ethan then at each other before the tall one sputtered some words:

"Are there more of you?" he asked, his body tensed, bracing for assault.

"No one's here but me," Ethan responded, raising his hands slowly.

"We don't know that," the tall one shot back. "We're going now - if you're telling the truth, stay where you are."

Ethan stepped away and watched as they inched back towards the edge of the plateau.

"All I want is my equipment," he half shouted after them. "I'll be on my way then too."

"Hey just wait," he shouted cautiously, one arm still held up.

Hearing this, the two kept moving, but the taller one slowed unexpectedly. A faint thumping could be heard deep in the valley. "Oh fuck," yelled the shorter one. "They're sending a chopper."

It sounded like it. They could all now hear the unmistakable whoomp! of rotors approaching from the hills towards Gravenhurst.

Immediately, they began diving for cover in the boulder field.

"Crawl under them," Ethan shouted. "The rock blocks body heat."

Just as he said it, a searchlight hit the trees at the plateau's edge as they burrowed madly in the dirt, hoping they wouldn't be clipped by its beam.

The machine shot overhead in a first pass, the grass around them lit up hot white as the searchlights engaged across the fields.

For a moment it hovered still over the field to the south, dipping and swaying and blasting static outbursts of radio chatter.

For what seemed an eternity they waited. It then circled three times before flying off slowly to an adjoining plateau. Whoever these people were, they had expensive toys and were well coordinated

Picking up his night visions, Ethan saw it was a jet black hawkish looking thing with no visible markings, sweeping low now through the valley, searching the base of the mountain, its beams dancing along the river banks.

"One of us must have triggered a perimeter alarm," he shouted. "Who are they - What's going on?"

But the pair just stood amongst the rocks, wiping dirt from their clothes.

"It will be tough leaving here not knowing where the sensor is," said the tall one finally, with a quick glance at his friend. "We deviated at the base from the path."

It was now 1:30am and the wind was picking up. They wouldn't be hit by the storm which was passing through the valley's far end, but it was getting cold.

"Are you going to let me know what the fuck is going on," Ethan said again, this time with more force.

"It's tied to the recent sightings," answered the tall one, who was now leaning his head back on a tree.

"What sightings?" he asked, feeling increasingly stupid.

"Of these....things...," said the shorter one. "They're monitoring it closely. Looks like they want to document it or even catch it."
None of it was making sense. Things? That said a lot. Why couldn't he have stumbled upon someone smart who knew how to communicate?

"You need to sit down and listen," the tall one told him "We can't afford having you misunderstand. None of us can."
He introduced himself as Francois, and started to tell his story:

"I first found out about it on the police scanners," he began. "My older brother's into scanners and about two weeks ago the cops got the first call. Out on Forrester Trail in Bracebridge - you know that area?"

He nodded silently.

"Anyways, this cop who was on patrol that night took the call. He went out there and spoke with a person who'd reported something in his back field. The dispatcher said he'd described it as a black humming box, about 30 feet wide and 12 feet high. Said it was about 50 feet in the air, just over the trees, but that it had been closer to the ground near his house. She said he'd sounded extremely scared. Told the officer to be prepared for anything."

Great. They were UFO idiots. He'd met a few at work over the years. Christ, he'd climbed all the way up there just to hear stupidity.

"Anyways, this is at about 10 at night about two Sundays ago," continued the young man. "The cop goes out there, guess he speaks with this guy and then I hear him screaming for backup with all this static in the background. I don't live far from there, so I take my bike to this pasture which overlooks the whole area. I'm there like two minutes and I see it, only it's changing shape, going in and out of this black cloud. Below, these people are running around and this man is lying on the grass, others trying to help him, dragging him away. I could see the cop dragging him back across the grass and this thing's giving off sparks and shining rays everywhere. I had to turn away, the arc was so bright. I could hear more cops arriving - there were about three squad cars. I looked back at this thing and it was now just a ball of pulsing light, giving off this kind of ozone smell. Then it shot straight up and disappeared."

The intensity of his voice was raising some alarm bells. He really believed what he was saying - and none of it was fazing the shorter one, who was staring at the ground, playing with his laces.

"I didn't know what to do - it was freaky, right?" Francois continued. "They dragged the man into the house and I could hear a woman screaming. Police were there all around the property. More police came. I stayed watching for about two more hours. An ambulance took him away. I went home at like 3:30am. The crazy thing is the papers or radio didn't mention any of it. I was told it's up to police to release info to the media, but they never did.

It was so fucked. So I went back the following day on my bike. Down on the property there were all these people with strange machines. A huge section of grass in the lawn was totally burned and they were setting up gadgets all around it taking samples. They were those people from over there."

He was pointing to the farmhouse, where the one upstairs room with the microphone still had a light on.

Maybe they don't know we're here, Ethan thought, looking back towards the young men.

Maybe they thought they were just animals.

"So I checked what I could find out about the man who was hurt," the young man continued. "My mom works at the hospital and said they had someone come in badly burned. Relatives freaking out when he died. She thought they were all lying - covering up for how he'd really got burned. Didn't believe a word until *these* guys showed up and had a talk with staff. She begged me not to mention it to anyone. Said the man died the next day and that his body was taken away by them. Flown out in a metal container."

He shook his head as if trying to escape from a bad dream.

"I stayed that day until one of the vehicles left," he continued. "I followed it past my own house then went in my backyard to look out over the whole town to see where it went. They ended up here."

So they were like him, thought Ethan, happened upon this place, but in a different way, interested in learning more - just like he was.

"My friend Mike and I started coming up here checking out what they were doing," Francois continued. "They have some weird stuff. They're interested in the far side of the valley against the hills. They've been interviewing people too. Well, that was after the other sightings. Other weird stuffs happening too. People appearing in backyards or banging on people's doors. Cops have no idea. By the time they get there, it's all over."

"Scanner's been goin' crazy for the past week and a half," he continued. " It's like it's intensifying. And these people over there do not fuck around. The minute something's heard on the scanners, they are there fast. Police refer to them as 'bingos' on the scanner. The minute they show up they take right over from the cops. Now police are not even responding to the calls. Scanners haven't been as busy though for the last three days. Total clampdown, but we know it's still happening. Saw it last night. They're trying to draw it out."

It was a lot to swallow. It was too crazy. Where could he even start?

In the bay in the distance the whitecaps rolled in towards the Lake Muskoka shoreline, crashing unceremoniously. Overhead they could see the lights from the chopper swaying out over the lake, making several passes, on its way back to wherever it was from.

Inside Ethan felt something stirring up, climbing out from the depths of his being into clear awareness. The stuff at the estate and now this. They all felt something.

The trees on the plateau bent gently as the wind picked up. They might have to deal with the edge of that storm after all.

"And what do you think 'it' is?" he finally asked them.

"Nobody knows," replied the tall one. "There are waves of it happening in different places right now. People say it can appear like anything."

"But you said this thing you saw looked like a box."

"It did to me," he replied. "But it changed shape. Whatever it is, it's fucked up. And deadly. I'm not even finished telling you."

"Last night my friend Mike and I did a stake out. We came up here about 10 and the thing appeared again, this time just as huge pulsating lights. There were five of them, flying around each other. Then they joined as one huge ball of light. The people in the farmhouse were watching - it was right above here in the sky. At different corners of the valley we saw flashes go off when the thing appeared. We think it's their equipment - some kind of correlation technology. We found one of the boxes on the ground this morning. It had a huge light sensor on it. We have photos."

"You're saying they're instrumenting the area then, documenting it," he said.

"Yeah, that and filming it," replied the tall one. "It's all they can do. Gather info bit by bit. You can tell they don't know much by how they're always arguing with each other."

His voice lowered almost instantly as the dull distant thumps became slightly louder.

"But they caught on to us," he whispered. "They tracked our cells when we found their box. Must have had a monitoring device with it to track cells in the area. Mike emailed me and they traced his email too.

Showed up at his parents place, scared the shit out of them with threats. We both destroyed our phones, but hid the photos good. We took footage of the lights too, but it's blurry just like all the footage on the net." He looked at his friend like they were silently deciding on whether to say more.

"Do we have to get into this part right now?" asked the short one.

"Yes, we fucking have to get it into it now," snapped his friend. "We all need to be on the same page. It's not going to be pretty if he doesn't get with the program."

Listening to this, Ethan sensed his already makeshift world fragment a little more, spinning off as his thoughts raced through rabid, fantastic scenarios. Like an unknown, incalculable machinery, a labyrinthine, unexpected manifold was slowly being revealed. *Clam it shut. Go home, get some rest.*

The tall one snapped his fingers.

"This thing is very old," he said. "Actually, it's timeless. They think we exist in time and space and that this thing doesn't. They call this here around us 'easy reality' because the thing can penetrate it at will, manipulating and changing things."

How did this kid know so much? He wished he'd never seen the men at the auction.

"Whatever it is can appear as anything, they think," he continued. "When it appears, it's only because it wants to be seen. They don't know why. There are theories it wants to set the pace in our collective consciousness - be the demarcation line between human knowns and unknowns, that way it can regulate us to control us, potentially mislead us."

"Mislead us?" Ethan asked. "What does that even mean?"

"Think about it," said Francois. "If it leads us with certain imagery, we make assumptions about reality like 'there are aliens and demons.' But you have to ask - what would we be thinking naturally about reality on our own without that imagery guiding our dreams, progress and science fiction? What realization or knowledge is it that it wants to guide us away from? Are we really destined to send robots to other planets forever in the hopes of one day learning more about physical reality or can we achieve mastery over it and learn to manipulate dimensions and space time ourselves? Remember: that which controls the information, controls the situation."

"Where did you get all that?"

"The Net," he shrugged.

His own thoughts kept swirling. They were like a great whirlpool, coalescing and merging what he'd experienced already and what the young man was telling him.

The kid was deep, but it was way too much to digest. They had to deal with the situation at hand.

Half dazed, he peered out from the boulders back towards the farmhouse. The light was off now. Glancing at his watch, it was almost 3am.

"Should we stay here?" he asked. "We could go back the way I came in. Do you have a vehicle? I could give you a lift..."

"We could try," responded the Francois. "No car. We got dropped off by Mike. Can you retrace your steps exactly?"

He didn't know, but it was decided they'd have to try.

At the rim, they began their descent, stopping at points to regroup and chart the remainder of the route. In 15 minutes they'd reached the access point at the river. They waded across and moved up onto the dark road. The blue pickup was still there, just up from where they emerged, gleaming ready in the mist.

"It's late. I can take you into town," said Ethan, fumbling for the keys.

But then Francois grabbed his arm, telling him to keep still.

"You have to be extremely careful," he whispered, crouching down to inspect the vehicle's undersides. Slowly, he crawled around the whole truck, checking each tire well.

Besides their own footprints the sand around them appeared untouched. Francois suggested they retreat back to below the riverbank and use the remote starter, which they did.

Click. The thing turned over smoothly.

On the highway, not far from Bracebridge, Ethan spoke with them quietly.

"You can stay with me for now," he said. "Might be better if they are already on to you – unless you want to risk going back. Might make more sense to really hide someplace they won't be thinking of."

"You're optimistic," said Francois. "They may be waiting for us when we arrive, but yeah, they know where we live, so who knows..."

As they turned on to Vankoughnet Road, the neighborhood looked quiet - the property did too as they headed up the long driveway through the woods.

Parking, Ethan thought of Saara for the first time that day.

It was early Friday morning and in another 24 hours she'd probably be on the island. It was hard to focus on the case now, it seemed several worlds away, almost insignificant even, given what he was learning.

'Only one world can fully occupy a person at one time'.

His old high school English teacher Brian Hayes told him that. Hadn't really known what it meant until now.

After showing them to their rooms, he drew a warm bath. Dimming the lights, he lit an incense stick and sparked a joint, mesmerized as the two smokes mixed with steam.

His mind drifted and a certain realization came: It was totally insane. All of it.

The summer itself had been out of control, but here in his inner sanctum he still felt protected.

Somehow they slept and it was around 8am when he awoke. The others were up already, down in the kitchen, making eggs.

In the bathroom mirror he studied his forehead creases, which seemed to be getting deeper.

Chapter 12

Ronnie still wouldn't talk and every time she tried to ask about it he just grew more distant.

Jordanna King was getting worried. It had been two full days of silence. He'd stayed in their bedroom playing SS Werewolf on loud, barely touching any of the meals she brought him. He'd never been like this before and she was starting to feel helpless.

Finishing up the last of the dishes, she peeked once again into the bedroom and saw that this time he was sleeping. It was four o' clock Friday afternoon and her shift started in another hour.
She'd just walk to work, no need to wake him. Maybe the extra sleep was all he needed?

At 4:45pm Ronnie heard the front door shut as Jordanna left to go strip. Tossing in bed, he found an agreeable position staring up at the ceiling and absently clicked off the TV - it'd been pumping out screams and machine guns all day.

Now it was silent, but images still flashed in his mind. For two days he'd tried blocking them out but they weren't budging. Instead, more old memories were surfacing. He'd thought he'd killed them all off long ago. They were screaming out for action.

In the kitchen he pitched what was left of Jordanna's meatloaf, as it had gone cold on their bedside table. In the bathroom he took a warm shower, then dressed and went outside for some fresh air. It was getting colder and he wondered if Jordanna had covered up.

Taking a long drag on his smoke, the pain still remained. Seeing that man had been enough to make him cry in private and Ronnie Watson did not fucking cry. Not since he was 10 anyway. That's when he became Ronnie Watson, not the weakling weirdo who'd been passed around orphanages like a worn-out football. No, he'd found 'the strength' and moved forward. That's what you do when you have nobody, get strong and never look back.

Finding Dr. Harold Waters had been relatively easy. A simple Google search and he had his address and lots of other details. The old cunt was all over Facebook commenting on shit.

A check with the local police license database he and his friend hacked back in May revealed the SUV's ownership. *Waters. That was his name.* He was just Dr. W to the kids way back when.

Packing some things, he was soon in his silver Camaro, racing through the streets to get it over with.

1015 Gorge Way. Should be easy to find. But these last few days hadn't been easy and his knuckles were turning white as he waited for the red to change at 4th and Landsdowne. When it finally did, he shot forward, catching a glint of light in the rear view off the Fabarm Marshall 12 gauge sticking out of the duffle.

The neighborhood near Landsdowne had changed in the last 10 years. Now on Friday nights, there were more punks and meth heads out than in years past. Gangbangers and addicts with no hope - the projects were breeding them faster than the City could handle. At least he hadn't ended up like them, he reminded himself, chomping on another cig. No fucking way.

Switching lanes, he pulled onto Gorge which was down close to the waterfront. 1015 was up on the left. A stately three floor affair. The Dr. had done well for himself.

Coasting to the end of the street, he idled in the darkness by a parkette. It was 7pm and most of the neighborhood was already quiet. At 7:30 he zipped up the duffel, straightened his hair and stepped out into the chill night air. A few minutes later he was standing in the backyard at 1015 after letting himself in through a tall wooden gate.

Placing the bag down, he pulled out the Fabarm. The steel felt bone cold in his hands as he maneuvered it around an old wishing well. There was a light on in the living room and through a window he could see Waters dozing in a chair as a TV droned. He must've been in his 80's or 90's now. Looked frail.

Unlatching a gate on the home's east side, he entered a short alley leading to a side entrance. Finding it unlocked, he slipped inside.

Waters lived alone, he'd got that much from his sister's Facebook page. In the kitchen he could hear him snoring in the other room as CTV aired a piece about safe trick or treating.

After locking the door and fixing the silencer, he walked out into the living room and shot him twice in the forehead. The body let out a moan, shook for a minute, then fell to the floor, dead still.

Turning off the TV, he marveled at how he'd always hated television. Something about the pointlessness of everything on it.

News was ok, but only for important stuff. He only checked in on the news a few times a year. Jordanna said he was like a diver coming up for air.

The rug was soaking up the blood, but there was way more than it could handle. Bits of skull everywhere too and his hand was shaking from the shots, which was slightly unsettling. No immediate satisfaction though. He'd known there wouldn't be. That only came when the memories disappeared. That's how it had gone with William Johnson.

God, he hadn't thought about him for years. Thought he would've been the last, not the first.

Something this time though made him pause before leaving.

Leaning the Fabarm against the wall, he ran upstairs to the master bedroom.

What he was looking for - the names of some of the others maybe? A picture or something? He'd know it if he saw it.

In the toilet off the bedroom he washed his hands, then went back in and started going through the dresser. It was full of knick knacks and pennies, a couple of old watches, socks and underwear. Not much else was in the closet either - suits, dress shirts, belts and ties.

A desk at the room's far end edged out from the wall. Beside it was a filing cabinet.

Opening it, there was mostly just personal medical association documents, some home insurance cards, golf memberships and a subscription to a senior's health magazine.

Above the desk though was a small wall safe he'd missed. The combo was in an old address book at the bottom of the cabinet along with a few social media passwords and credit card info.

Cracking it, he found an old leather binder atop some banking information. He took it out and emptied it on the bed.

Its documents were old and fraying at the edges. The words 'Muskoka Centre' appeared on some. It wasn't his group, but he was getting warmer.

Gathering them up, he placed them back in the binder, zipped it, then threw it under his arm.

Wiping everything down with a towel, he retraced his steps through the house, leaving it just as he'd found it, save for the corpse and pooling thick blood. They'd never trace the gun.

It was just after 2am when Jordanna got home. Tiptoeing into the bedroom, she snuggled up close, wrapping her warm arms around him. This time, instead of a cold, lifeless body, she was greeted with a tender embrace and some half-asleep murmuring.

Well, that was different, she thought, hugging Ronnie even tighter.

In the morning, it was even more apparent something *had* switched his mood.

Over breakfast he talked excitedly about an upcoming tournament in Orillia. Then, clearing the table, he actually started running water to do dishes. She thought about this all over a bowl of love crunch.

Asking him about the last two days seemed almost pointless now, but she couldn't help it:

"Babe, I don't want to sound like a broken record, but I need to know what was bothering you," she said cautiously. "I mean, it's great you're feeling better, but it's not normal to go distant like that for no reason."

The dish clutter came to a stop and she could see he was upset.

Head down and arms tensed, his knuckles clawed the edge of the sink.

But then, after a few seconds, his shoulders became more relaxed and he mumbled something like "it was no big deal."

Turning to face her, his pout turned to a wide smile.

"*I know*," he said. "Let's go up to Parry Sound today and check out some of those spots we haven't been to yet. We could go for a booze cruise, check some shit out and go out for lunch."

It was avoidance, but there was some movement, which was always good. Maybe if she went along with it she'd pull it out of him when he was drunk. That's what the booze cruises were - he got drunk and she got high - they'd been doing it for years.

"Sure," she said, camouflaging her concern, "we haven't been up there in awhile."

While he showered, she made the bed and aired the windows in the musty bedroom. Pulling the sheets out to bring them in properly, a leather binder that'd been tucked between the mattress and the frame came out.

Opening it, she read the first page of some old worn out papers that were inside. The header on one read 'Muskoka Centre: Group 11C-222'.

Dated May 15th, 1981, the introduction outlined a new therapy regime for adolescents exhibiting anti-social behavior:

'It is proposed to continue research on problems critical to a clarification of the fundamental aspects of the stimulus-response relationship in biological systems.'

And then:

'Studies will be conducted on the geography of the brain in selected subjects to determine the locus in which stimulations will produce specific reactions.'

In the subsequent pages there were pictures showing children in beds hooked up to wires being administered drugs intravenously. Hearing the shower stop, she quickly stuffed it all back inside and placed it back beneath the mattress.

After hitting the liquor store, they ended up visiting Honey Harbour instead of Parry Sound after getting lost in a residential maze in Swiston, which she thought was basically the asshole of the world.

"For fuck's sake, Ronnie, we can't keep going around in circles," she said. "Get me to a highway!!"

"Ok, ok," he agreed, cock eying the map and spilling pilsner all over it in the process. "I just don't get why the road took us here. What is this - Koonstra Street? That's not even on this thing. Ok, whatever. Take a left at the next intersection. That'll get us to Highway 12."

"I'm starving," she continued, turning onto 12. "Think you can lead us to food?"

"Yep. Why don't we go up there to that Denny's? Over there on the right."

She'd make extra sure not to ask for more directions. She had shit to do. Since he hadn't been working, she'd started babysitting, sometimes at the drop of a hat and her aunt had texted her while they were lost.

"It's alright babe," he said sleepily, finishing a dry, stale tuna melt. "You go do that and I'll work on my game. Jeff's going to run me through the paces tonight on Foresight. It's the new one from Nevada."

At 7pm he dropped her off at her aunt's house in Orillia which was about 25 minutes north of Barrie.

"See you at midnight," he said, planting a big smooch on her lips.

Back on the road, he checked his watch and gunned the motor. At Highway 12 he turned west barreling back through the now foggy hills towards Penetang. Lighting a smoke, he fidgeted in the vinyl seating trying to grab the paper he'd stuffed in his jacket.

'Dr. Ian Somatara' it read. '48 Clayton Court.'

Finding the place was easy. He'd seen the home earlier with Jordanna. It was another big one. And in a less dense neighborhood.

This time he parked further away, on the other side of a field. 'Stream Chase', it was called.

It was colder than the previous night and he was glad he'd worn layers, although this didn't include proper footwear. Halfway through the field he'd already endured a few soakers.

The wetlands ended abruptly at a set of well manicured embankments. The home he was looking for - a large two-story with a faux cupola loomed over top of one and he started his ascent.

At the top he hopped a small iron fence into the backyard, pausing behind a small bunkie that faced the home behind a large pool. The yard was silent save for the soft hum of a pool spider making its rounds.

Squinting, he could see there was a west entrance to the backyard opening beneath a large brown awning. Side entrances were his thing. Even with gaming he always had the most luck with them.

His sneakers squeaked as he snuck along the lawn at the pool's edge. Once past the garden, he kept to the wall and made it to the side door.

Locked, he found a nearby window well, knelt down and peered through its mud stained glass. Using his pocket knife he jimmied its screen off and pried open a pane. He went in head first, falling about four feet after squeezing through, slamming his left cheek hard into a cement floor, softened only slightly by a dark shag carpet.

Thankfully, the home was quiet and he wondered if the doctor was in.

Pitch black, there was no telling how big the basement space was save for a dim nightlight flickering faintly on a far wall.

Waiting a moment to collect his bearings, he crawled towards it, to where he could just make out what looked like stairs. Reaching out, his fingers traced the edge of the first step and he slowly stood up, ready to climb.

Then Wham! Something hit him hard in the chest, sending him flailing back, careening through the room, disoriented and seeing stars.

His head cracked against a glass table edge and he immediately felt sick, curling into a ball, then vomiting in convulsions, clutching his searing, throbbing chest.

"*You fuck,*" said a voice and suddenly there were lights.

A blurry figure raced towards him. Throwing his hands up in a feeble attempt to stop another blow, it was too late. Down it came, with a metal chair this time, crushing his right shoulder upon impact.

"*Fucking little shit,*" the voice was saying, and he could see tables being flipped as the figure moved in for the kill. Without thinking, he grabbed a small ceramic bowl from the floor and slammed it straight into the face of his attacker. A howl rang out and the figure fell, gyrating in wild spasms.

Leaping to his feet, right arm swinging like a rag doll's, he jumped on top of the man, pressing one side of his skull with his good shoulder, then bashing it repeatedly with the jagged end of a splintered table leg.

He felt the body's strength recede with each blow until it grew limp, then wet in the carpet.

Even when he stopped he wasn't sure if it was Somatara.

But there in the bright fluorescents he could finally see outlines of the once familiar doctor's face come into focus, staring up at him through smashed glasses, crushed cheeks and broken, mangled teeth.

"Do you know who I am?" he screamed down into the bashed and bruised mess.

Staring up, a toothless smile half formed in the head's bludgeoned, torn lips.

"Y'thuh," it spat, pools of blood pouring from the corners. "Y'thuh....."

"That's fucking right," he replied, breaking the leg right off its hinging. *"That's fucking right."*

"Sh...the..., shhhthe really, reeeeeallly, li, liked youuuu...." said the skull, it's awful, desperate smile growing wider.

Bringing the leg square down on it, they were the last words he heard.

Repeating the move maybe 30 times until he and it were breathless, he fell back, exhausted and void, closing his eyes as tightly as he could.

"Yesssss," he spat, wheezing and clutching his chest, a wild pain singing from his dead arm as tears began flowing uncontrollably.

"Yesss....." he repeated again between sobs, his face drenched in salt and sweat. "Yesss, yess, sh, sh, shhhheeee did."

For two hours he lay still, breathing in calm shallow breaths, there beneath the fluorescents, afraid to look anywhere besides the ceiling. At 11:30pm he fought the room and rolled over, pulling out his cell with his one good arm.

"Babe - I've had one too many," he texted. "You'll have to get a ride home from your aunt. Sorry about the inconvenience. I'm staying here tonight and will be back in the morning. Love you."

Chapter 13

Bundled in her RW & Co trench, skinny jeans, white silk scarf and shades, Saara sat quietly on a bench at the public docks in Baysville. She'd arrived an hour early, time enough to go over her plans and think more about the case as she waited for the ferry.

Others seemed to have had the same idea and she watched as people strolled lazily along the walkways.

A cool front had moved in overnight, requiring some last-minute packing with the additions of sweaters, hoodies and pullovers. This had meant a couple of extra bags, which she'd piled around the bench at her feet.

Mid-lake, just below the horizon, she could see the tip of the Mohawk Belle Steamship jutting out of a morning fog bank, an almost mythical sight in the mist as its horn blew signaling noon. She was coasting inland from her first cruise of the day preparing to board the new arrivals at 12:30.

While it was still early, Saara decided some fries would tide her over until the trip. Johnny's Ice Cream Hut had popped up about a year earlier on the main walkway to satisfy the tourists' insatiable cravings for sweets.

At the counter she inquired about how business had been that summer.

"It was great," responded Johnny breezily. "But I could do without all the criminals."

Middle aged and snotty, Johnny wore one of those little 50's sailor hats which hid what was left of some patchy black side hairs on both sides of his head.

His rock star grade leather skin also impressed her and she could almost see a cigarette dangling from the edge of his mouth as he scooped deeply into a freshly opened tub of Kodiak Fudge for a youngster ahead of her.

"*That's* not a very nice way to refer to tourists," she replied sarcastically, before parroting a local shopkeeper mantra: "They're the lifeblood of the local economy."

"Didn't mean them, I meant the criminals," said Johnny, suddenly eyeing her up. "Lots of crime here in the bay this past summer. Some of it serious."

Being with the paper she'd already heard a little bit about it. An upswing in pickpockets, vandalism and vehicle thefts, as well as hookers. She listened as he recounted that list, adding a couple of muggings in for good measure.

There was 'a different crowd' going to the island these years, he said, "the rich. Big flashy boats."

"It's under new ownership," he said."I'd have people filling up with gas here talking about all the wild parties. Between that and the vandalism, it's been a parade of craziness all summer."

"So it's been pretty bad," she concluded.

"Does a frog have a watertight arsehole?" asked Johnny.

Paying for the fries, she strolled out onto the finger docks, watching as sailboats bobbed in the now shimmering waves. The sun was finally coming out and the thought of being away for a week was relieving.

At 12:30 she boarded the steamer. It would be a cruise for the better part of an hour, so she hiked up to the top deck bar for a gin and tonic. The boat was full and children were everywhere, running the halls, climbing benches and spying through portholes. Their parents seemed in a constant state, endlessly searching and calling their names.

In a quiet booth, she leaned back and exhaled a sigh of relief, her thoughts already mingling with the ship's gentle lilts as it navigated the waves.

They settled on a point in time early in the case, just after the girls disappeared when she and Ethan had made the initial decision to pursue things together.

On one of those early nights she'd stayed at the estate for the first time in a room overlooking the front lawn. Below its second-floor balcony was the Noctivagus garden and just beyond it a slight indentation in the hillside, populated with thick maples and oaks.

Further on between the woods and the river lay a soft ultramarine bank of moss and that night - it was mid July, she'd lain awake listening to the song of a whippoorwill in the marsh.

In the stillness its gentle, firm, coos were hypnotic. Sipping her gin, she couldn't help but notice how it was this memory that came into focus now, just as she was starting to relax.

Footsteps in the garden that night - it must have been around 11:30 - had broken up the distant song and she'd jumped out of bed to investigate. The moon, incredibly vivid, had lit everything in brilliant silver tones and she'd stood on the balcony listening as the steps came closer, crossing the cobblestone path through one of the garden's main trellis areas towards the gate. Its rusty hinge creaked, and it was then she'd become slightly worried, as she knew Ethan was asleep in the adjacent room snoring loudly.

Tiptoeing to the edge, she'd peered down and seen a tall dark figure - a man - bent over examining a box on one of the white iron garden tables. He was in no way attempting to conceal himself, which was weird, as he stood confident and relaxed in a black velvet smoking jacket, a pipe in one hand, its smoke curling up past her in the still summer air.

Breathing in the intoxicating fume, she'd watched as he turned the box over as if looking for an opening.

She hadn't known if it was a dream, but suddenly he'd turned at the sound of a breaking twig down near the river. Beyond, in the moss bank, which was completely enshrouded at that hour in fog, figures could be seen walking in a column carrying torches. Gently he placed the box down, unaware of her presence, and crept over to one of the garden pillars, watching the procession and following it from pillar to pillar as they shuffled by.

She didn't remember seeing him leave. Didn't remember anything beyond that really, just that she'd clutched the cold metal balcony railing when she returned after finding herself in the garden half naked. Never mentioned any of it to Ethan even.

The boat's bar area was now filling up. A few couples and spinster solitaire types. Ordering herself another gin and tonic with lime, she grabbed it from the bartender and headed back out to the deck.

Outside, the big island was just coming into view. They were emerging from a tight channel that lay between a smaller island and a craggy point stretching out from the mainland. As a child she'd sailed the lake in the same ship with her mother and had always loved this spot.

The same two cottages were still there, perched atop the mainland jetty, hovering over the watery pass like guards monitoring the divide between two lands.

Of course the small island now boasted an ultramodern cottage, complete with three black speed boats tucked away in a cavernous boathouse. It was the last way tier in her mind before Bohemian Island and it dawned on her that a new and potentially dangerous chapter of the investigation was about to begin.

She shouldn't worry about Ethan, she told herself, playing with her tiny drink umbrella. Determined to start the week with a buzz, she headed back in to order another.

In the doorway she collided with a tall red-haired woman who'd made for the entrance at the same time. Stepping back to allow her ahead, she watched as this exotic creature, all taut-cheek bones and tantalizing allure, did a double take, her wide green eyes catching her own with a curious look.

"Saara Khan - Well, I don't believe my eyes - it's me - Rebekkah - Rebekkah Charleton from Wynnford Heights."

Smiling back, she hid an immediate slight annoyance at being recognized by anyone - it was supposed to be her own private trip.

"Of course, of course, how long has it been - nearly 20 or more years?" she found herself saying.

"I never forget a face and *yours especially*," replied the woman. "You are as beautiful as ever. Are you with anyone? I'm taking a week's vacation on the island - need some R & R. Will you be staying as well? Can't believe I've run into you."

This beautiful former grade school 'friend' was going to pose problems, she thought, as she continued to force beams of surprised happiness.
"Why yes, I am," she replied. "I'm much the same as you, just a vacation - funny running into you here after all these years."

Still stuck in the entrance, they quickly found a booth starboard side and settled in with their drinks.

A volley of chirps established parts of her acquaintance's story. Rebekkah had been married with no children but that had ended badly five years earlier. Now an insurance adjuster working in Toronto, which was roughly two and a half hours south of them. She too had remembered childhood visits to the cottage country district fondly and chosen this vacation following the recent death of her 84-year old mother.

Before Saara could speak, the Captain's voice crackled over a loudspeaker to say the ship was arriving. Gulping down their remainders, they gathered their purses and agreed to continue once they were settled.

On the dock, photographers busily snapped photos of the arriving guests while a small brass band played something light.

Rebekkah was playing the country travel thing to a hilt, having brought a huge, vintage travel crate with her. Saara watched as she moved on ahead beneath a large yellow sun hat, dangling a cigarette between carefree fingers.

Their luggage wasn't far behind, travelling towards the main lobby in a bulging golf cart operated by an employee dressed in the island's standard red and blue uniform.

The plan was to meet up in a day or so for dinner and they parted after checking in at the lobby front desk.

Wandering through the large entrance hall towards the elevators, Saara took in the gorgeous pine flooring and high arching rooflines. The Ojibway motifs seemed to reach out to her, as did the stunning art and sculptures dotting the hotel's low-lit hall spaces. She watched as Rebekkah's hat floated off through a bustling corridor amidst businessmen and holiday goers at the lobby's far end.

Her own room was up on the 4th and stepping out of the elevator, she followed an attendant to room 415.

The room was a spacious delight complete with queen size bed, snazzy off bathroom and a reading room for guests. The floors and walls in the bath were tiled in Tuscan marble and granite and for a moment she took it all in as the bellhop left her things in the bedroom.

Tipping him, she closed the door gently, then turned, ran and jumped on the bed. This would be her home for the next seven days and she was going to make the most of it.

The room's wall sized window curtains were half open revealing an extended view of a dark autumn lake and its deep forest hillsides. The panorama overcame her and she suddenly wished she had someone to share it with.

After slipping out of her clothes she drew a hot bath. It was a trip ritual. Christen it with foamy luxury. Soaking, she thought about the hotel being ancient with twisting, mysterious hallways owing to its octagonal, many leveled design.

It seemed one of those places where if you weren't watching you could get lost and not find an elevator for at least twenty-three minutes.

It was old. That part was fact.

Skimming one of the room brochures she read how it had been around since the 1800's with several wing additions since. With the help of some old black and white photos in the brochure, she imagined what it had actually been like back during its heyday, at the socialite parties, lake regattas and what not.

She'd noticed the halls were lined too with vintage pictures of gatherings and scenes of fancy dress. ballroom dancing and moonlit soirees. Some big names had played there too - Doc Holiday, Chester Baker and even a young Jimmy Page when he travelled with the Yardbirds. As she dreamed, she envisioned the bands making their way north to the hotel from the city, first by train, then steamship, then by limo and foreign-sounding cars.

Through the walls she could hear the tall pines playing a slow waltz of their own as bustles of leaves danced across the lawns.

The original hotel had character and vacationers were still drawn to it partly due to its mythic Muskoka reputation and ambiance. Sinking into the suds, she lit a joint and imagined a giant wind face blowing gusts of O's outside and it didn't feel out of place.

She'd use Rebekkah as a foil if need be, might come in handy as a cover. She could gather info and hang with her from time to time, no harm in that.

But where to start. There was still no call from Ethan and he wasn't answering his cell.

At six she went down to the hotel's main dining lounge, a circular room which had been built around a heavy central wooden beam. The tables were located around its perimeter, each with an expanded view of the front lawn and beach areas.

During her meal she poured over an island map. Her seat overlooked the hotel's south end and according to the dotted lines, the original supply entranceway to the hotel's main complex was still located there replete with original docking system. The restaurant's kitchen was in roughly the same area and she hoped to scope this spot out while out on reconnaissance later. It was likely that the women would be brought to this end of the property, she thought, and not the main docks to the north, so as to not cause suspicion.

Over a few glasses of Pinot Grigio, she searched the shorelines. It was getting dark and the dining room candlelight was competing with the outdoors for her attention.

Eating hurriedly, she billed the meal to her room and took advantage of the dying light for a walk through the grounds.

Slipping out a side door off the lobby, she found her way down a winding staircase to the lawn, to a set of bowling greens. Strolling towards a boardwalk that followed the shore, she could see a group of chefs had gathered outside the kitchen near a smoked salmon shack. Amidst bilious cigar and cigarette smoke, they were on a break, enjoying a few evening drinks.

Anyone being dropped off here after dark would have easy access to the entire grounds.

Looking back up at the hotel, she could see her own lonely room up on the fourth.

Good. There'd be a direct line of sight for anything coming or going.

Back in her room the vigil began. She even had a small bar fridge for company.

Chapter 14

Ronnie stared at his wounds, as the cool autumn air worked futilely to soothe them through the open car window.

It was getting colder and he looked to see if the blanket he'd taken from the basement couch was drying. Nope, not yet. He might have to use his own shirt to stop the latest surges of bleeding.

He'd headed north from Somatara's home at noon when he'd awoken. Now in the small village of Bala, he'd made it to the Moon River where it divided the town at the old railway crossing.

Jordanna had sent several texts before his phone died. He'd responded to one, saying not to tell the cops.

The three deep gashes in his shoulder throbbed but the rest was numb, flopping like a broken horse leg and he wondered when the decay would set in. He'd parked beneath the rail line to clean the blanket which had been caked in blood, plus mud and pitch from the marsh.

It was a relatively secluded spot. On one of the tunnel's graffiti covered walls he'd spied an electricity receptacle, which to his surprise worked. His phone was charged and he bit his lip as he punched in Jordanna's number for a second time, against his better judgment.

"Baby, I can't tell you where I am," he explained over the screaming. "I'm hurt and there's still something I have to do. I need you to have faith. I'll tell you everything when I get back."

"Bullshit," she wailed. "This is so serious. I want to be with you right now. I need to help you. Oh my god babe, what is happening? Tell me where you are so I can come and be with you. Baby, pleassssse..."

He imagined her crying, standing there, chain smoking in the cool blue of their apartment.

"Charlie misses you," she sobbed, "Please come home. I'll come and get you right now"

"I'm going now," he said simply. "I'll call you in a bit."

With that, he ended the call. There was nothing he could tell her yet.

Lighting the last of his cigarettes, he watched as the blanket swayed on the tree branch he'd hung it on, like a truce that wasn't working.

The cell service was patchy, but he'd seen Barrie Police were investigating their first murder of the year after being called to a waterfront address that morning.

Pulling the makeshift map he'd made onto his lap, he pondered his next destination, but stopped short when he suddenly couldn't breathe. This caused him to drop his cell out the open car window into the dirt.

There were waves of nausea and he shuddered as, for the first time in over 25 years, a long repressed image danced into his mind.

Floating there in the darkness of the trees at the old centre, it was staring down on him, from directly above, in that rotting, rusty playground.

NO!, No, go away, he moaned. *GO AWAY!*

Snatching the still wet blanket through the window, he wrapped it furiously around his arm as his body shuddered in violent spasms.

It was a face he'd never wanted to see again, but it was there, in the branches where it always was during his lessons. Symbols now - too many of them, flooded his mind as his body engulfed in sweat.

Listen to her. Listen with your mind.

I don't know how. Make it stop.

What is it saying? Can you understand it?

I can't breathe. I'm dying, make it stopppp. Make her stop...

Slashing the dash with his keys, he howled out in pain, head spinning as he tried catching his breath.

Focus, just focus. The tree. I like trees. It's a strong tree. I'm under the bridge in a car. This blanket is warm.

Everything... is alright.

Chapter 15

Ethan closed the rattling shutters in the kitchen for the second time that day. After getting to know one another, it was now 7pm Sunday just after dinner and the storm front that had threatened rain the last 24 hours was firing its first shots.

Francois Charlebois, from Kingston Ontario, he'd learned, was into triathlons, scanners and girls, while Ivan Wolfewicze had moved to Canada from Serbia when he was 7, escaping a life of petty crime and poverty. His specialty was computers, but it was their shared love of scanners that had brought them together. Both were impressed with Ethan's credentials, Francois especially. His father had been a newsman early in life, before trading in his press pass for an IT degree in the 80's.

They were now in the main living room. Ethan struggled to balance a heavy wooden box he'd pulled from storage in the garage. It was an early model scanner, a relic of the late 90's, but it was digital, just barely. Francois thought it might still do the trick.

After plugging it in and switching the on button, sure enough, the thing lit up, coming to life in a crackling hum via some empty channels until Francois punched in the local cop feed.

They were relaying info about an incident that was still in progress:

"Badge 2021," crackled the dispatcher. "I'm just re-reading the occurrence about this Victor. Went to Quebec for a school trip in June, met a girl there who goes to another school here in the district. Came back, was at girl's school wanting to see her. Complainant is her mother who doesn't want her seeing him."

"What's the last name on that?"

"That's Stanford, Taco, Alpha, Yes."

Francois set the machine down triumphantly on the coffee table.

"We'll keep this on," he said. "There might be something. The great thing about this wave is it's not too far out into the country. Lots of them are."

"What are 'waves' again?" asked Ethan.

"The sightings - this thing materializes over time in waves of sightings. Not everyone calls them in. A lot are being reported though. It's partly due to the timing. Many occur in the late evening, which is different from the early morning ones which are far more frequent."

The voices faded in and out in the background throughout the evening. It was mostly run of the mill stuff - accidents, domestics, break and enters.

They agreed to take shifts monitoring it. Francois between noon and 6pm. Ivan from 6 until midnight and Ethan from midnight until morning.

At 5am Monday, Ethan awoke with a startle when a bird hit the window. Still on the couch, the message light on the old wall landline was blinking. It was Saara. Said she'd had trouble connecting with his cell.

As far as voluntary house arrests go, things were running smoothly. The plan was to visit the next sighting while it was in progress - if they could. Francois said the wave had held strong for three weeks and from what he'd been able to learn from the Internet and a few obscure books, they lasted on average between four and five weeks.
That evening they hung in the cellar in a room that had been transformed into an old style pub a few years earlier.

Its large kegs and mahogany bar, which had been rescued from a steamship wreck off one of the lakes provided a comforting departure from the gloom of the main level. Ethan had its interior lit in vintage gas lamps and had built the stairs and floor with slabs of granite.

On the walls hung pictures of old boat captains who'd navigated the nearby waterways in the late 1800's.

"If there was ever a time in my life as up heaved as this I cannot remember, but it is exciting, yes?" Francois asked, amidst sips of vintage Bordeaux Ethan had pulled from an aged oak casket.
The young man watched as their host shuffled a faint a-train across the floor to the bar, like he was in some French discotheque of the late 70's. This sub annex of the main estate home was built in 1834, before the skirmishes with the Ojibway and it had a colored history. The original owner had used the room as a tarot card parlor, and, according to legend, it had seen its share of visiting dignitaries from throughout the province and even abroad, who travelled there for readings.

For the first time since they'd all met, and likely due to the drink, Ethan had begun to feel somewhat at ease. His older years took in the youth and slight frivolity with a commanding, appreciative gaze. Ivan had occupied himself with the pistol collection inside the glass cases lining the west end of the room.

It was here in the annex that Ethan had prepared his initial office years earlier before deciding midstream it was better suited as a man cave.

Francois sat down on a plush, bearskin rug in front of the bar and motioned to him for attention. "You wanted to know about them, where they are from, who they are?" he said. "I can tell you all that because my mother did some snooping while they were at the hospital."

"First she'd noticed they were taking shifts with the patient and she had seen one of the team - a man - leave a bag by his chair when he went to the washroom and she looked through it. She found a map that had three points on it - the area covered a triangle stretch of hundreds of miles around our area. She jotted down the three districts on the map, committing to memory the locations of each point. She also saw a piece of paper that had the words 'Rural Factor' imprinted upon it. There was a gun in the bag. She got scared and stopped rummaging."

"I took this info and searched it all on the net," he continued. "But I was smart enough not to type "Rural Factor" on any search engine. The map locations were the key. I searched each area and typed the word 'sighting' as well in the queries. I found out a lot that day. Each area had had waves of sightings within six months of each other. In some of the chat rooms where the sightings were mentioned, some of the people in the different towns reported meeting with the same types of people afterwards, people who seemed to know a lot about what was going on. I went and visited a few of the witnesses. One guy told me that after he saw an egg-shaped object land in his field some people visited him and set up strange machines in the cornrows for several days. They told him some story he knew wasn't true. That it was a government prototype and they were checking for residual radiation, but he said it was more like they were waiting for something to show up. They stayed in a guest cabin on his property and had black SUV's.

When they left it was right after he saw the woman in the group take a call that seemed important. He overheard one of them mention Muskoka, which it turns out, they came to next. They are not government, but some kind of corporate contractor for them. Scientists. One of them has a PHD in astrophysics. Another's specialty is epigenetics."

"That's still an emerging field, right?" asked Ethan. "The study of the effects of historical events' on current personality via DNA?"

"Yes," replied Francois. "They are very interested in time. Vast stretches of time, which, in another dimension would be the flickering of instants. From what we can gather, they believe it is consciousness itself that is the phenomenon - that we are but a subset of reality and that everything is in consciousness. That's not all - during these waves or flare ups, other shit happens too. Here, in my bag I have a document we stole from the team..."

"Wait a minute," said Ethan. "Stole? How'd you manage that?"

"Just read it," replied Francois, shoving the papers into his hands. "They look at everything – weird occurrences – it's more than just objects in the sky they are interested in."

At the top of the first page was a reference heading number: RF - 317 08.23.15., beneath which were point form notes under a heading that read "Witness Statements - Ontario".

He read the statements. Some of the locals mentioned he knew by last name.

"A man came to the door dressed in a tight-fitting glowing body suit," read one. "Banged on door, was holding some kind of baton. Disappeared in the air in front of witness. Family dog was missing, found later mutilated in backyard. Several pets reported missing in neighborhood"

Looking up, his perplexity must have been showing.

"People start seeing things during these waves," said Francois. "On the second page there's a whole list of other effects people are reporting - teleportation, manifestations and psychic knowledge, even time slips. What people are seeing are what they are experiencing personally or seeing through their own 'lense'. The team believes the phenomenon either distorts itself to suit the intuitional imagery of a witness or the witnesses are seeing something so far beyond what their minds can comprehend and interpreting it through their own preferences. Some believe it's a mix of both. The objects/people change shape too. If you keep reading, people are reporting some whacked out shit - ghosts and fairies. Crazy."

Laying the papers on the coffee table, Ethan stood, collected some dishes and said he'd be back after some cleaning up. On the staircase, his heart sunk heavier.

In the kitchen he leaned against the island wondering how he'd manage. The case had been developing and he needed to be there for Saara, but how could he now with all this?

Opening another bottle of red, he ran through scenarios. Maybe they could all stay at the estate until the wave blew over. He had enough food if needed. Raising a glass to his lips the internal monologue continued:

Did this have anything to do with his own experiences? His eyes stretched out into the hall by the library.

Wine in hand, he moved towards it with the intent of entering for the first time since the occurrences. Flicking the lights, the familiar, once comforting musty scent of old binded books manifested. In the corner the window curtains were still drawn back and he went over to close them.

In the centre of the room, he stood by the chair and lamp and took a good look around. No signs of life, he concluded, as if to provide himself reason for leaving quickly.

He still had many questions for the two young men. So much of what had happened there in the last week seemed associated with the more widespread events they'd described. He wondered if there were others like him, people making no mention of the events they'd experienced for fear of ridicule, existing in private limbos, worlds shattered by profound disruptions of normal causality.

His mind retraced all he had learnt. He couldn't really understand it, the intermingling lives and breathtaking collisions between the known and utter mystery. A profound tapestry was unraveling before them and its implications were startling.

As he mused, voices could be heard coming up from the cellar through the vent grates.

They were having some kind of argument.

There was a faint must too — or was he imagining it? Leaning over the grate, he took a sniff. Yes, there it was. Like sulpher, not too strong, but there.

At the stairs he smelt it again. It was definitely coming from the basement.

"It's gone," he heard Ivan say, as he rushed back in to the subterranean den.

"What's gone?" he asked.

"There, there was a mist hovering in the air between us," said Ivan. "It felt... alive."

His eyes shot at Francois who confirmed what had happened in a nod and wide, vivid stare.

"It's in the house," blurted Ivan, backing up against the wall, arms folding tightly around his chest.

He had to tell them.

"I think I know what is happening," he stammered, setting down the wine which had been spilling the whole time.

"I've been experiencing things here too," he said cautiously, though he didn't know why as both men had seen much, much more. "So far it's been harmless. Scary, yes, but harmless."

"It was speaking to us," screeched Francois. "But inside our heads. It was just this steam that turned black right here. It was like it became us."

A palpable unease had gripped the room. He decided to tell them everything straight up.

"Now we're stuck in here with this thing and we can't even leave," moaned Ivan, eyes darting wildly between the bar and the doorway.

"It, it..asked me to go with it," he stammered. "I actually started seeing it, but through its own eyes"

It was certifiable, he thought, turning his gaze to Francois who also looked agitated.

But there was something, the smell was getting stronger and it felt like the room temperature had dived 20 degrees.

Following their line of sight, he turned, looking up into the corner above the door.

Something was moving there, almost translucent, seemingly seeping in from the wall itself.

Frozen, they watched as the opaque moving shape turned rapidly from a faint mist to something much darker and larger.

Within seconds the whole room was engulfed in a thick inky darkness.

They took the stairs to the kitchen, slamming the door behind them.

Chapter 16

I

"Get in the living room," yelled Ethan. "I'll wait to see if it comes up."

As the others scrambled, he pressed all his weight against the flimsy wood barrier.

This thing could go anywhere, might already be up there with them, he thought. Listening, he couldn't hear any noise, just the industrial hums of the cellar furnace and kitchen fridge.

Maybe they had just imagined it. Maybe that's what this all was - group hysteria?

He hoped so. He wanted desperately to just walk in the living room and knock some sense into them, thank them for their wild stories and send them on their way. Like they always did with schizos at the paper. *Sure, you had a brain implant. The CIA are really interested in you, because you are so fucking important.*

But what was that - something moving - fuck, the fucking shutter.

Abandoning the door, he leapt to the window, slamming its shutters which the wind had pried loose yet again. *It was just the wind. That's it. Wind pushing fog through the vents. Get it fixed this week. No problem.*

"Do you see anything?"

It was Ivan, still moaning from the living room.

"Nope. All good. You?"

"Nothing so far," replied Francois. "Should we come to you?"

Staring at the door, Ethan willed it not to move. He didn't have to, it was silly of course. They needed to leave though. All of them. Get out, enjoy some nightlife. To hell with being scared. And the team? Wild imagination.

Satisfied normal reality reigned, he joined the others in the living room.

He'd make his case slowly. Maybe change the subject over the following few minutes, show them his record collection. Francois liked music. Had told him so earlier.

"We are *not* going back down there," blurted Ivan, still clutching his chest.

"Yes, that's probably a good idea," he told them.

Francois seemed in a much more receptive state, about two rungs below the panic his Russian buddy was exhibiting. He was his in. Just had to massage it a bit...

"Yeah, downstairs is off limits," he found himself saying.

Reinforcement, it always worked.

"Let's just wait a bit here. Always good to be on the main level. Good if we have to get out quickly."

Why did he just say that? He could tell by their eyes it'd just made things worse.

"You were saying you saw something here before?" asked Francois. "Why didn't you tell us??"

"I thought it was just, I mean, I think it was something like you said, but y'know how you can think you're seeing something. It's an old house and me being here all alone."

Fuck. they weren't having it. Just shut up. Listen.

"Oh no, you aren't not going to tell us now," said Ivan.

"You have to tell us everything," added Francois. "We told you what we know."

This was fucking stupid. What was it - 2am? And here they were, grown men, arguing about ghosts.

"Okay," he began. "Just chill. But let's at least take into consideration we've all had a few and are pretty stressed. We have to figure out what's real in all of this and what isn't."

That sounded good. Now what? Tell them about Jack?

God, *he was* losing it. And this was the limit, where everything scattered into chaotic irretrievable disarray.

He settled on that he'd 'seen a few things'. It wasn't a lie. Hadn't everyone?

"What things?" demanded Francois, suspicion rising in his voice.

"Oh, shadows and noises - that kind of stuff."

Before he could continue they really did hear a noise. A doorbell. His doorbell. Really? Who the hell would be ringing his doorbell at this goddamn late hour?

Bringing his fingers to his lips, he went to find out as the others just stared incredulously.

Yep, there was a figure out there. Not too tall. Looked like a man?

Nervously, he turned the handle and the door opened revealing an elderly gentleman wearing a raincoat and galoshes.

"Can I help you" Ethan asked, recognizing him instantly.

It was old Mr. Hawkins. His mouth dropped saying his name in his head. Because it couldn't be. It was impossible. He was the estate's gardener from before Morton Lodge took over. He'd *died* in a car accident not four years ago out on the Vankoughnet Road.

Seeing him, Francois let go a scream. As Ethan turned to let him know he knew him, he saw the young man had also turned deathly white.

"No - you can't be here, nottt youuu..." he was babbling incoherently.

"Who - Do you know Mr. Hawkins? How do you know Mr. Hawkins?"

He was catatonic. Ivan looked shocked too. Turning back, their visitor had now somehow disappeared. Did he come inside? *Oh fuck, was he in here with them?* Had he only *dreamt* he'd died? Maybe he was just finishing some work...

Closing the door, Ethan turned towards the others, but they were gone now too. He was feeling sleepy – was his mind running away with itself? He hadn't felt tired a moment ago.

Closing his eyes, he started to drift. Can't sleep now, have to find Hawkins, he could be doing anything in here at this hour. He could be harming the others...

II

Ethan awoke in the cellar. The lamps were still on and the record machine was still playing that KISS Live album Francois had been so fascinated with.

Struggling to his knees, he reached out blindly for firm footing, disturbing a vintage dish that was on the bar in the process. Staggering to the beer fridge, he grabbed three bottles of water and flung two to the others who were passed out on the floor.

Overwhelmed, they must have all succumbed to a deep sleep. They'd been enjoying a few jokes, was the last he could recall. Or had they been upstairs?

Now he had a splitting headache and felt like puking.

It was 4am and in the bathroom he searched for some aspirin. In the mirror he saw that a strange red rash had formed at the top of his chest.

Pulling back his shirt to examine it, he could see it was triangular and comprised of small dots rising from the skin's surface. Running his fingers over it, it was like the flesh had melted and fused back together in welts.

Pulling his shirt off, he turned around, positioning his back towards the mirror. The tips of his shoulder blades had the same peculiar rash lines which itched and stung. At the medicine cabinet he grabbed a topical balm and applied it to the marks. Checking his clothes, it was puzzling: His shirt wasn't burned in any of the corresponding areas.

Eyes bloodshot and vacant, he was overtired and extremely weak. In the den he fell back to sleep in a chair, slumbering through right until noon.

But he was the first to rise, quietly setting to work before the others came to.

On the internet he found several sites purporting to only contain reports of verified sightings. It was obvious nobody online had any real information. Nothing rang true with their situation anyway.

Once awake, the others joined him around his desk. Francois quickly halted the exploration by hitting the power button.

"This will get us in deep shit," he said, unplugging the laptop.

Ivan had marks on his back too. Francois didn't, but he had what looked like the same type of rash on his left cheek.

"I need to see a doctor," moaned Ivan, scratching at his welts.

"Leave it alone, it's fine, you are just losing it," snapped Francois. "None of us can lose it. We just have to wait this shit out."

That evening, they thought they heard the rotation of chopper blades, but each time it turned out to be nothing.

Alone on the porch Ethan smoked pot until late, immediately re-dosing each time the buzz faded.

The night sky seemed deeper now, more ominous, like part of a larger picture unattached to normal life, primordial.

How he felt about the estate had changed too. It wasn't his anymore. At best he was its guest, trapped inside as if in a cocoon of which he understood nothing. There were palpable, unknowable things and no control beyond the pure experiencing of it.

At 3am, he decided to head in. Asleep on the couch, Francois snored loudly. He didn't know where Ivan had landed.

Climbing the staircase, a quick flash from outside stopped him cold. It was a vehicle approaching through the woods up the driveway, fast.

Half-yelling 'time to go!', he yanked Francois from the couch. Still asleep, the young man careened through the living room furniture as they pulled themselves desperately through to the hall to the side door.

Hitting the back lawn, they made for the woods. Behind them they could see lights swarming through the Estate as other vehicles screamed up the driveway.

Hopping the iron fence at the edge of the property, they took the short trail through the woods towards the boathouse, Francois followed blindly through the darkness, still dazed.

"We'll make it to the river," whispered Ethan, pointing out the direction.

In the dense bush, they could hear bursts of radio chatter as the team scattered out across the lawn after them, search beams bobbing like frenzied wasps. In the distance, chopper blades.

"Keep down," whispered Ethan. "Low, we're almost there."

Past the boathouse a 20-foot bluff rose up from the Black River. Ethan was first to leap.

Down they plunged, knife jacking the rapids with two heavy splashes, the frigid water scoring them as they sunk deep in the rushing black.

They were met with searchlights scouring the surface and banks when they re-emerged, tumbling in the rapids, foam spray glistening in the moonlight as they merged with stronger currents.

For what seemed an eternity they floated in the dark spray, until they were far from the estate property.

A sand bar jutting out from the bank caught Ethan's upper body, knocking the wind from him, an unfriendly ally against the swift currents.

Reaching out he grabbed Francois, pulling him in closer.
Clawing sand to maintain their position, they inched further up into the thick mud, securing a foothold until they collapsed face first, wheezing with chills.

It was Monday around 5am.

Chapter 17

Ronnie's right arm still wouldn't move.

He'd slept in his car by the Moon River and the noise from the rapids had kept him awake all night. Soon it would be dawn and he'd have to start moving. The wait hadn't helped. He knew where he was headed and with the arm's condition not changing, the pause hadn't done much but put off the inevitable.

He pulled a wad of cash out from where he had it wedged beneath the seat. It was enough to live on for about two weeks if he needed it. Don's Bakery would be open soon over on Highway 169. Then he'd be off to find Fred.

Fred Martin ran a bait and tackle shop in Milford Bay and he'd have it open by 9. He imagined the startled look he'd be giving the old codger when he walked through the door. Fred would be in his mid 80's now and they hadn't spoken in years. Not since the last time.

"You're right Fred, I'm getting too old for this," he sighed, staring back at his bloodshot eyes in the rear view. Fred wouldn't like it, but he'd understand. He had to. He was the only one left who could.

At 8:40 he pulled the Camaro up outside Don's, parked and went inside where he bought a breakfast sandwich, coffee and two scones.

He'd save one for Fred - it might help ease the shock.

By nine thirty he was pulling off highway 118 West onto Little Trout Road. 'Haavenaar's Bait and Tackle' was only a mile up ahead. Nothing much had changed since he'd been there last, which must have been the mid-90's.

The senior was at the gas pumps outside the store as he pulled onto the property.

Looking up, he didn't immediately recognize the vehicle. Instead, Fred Martin turned and petted a hound that was laying on the front steps and went inside, leaving the front door swinging slightly ajar.

Ronnie parked and followed him in.

A soft jingle sounded as he entered and there was Fred, peering out from behind the same old dingy counter.

A peculiar smile spread over his face when he saw him enter.

"Thought I'd never see you again," he said, his gin soaked voice already wavering with emotion.

For a moment they stood quiet, just taking each other in.

Brushing away his tears, Ronnie couldn't stop the rest. Not once he'd looked in the eyes of the man who'd saved him all those years ago.

"I, I'll not stay long," he said, trying to maintain control. "I, I jus' need to know about something."

The old man's look changed to a grimace when he heard this, before turning to one of grave concern

"It's, it's about her," said Ronnie, finding it hard to keep talking. "And uh, where she is. If you know."

"Oh my dear, dear boy," said Fred, shaking his head slowly, his voice cracking like old dried wood.

He had known it wouldn't be easy, he reminded himself. What had he even been thinking, he thought, watching as Fred's stern look appeared almost paralyzing, like his emotions were gearing up to tear both of them apart.

"That's a question I never wanted to hear you ask," said the tackle shopkeeper quietly, eyes welling up in a mix of pain and fear.

It was to be expected. He hated doing this to him.

"Come now, what has brought this thing on?" asked his old friend.

"I can't say Fred. But I have to do this now. It's time."

"You just let *time* take care of it boy," Fred yelled. "This is time's job. She'll be done soon enough. *You aren't going anywhere to do anything.* Look at you, you can hardly stand yerself up. When I saw you last what did I tell you? That it was *nature's* turn - she was going to take care of it and you agreed. What did you say? Told me straight to my own two eyes. *You said it was nature's turn and that it was over.* Well, over means *OVER*. *Done.* That's what this thing is."

He slammed his fist on the countertop, the lotto cards and lighters fell from their casings down onto the floor.

"No one's gonna be there to pull you out this time if you go an' try to do this thing," he continued. "I'm too old. *No one else boy.* You got that through your thick skull?"

The words were being spat out now, the ones that weren't being held back.

"You gonna go and do this and then all that work we did - what is it going to amount to? You's *alive.* That's all that matters here. Those other things are not natural - you know that."

He took it all in, waiting for Fred to pause. God, he needed this to work.

"All I want to know is some, some clue," he gasped, wiping his cheeks slowly. "Anything you've heard or seen. I don't want to do this. You know that. But Fred, please. Help me. I can't stop until this thing is done."

"'*Can't stop*'," said Fred, rolling his eyes at the ceiling. "You gone and forgot 'bout what her old beak does? *You gonna tell me that?* You of all people...."

"*I know* what happens," he snapped, finding the anger inside him again. "Fred, I love you and I will never forget what you did for me and Sam. Never. But for all our sakes, please just let me know. For Sam's sake. *For Sam, Fred.* The one we promised to. The one promise we never kept."

The old man's head sank until his chin dug deep in his chest. Stretching his hands forward he gripped the front ledge of the counter, digging his nails into the corroded linoleum and board.

He let out a long, mournful sigh.

"No. No, I'm not going to do this," he repeated, shaking his head. "This is not happening. You are not asking this."

"*I am asking,* Fred," he whispered. "I'm asking because it's all I've got left. I'm stronger now. Now's the time."

He saw the pain he had conjured and how the old man had made peace with knowing they were both safe. It must be killing him, he thought and for a minute he felt like fleeing back through the front door.

Fred's eyes suddenly looked up and straight through him and it was like he wasn't talking anymore. Something stronger was.

"Three, maybe four years ago," he began, between two long mournful sighs. "I was out Longford way. Back in on Saw. Fishing trip, just me and buddy. Thought I got a sense about something of that kind. But goddamnit I knew to get the hell out of there and high tail it and so did the dog."

"*So did the dog,*" he repeated, tears streaming down his pock marked cheeks, the lotto cards bouncing beneath his shaking clenched fists.

"Look at him," he said finally, motioning towards the old hound in the corner. "The dog's got more sense than you."

"Thank you," he replied and bent down to pet the old creature. "Fred, thank you so much. Longford - that's about 12 clicks past here - towards Lake of Bays, is that right?"

Fred nodded.

"I could be there tonight," he continued. "Was it strong - what you felt? Of course it was. Anything out there where it could be? What were your thoughts?"

"I thought it might be at the reserve, but there was no one there at the time in late fall," he said. "I was thinking it had to be over in the Lake. There are places all along the west shore there now. But I tell you boy it was *sickening*. That feeling. *Sickening*."

"It's a start," said Ronnie, nodding. Gingerly he placed the paper bag with the scone in it down on the counter.

"Come here boy," Fred beckoned, straggling out from behind the clutter of fishing lines and old rods.

Pulling him close, they hugged warmly. Ronnie loved the old woods smell of Fred's clothes and held him as tight as he could with his one good arm not ever wanting to let go. For years that smell had meant hope.

"You just remember that none of it is real boy, not in the normal way," coo'd Fred softly. "You remember that when you're out there. Remember the way I learned you."

Nodding, he nuzzled his cheeks deeper into Fred's thick flannel hunting jacket.

"I know," he said. "I always will Fred."

Without looking up, he loosened from the embrace, turned and headed towards the front door.

"You know Sam's in a place where it don't matter anymore," Fred called out after him. *"Sometimes I wonder if that's the best place for all of us."*

He watched him through the rear view watching him leave through the screen door. Finding Longford wouldn't be hard, he thought, guiding the Camaro back onto Highway 169. He'd wiped away his last tear while leaving and the road was clear.

Finding her though wouldn't be easy.

Fred could've sensed another one - it was possible. They'd heard stories during their time at the centre. Rumors amongst some of the others who'd been there prior to their time.

Sam said she'd seen one. It was older, bigger than her. Was assigned to a pair of other children who disappeared before she got to know them. They must have been about 11 and 8, she'd said. The old one always wore dark clothing, she'd said. Seen it mainly outside in the grounds with the doctors. Never up close.

But they'd said it'd never come back during their time.

God, Sam.

He hadn't thought of her in years. She'd never really left him though and he could see her long blonde hair and impish, innocent face.

Always smiling. It was that smile that'd helped so much back then. He could see her perfectly now as the memories surfaced - standing in their room by their small table and chairs.

He'd been older than her, but not by much. Old enough to sense more about the danger they were in, but he'd clung to her innocence, even when he knew it was not enough.

Funny how that and Fred's help *had* turned out to be enough, despite everything that was occurring.

"Let's play the rainbow game", she'd say, bringing her hands together in a small triangle. He'd taught her it, supposed he'd learned it through one of his foster parents. She'd loved that game and they'd play it for hours and hours. The fingers were colours of the rainbow and they'd open and wiggle when the storm had passed. That stupid game.

He remembered the fear they felt when they'd come take her out for the lessons.

He and Fred had never learned where she was from or what had happened to her parents. Like so many there, she was a forgotten, discarded child of the late 70's. There from before he'd arrived. He remembered seeing her that first day - a small blonde burst of sunshine, dancing in the grey underground hallway, walking with the doctors.

Fred had thought she was from Norway. Something about her features, he'd said.

Longford was a reserve, but not a native one. In the late 60's about 250 acres of pristine lakes and forest had been bought up by wealthy American interests and turned into a wilderness paradise for tourists.

They came up from stateside to rent cottages, go on guided fishing expeditions and tour the lakes on restored steamships.
About 28 families would return annually during its heyday - that number would likely have dropped in the ensuing years as it was still very cliquey.

He'd known a few who worked there down through the years. Most from the time he'd spent there. Fred had worked there after his time at the centre too. Odd jobs mostly, closing and opening cottages in spring and winter, securing boats for winter storage and acting as a security guard when need be.

'Longford Reserve - 12 kms' read a sign on the right and something else in him stirred.

It was the lush dark woods he used to love. Mainly between Saw and East Muskoka where he'd hiked the trails as a child, but never on his own in the fall.

The main part of the park would be vacant now that autumn had taken hold. Some could still be at the more remote cottages. The place encompassed about 900 miles of woodlands.

Might have to deal with security, he thought, remembering the spot where he and some friends had learned to do break-ins.

Should be a section of fence a ways from the main entrance, he remembered as he neared closer.

Fuck, the arm still throbbed. Pain was getting worse and the numbness had spread up past his shoulder too. Probably lost the use of it forever. Fucken' thing.

He'd need to park somewhere secluded.

Ahead there was a clearing just off the road, no more than a small meadow. It was perfect.

The main entrance gate he'd remembered was about 50 yards ahead. It'd be locked, but here where he'd parked he could hop the fence and keep the Camaro hidden. No other tire tracks either, which was good.

After parking, he reached into the duffel on the back seat and pulled out a small white cardboard box. On the top was printed K-1301-DCB-1. He hadn't needed one of these in awhile.

Opening it, an aluminum foil-wrapped slide containing three light blue encased pills fell into his hands. Popping one open, he put it in his mouth and chugged on the bottle of water he had going. A cool wind flowed through the meadow and the hills ahead were a gorgeous site in the autumn haze. If she'd been near there recently he'd soon know it.

The trail to Saw was just a few kilometers away.

Chapter 18

Ivan was seated at a long wooden table in a room lit by oil lamps, their light gently illuminating his face and those of two others.

At the end of the table was an older man dressed completely in black, a pair of burly arms folded against his barrel chest. He was teetering back on his hind chair legs while to his right a young woman sat, a long black haired beauty with dark chocolaty brown eyes, who peered up at him from time to time as they waited.. She was dressed in a white silk dress and a headband encrusted with tiny red jewels.

How he'd got there was still a mystery, but it had been over six hours and he'd almost stopped trying to figure it out.

After several moments, a heavy door swung open and a tall man with brown hair entered. Jack, the master of the estate, was flanked by two blonde women. Each took their places around the table.
Jack picked up a green folder, scanned some of its documents and quickly handed it to the black haired woman. She opened it and looked up at Ivan squarely.

"Ivan Wolfewicze, this is your name?" she asked demandingly.

"Yes," he answered.

"Interesting," she replied, looking back at the master knowingly.

There was a cat like way about her, he thought, watching as she shifted in her seat with an alluring poise. Primal energy. There'd be getting nothing by her if he wasn't careful.

Earlier, Jack had shown him around the grounds and it was an altogether more mysterious place than it was in 2005, whenever this was.

He'd yet to ask, but he had guessed the late 1900's. Jack told him they'd perfected a method of travelling to certain times of their own choosing and that the property aided him in doing so, but he'd kept tight-lipped about how this occurred. Ivan's last memory was of falling asleep in the estate's living room by the fireplace hearth while Francois drifted on the couch. Then, there'd been disruptive flashes - images of a skull and feather on a tree. This fleeting memory had returned to him several times over the course of the day.

Jack spoke in an indifferent tone now, shifting his powerful large frame, saying they all faced a difficult task.

"The skirmishes in the hills are increasing and the local barrister has good word the Ojibway are sending their medicine men out onto the cliffs at Deer Lake," he said.

This native dimension seemed to scare him and Ivan watched as the master tapped the table with his index finger several times while making this point.

Earlier Ivan had thought he'd heard Jack and another man discussing how medicine men were summoning spirits to help halt the British approach, and that this was causing problems for their plans in future times.

Other pieces had come to him more slowly. The medicine men had also set up camps near Britt and Minett. Information from Jack's spies had been of no use, as they weren't adept in deducing spiritual warfare, so Jack's mysterious Orange Order had been called in.

Puffing his pipe, the master stared through his smoke at the others as it curled up slowly, dispersing along the low ceiling.

The black haired woman pulled out a map, running her long fingers over lakes and rivers like she was plotting a route. Over and over her fingers poured, until, finally, they landed at a specific point.

"When I was young, my father would take my sisters and I to *this* spot on the Moon River where he said the Ojibway would meet in the fall for invocations," she said. "Father and his Orange cohorts would search for instruments and debris left behind, which would indicate the nature of the powers they'd summoned so as to predict their next moves. We'd wait in tents, but I remember he said this location never failed them."

"It was known as 'the haunted ground' - 'Mkjininnk' where the veils between the worlds grew thinnest during the phenomenon," said Jack, his pipe wobbling.

"We can access it only at night though, as their scouts are in those woods near Brant Island and they are ruthless," he continued. "We could take the trail to the banks of Bala Bay and paddle in from there. An outfitter can equip us with canoes in Torrance."

The older burly man nodded, thoughtfully stroking his rough, bushy beard.

"I presume you've checked the status of our friends to the north," he asked, in a rich baritone voice. "No plans of their own while we do this?"

"No," said Jack. "This is in keeping with their plans too, which for the moment are 'see what we come up with'."

More talk ensued - a lot of which Ivan didn't understand. Jack then nodded at the other four signaling for them to leave. In moments, just he and Ivan remained.

Closing the door, Jack invited him to move to another seat, a leather armchair. Taking stock of the rest of the room for the first time, Ivan sat himself down in it looking up as his host lit yet another pipe.

Before his captor could start, he launched into a bitter tirade:

"*What the fuck is going on here?*" he demanded, his neck vein surging.

Staring back in silence, the older man took in his fierce eyes as if to gauge whether the long or the short version would better suit the occasion.

"You will have your answer if you listen," he said. "We came upon a method early in our experiments - stole it actually from the Ojibway. It will take some time to sink in, but it bends all of this - time and space. A complex ritual fraught with danger. Thankfully for us *and you* it's also reversible."

"Thought", he continued, tapping his left temple, "is the key."

Ivan glared. He was either a genius or a madman, but he still needed to know more. And he needed him to think he was desperate.

Starting again, Jack was seemingly enjoying the moment.

"We don't make these sojourns lightly," he said. "Someone from your time, *you*, must accompany us in the coming days in order to have knowledge of the rite - in order that you can reverse it in the future."

"Why don't you take care of that," he snapped back, coughing nervously for effect. "You seem to be everywhere."

"Insurance," said Jack.

The master paused, his voice taking on a more wistful tone.

"If something happens to one of us in your time, we need you there to act in our absence. You'll see. We need you to help us apprehend a woman whom you will learn more about soon. But you must be hungry now, no? Shall we eat? We can discuss this again over lunch. You can learn all about the things we have accomplished. More about our aims."

Together they left the room, entering a dark hallway which they took towards another heavy door. The dining room was where it still was in the estate of 2005, close to the front of the main home. Here it was heavy with mid-Victorian veneer and furnishings.

Jack checked in with the kitchen and arranged for two club sandwiches and a bottle of Merlot from the private cellar.

He had a hand in a vineyard in the Niagara region, he said, and today they would sample a vintage from four years previous.

Through the room's bay windows, the two men gazed out over the front of the property which even in this time had a budding garden, although not as big as Ethan's.

Several workers could be seen mending fences. Overall, the estate appeared humming with life.

Jack asked if he had ever heard of the Orange Order.

He said he hadn't, but that he was interested in anything that would get him back home.

Reaching up and grabbing a folder with several dusty newspaper clippings from the edge of a high mantle, his host placed them on a desk in front of the room's huge stone fireplace.

"Here," he said. "Read through these while we await for our food. You'll have more questions."

Yellow and frayed with age, the clippings were from two papers mainly - the Gazette and the Banner. They told the story of the formation of Orange Lodge 2214 Oakley Ward, its various members and activities. One clipping, dated Aug 17th, 1884 chronicled a Ward picnic at a place called Tretheweys, located by a waterfall on the south branch of the Muskoka River.

Another outlined new Lodge members in the fall of 1901. Magical order this, people in archaic regalia that.

"Really?" enquired Ivan adopting a faux sarcasm. Closing the folder quickly, some of the clippings spilling onto the carpet.

"How about some straightforward information," he continued. "Beginning with what the fuck you guys are really up to?"

Smiling, Jack pulled at his pipe and with a wave of his hand, the young man began to feel ill. Staggering to a chair, Ivan fell, clutching his throat, unable to breathe.

His weight flipped the chair and he crumbled down in a heavy heap facing upwards gasping for air.

Looming over him was Jack, still smiling, still smoking as Ivan's fingers dug desperately into a carpet, ripping at its edge tassels as his convulsions quickened.

His heart was pounding so hard now it seemed close to exploding.

Then, Jack held up his hand, stretching two fingers towards the ceiling.

At this, the invisible grip's intensity eased a little, at least enough for some air to return. He was wheezing now, tossing his head to and fro, cheeks smeared with hot, spilt tea and cat hair.

"Did you like that?" asked his tormentor.

As some strength returned, he leaned up on one elbow, flushing with anger.

"Oh come now," Jack mocked, "Don't look so upset. Go on, get up and take your seat. You know I've snapped the necks of men much larger than you using the same technique."

Striking a match on the fireplace, Jack's freshly lit flame threw a rosy glow back upon his face as he again lit his pipe.

"You know our enemies won't be so kind if they find you," he said. "Ahh, *but who are they exactly* you must be wondering and what mess have you been brought in to? Sit and I'll tell you. You won't be familiar with any of it, but if you listen you just might survive and be able to return home. We are a magickal order in the grips of a terrible battle with another - a rogue Ojibway Midewiwin. They are encamped in our hills, basically surrounding us at present, and have won the allegiance of the greater Ojibway tribes of our District. It's a most terrible situation, as they are, for the most part, the noblest of the Indian races. How this all came to be stretches back into history, a number of skirmishes and mistakes on both the English and their sides creating a most unsavory politics. I was seconded from England to create the lodge here in 1899 and have been running the operations since."

Pausing, he watched as the young man mulled it all over.

"How you enter into this is complex, but central to our latest efforts," Jack continued. "We need you as a time marker for a powerful ritual we will be staging at Bala Falls. You don't need to do anything but be present. Following that, if all goes according to plan, you'll be returned to your home time.... strange as it is. We were going to hold it in our barn but plans changed."

"Your value in this is as a 'marker'," he continued. "People can't shake their time, they are 'in its mold' psychically - thoughts, mannerisms, sensibilities - all are of your time and therefore people are good markers in rituals where we want to invoke specific times. Everything is consciousness. In you, we have 'a time instance' of yours."

"But I've read true magick can only really nudge things," replied Ivan, catching him off guard with the insight.

"I've read that true reality is so densely packed with information that anything done in space and time can only reinforce certain possibilities in the informationverse - a term *you* may not be familiar with."

"I see you've got a good grasp of the basic concepts," returned Jack, smiling. "You'll find that concepts though, for the most part, are useless when it comes to making things *work*."

"What happened to you and your throat just now 'worked' due to my exact observation, intuition, time and practice - the combination of all of those elements really. I could waste my time on concepts about anything and everything, it doesn't mean things will work. All intellectualism is merely a sideshow. It's an entirely different language of mental causation, an entirely different universe. Things happen *for reasons*. Concepts are like ghosts looking for a home. Reasons form the ground of being."

"Nevertheless," replied Ivan. "For the brief time I was enthralled with magick I never saw results that were enough to cause me to believe any of it worked easily. And yet.....here I am. I suppose I'm not dreaming, so something's happened. Is this reality we're in now as 'real' as the one where I'm from?"

"That is open to some interpretation - you might see it simply as the result of certain conditions being brought together," said Jack. "Some things remain secret. This is true of all times."

Bending forward to collect the scattered clippings, the magician placed them back in the folder, closed it and returned it to the mantle.

"Had you read those thoroughly, you would have learned several of us have died, viciously in some instances, at the hands of the rogue Midewiwin," he said. "And that it's a deadly situation we now find ourselves in. I'll let you read them later. For now, you are my guest - but remain on the grounds for god's sake."

Nodding and resigned that he'd be here until he was no longer needed, Ivan watched as he left the room.
When he'd gone, he got up out of the chair, stood by the window and pondered the situation. His thoughts rested on the Midewiwin. Turning, he scanned the rows of titles on the room's bookshelves, his eyes coming to rest on a bright red volume entitled 'Ojibway Lore - Tales from early Muskoka'.

A thick tome about an inch and a half thick, he pulled it down and thumbed its pages for any mention of the secret society. There were some accounts that touched on the sect, but details were scant, mainly brief mentions of ceremonies and rituals.

One photo within its pages caught his eye. It depicted an Ojibway ceremony in full swing and what looked like a medicine man holding a rattle over a fire in the centre of a large circle. At the circle's edge tribes people looked to be in the throes of a strange ecstasy, many with their eyes rolled back and arms outstretched as if receiving spirits.

Unaware of it at first, his attention had also focused on his left hand, which was caressing the strange feather in his inside coat pocket that he'd been given several weeks earlier. He hadn't thought much about it since that time and couldn't really remember how he'd come to acquire it. Had he just found it? But why would he pick up such a thing - and then keep it?

Wondering about this and the photo's uncanny figures, a bell suddenly sounded, snapping him back to the moment.

Jack had returned with a maid from the kitchen who was holding a tray of hot sandwiches.

Chapter 19

I

It was 3am when Saara was startled awake by laughter coming from the grounds below.

Peeking out the window, she saw three well dressed men and two scantily clad girls stumbling across the lawns towards the hotel. At one of the finger docks there was a moored white bow rider with a man still behind the wheel.

Throwing on a sweater, she grabbed the small ice box from the bar fridge and headed for the elevator. If she was quick, she might beat them to the ground floor side lobby and follow them from there.

At the end of the hall, she swung the staircase door open but stopped short of heading down.

Three floors below, they had entered the stairwell. She waited as they climbed, reaching the third below her. Another door opened and the voices became muffled.

Waiting, she descended the stairs and pried open the exit door ever so slightly. They were midway down the hall and she could hear one of the men looking for his room card.

"And.... Card 304, we have it," he slurred.

"Mmmm...," answered one of the girls.

The room door clicked shut and they disappeared from sight. Taking the stairs to the ground floor exit, she entered the side lobby. No hotel attendants were around, so she continued on outside wishing she'd thrown on more than a light sweater.

Keeping close to the vine covered walls, she stepped cautiously along a cement path between the hotel and a line of hard maples. Through the trees she could clearly see the boat, its driver's bald head was shining in the moonlight and he was smoking.

After a few minutes, one of the back-kitchen doors opened and a man in a hotel uniform appeared, walking out to join the driver at the dock. They appeared familiar with each other and the uniformed man lit up a cigarette of his own

"Does Mark have many boats?" asked the driver.

The voices were low but clear.

"Yes, he brings out a different one every now and then," replied the employee. "Had one of them here last week - a Cobra 270 Python. Took a few of us for a ride."

"When you see him let him know I want to borrow it," laughed the driver. "All I ever get is this thing."

"Hey, at least you get a boat," came the reply. "I'm stuck here the whole time."

"How long is this one?" continued the employee.

"A few hours, then it's back to Barrie," said the driver. "Ron keeps it simple."

"Well, back to the desk," said the employee, flicking his butt in the lake.

"I'll be here," said the driver.

When he was gone, the man in the boat stepped out and stretched, walking to the end of the dock where he stretched some more.

Back in her room, Saara grabbed a notepad from her luggage and wrote everything down. At 4:30am, she pulled the duvet around her and reached for the side table lamp, remembering she had to try and get in touch with Ethan the following day.

In the morning, she awoke feeling hungry, so she put herself together and ordered breakfast from room service, running a couple search engine queries for Bohemian Island and 'Mark' while she waited. The hotel's owner was named Mark Edmonstone. In a local puff piece about tourism that spring he'd been quoted as saying he felt the "time was right" for more expansion at the resort. The article had been published by her paper the Gazette.

Searching Facebook she was able to find a good picture. Handsome and strong featured, he had dark hair and thick eyebrows. A physically powerful looking man with a magnetism, if the picture was anything to go by. Uber rich, he exuded a confident middle-aged smile, standing by a woman on the steps of the hotel's main lobby.

The island's website suggested he'd inherited the hotel business when he was 37 from his father Andrew Edmonstone who'd passed away in 2001. This had followed his son's 12-year military career, at the pinnacle of which he had held the rank of Colonel.

Searching Edmonstone Sr, she learnt he had come from a long line of shipping magnates out of the UK, none of his companies were called Siren, as far as she saw, but it was something.

After breakfast she was ready to expand operations, donning some of the garb she'd packed including a wicker hat and red sundress.

In the main lobby a suite of offices extended behind the check-in counter, but she suspected Edmonstone's was elsewhere. She sat for a while on one of the lobby couches by a huge granite-slabbed column reading a complimentary newspaper and watching to see if she could spot him.

Probably off in Europe having the time of his life, she thought.

But the uniformed man had said he'd been there last weekend. So she waited. It was her second day and she had to make every bit count.

Later, strolling through the halls there was still no sign of him or anyone who looked like they could lead her to him. While lounging lakeside after lunch she overheard a bartender complain about having to be at 'the gala' that evening. It was being held in the ballroom for some local charity. The local mayors and MP would be there. Would Edmonstone attend too?

When her second whiskey sour arrived, she tried to learn more:

"There's a gala here tonight?" she inquired of her waitress.

"Yes, it's about establishing 10 acres here as a nature preserve," she answered, maneuvering a pink napkin just so. "The hotel is making a big donation. Guests can go for the public part. I think it's at 5pm, but you have to buy tickets for the actual gala."

"And where do you buy those?" she asked.

"At the front lobby desk. I think you can order them too, have them sent to your room."

A donation meant the hotel bigwigs might be there, but she wouldn't be buying a ticket.

Experience had taught her that mostly vacuous, glad handing social parasites would be there. She'd probably know them all and have to sit next to one of the bigger bores. Luckily, she'd made plans for dinner with Rebekkah in the hotel lounge at seven.

Nodding in gratitude at her generous tip, the waitress left Saara to her thoughts.

It was now around 3:30pm and she'd be busy after dinner, especially if a new slew of girls returned by boat. This time she'd have to be more prepared.

Ethan still wasn't responding which wasn't like him, especially when things were getting serious. They hadn't left any trail for others to follow, but in her wildest imaginings she wondered if the cops had picked him up on some trumped up charge, maybe about meddling in the case, just to make a point.

At 4:45pm she made her way to the ballroom, which had been done up in a spectacle of ribbons and h'ordeurve tables. Chefs were already lined behind them slicing brisket and laying out sandwiches while hostesses made the rounds with sample trays of fine foods.

Near one of the empty tables she munched on some delicious escargot and watched the room fill. Her predictions hadn't been far off.

Many of the attendees she recognized - the usual attention whores from across the Province. She spoke to a few, allowing them to presume she was there as the press.

Avoiding others, she took a seat in the middle of a half empty row of chairs and waited.

At 5 the clamor subsided, and the lights grew dim.

The hotel was donating $25,000 and there, flanked by several aides, stood Edmonstone, centre right of a makeshift stage, dressed sharply in a royal blue suit.

After a brief introduction from the Hotel's Director of Planning he made his speech. The words flowed freely, but like most politicians, they could have been about anything.

Nothing about the new island golf course which saw 150 acres clear cut last year though, she thought, finding Edmonstone both a touch facile and attractive.

Others took the stage for a group shot afterwards with the big cheque. Edmonstone's aides remained close as he shook hands and chatted with the cocktail crowd.

It was now 5:30pm and she watched as one of his helpers took a call in the hall where it was quieter. Edging closer, she idled by a coat rack, her own phone by her ear and eavesdropped.

"Yes, we will be there tonight at the arranged time," he was saying. "We are close to finishing up here."

"No," he continued. "Same as usual, but, you know, they may have to soldier up. These are important clients. Yes, 10:30 is perfect."

Looking back, his boss was trying to manage a charming departure from a crowd of local Rotary Club members.

When the aide returned, they left promptly through the main exit. From a distance, Saara saw them make their way down the hall and out a side exit to the parking lot.

Through a window she saw them move towards a fleet of jet black sedans.

One pulled out slowly and they got in. It headed through the stone gates at the front of the property, then down Arney Road.

What was happening at 10:30pm, she wondered.

Anyway, it was time to freshen up for Rebekkah.

II

At 6:45pm she'd found a seat in the restaurant's low lit lounge just before her old friend arrived, gliding in spectacularly in a pair of red high heels, and a sultry black foil dress that was wrapped tightly around her svelte, lean figure.

With a quick brush of her long hair she sat down at the table smiling darkly.

"I thought I'd never get out of that meeting," she said, glancing at a diamond encrusted watch. "Hope I didn't keep you waiting."

They ordered vodka and orange juices and the maître d' brought them menus, suggesting they take a window seat in the restaurant should they be having dinner.

"Oh, and what meeting was this," Saara asked innocently.

"They have this deal where you have to sit through a two-hour condo sharing spiel - they try to get you to sign a contract right there, which I felt was pretty pushy," she replied, pulling a stray curl from her eyes. "It's part of the vacation deal I took. You get some perks - massages and a free boat tour if you sit through one of the sessions."

"And I haven't seen one fuckable man yet either," she continued, sighing like a slow setting dusk. "I'm sure there are some though. You had any luck?"

The poise in her voice was polished and visually, Saara could place its confident origins. A creature who got her own way every time, no doubt.

She returned her friend's stare with a cool "not yet" dreamy roll of her eyes. "It's only been a day though," she added with a fake giggle. "Meowwww..."

Laughing, Rebekkah's irises grew as large as moons and she stared back with a soft lick of her lips.

Definitely not girlfriend material, thought Saara and the needle of the polarity between their two obvious alpha personas was already flitting madly. It remained to be seen whether it could reach an equilibrium.

The strange woman's stare was pulling strings deep inside her and she found herself shifting in the plush leather seating.

Deftly guiding the conversation back towards dinner, Saara held one of the menus up to the light and read aloud: "Veal Milanese - squash, arugula, hazelnut salad - $30. Prosciutto wrapped halibut $28. Lamb shank, braised until tender, sweet potatoes, parsnip, pecans."

"It all sounds sumptuous and exquisite," said Rebekkah, setting down her drink, then folding her hands as if in some prayer. "Let's go get a table."

Nodding, Saara rose. As they started to move, Rebekkah said she had to visit the toilet to briefly freshen up.

"You grab one," she urged, handing her her half empty glass.

Seats were still available and Saara secured one with a great view of the lake. On the water, the ferry puffed smoke making for the mainland, while hotel employees cleared the grounds of the day's leftover towels and awning chairs at the beach.

It caught her by surprise then, when a hostess suddenly appeared touching her arm.

"I'm..., I'm sorry to interrupt, but I have something to tell you," she stammered in a hushed tone.

"Yes, please do, what is it?" she answered.

"It's just that, that woman... Well, how well do you know her?" she asked.

"I just met her recently while I was coming here by ferry but I guess I knew her a lifetime ago too. Why?"

"Well, earlier today one of our cleaners was in the bathroom and saw her purse while it was open and she has a gun," whispered the woman. "You look like strangers, and I know you from the paper, so I felt you should know."

A small panicky explosion went off in her mind as the image of the purse weapon formed.

"Yes, yes thank you," she said, patting the woman's hand and staring intently, signaling that Rebekkah was approaching from behind.

"If I remember I'll remind myself to ask you," she added, nodding as the hostess backed away.

"Remind about what?" asked Rebekkah, taking her seat.

"Oh, I was just being told about the boat tours they have and was trying to remember the deals I'd been told about. Apparently, there are some really historic ones you can go on."

"We could go together," said Rebekkah. "I'm supposed to take a cruise tomorrow afternoon on the Chikamuk. It's a recently restored steamship that plied the lakes back in the 1800's. I think we board at 11am. There's lunch with a famous chef who'll be serving the catch of the day. I think it hits some of the other islands too and it lasts two and a half hours. Weather should be great. Forecast calls for sun."

Nodding calmly Saara said she'd have loved to, but she'd already made plans.

"Let's order," she suggested, quickly changing the subject. "I'm famished."

Scanning the menu again for the most basic thing so she could keep thinking, the part of her brain Ethan called 'the Reptile' remained screaming.

Appearing as if she'd not picked up on any irregularity, Rebekkah quickly settled on the Carpaccio.

Was she an undercover?, wondered Saara. Not likely, they tend to keep things uncomplicated and wouldn't interact with anyone outside a case, unless of course, she *was* the case, but how could that be? Maybe the gun was for protection? No, it had to be more than that. Both of them were on the island for a reason.

"I'm really not all that impressed with room service," Rebekkah was saying, "I ordered a Long Island ice tea last night and it took them twenty-five minutes."

Then she became animated, relating an experience she'd had in the hall outside her room.

"I actually met the actor Donnie Wilkins," she said. "He was bringing his luggage to the elevator with some girl who looked like a stripper. Autographed a page in this book of memories I have that I collect in my travels."

"Oh wow," she replied, still lost in thought. "I saw Vicious Intent last month. He was great in it. Wonder if he's staying long. He's got those dreamy eyes."

"Yeah, that's what I noticed right off the bat," laughed Rebekkah. "I came around the corner and recognized them right away. It was almost like we'd met before too y'know, but it's just from seeing his face everywhere."

She fiddled with her red hair, like she was trying to remember something.

"You know, it's odd we'd run in to each other here. The last time I saw you was on that train to Toronto about 20 years ago. Do you remember? I was getting on in Barrie. It was only for about 2 minutes. You were with some blonde guy."

"That would have been Eric, my boyfriend at the time," said Saara. "I vaguely remember. Before that it was back in public school when I suppose we last saw each other."

"Yes, wasn't that a trip," Rebekkah laughed. "You were always into so much stuff. Badminton, lacrosse, swimming. I was never into anything except guys and partying."

"Hold that thought," said Saara, pouring herself a refill of water. "You'll have to excuse me now for a minute I have to visit the ladies room."

"Sure," said Rebekkah. "I should let you know though, I have to take a call early tonight. Maybe we can meet for a party night later this week?"

"Yeah, we'll make plans when I get back."

In the washroom, she squatted in a stall and tried Ethan's cell. Still no answer. Where the hell was he?

She wanted to just sit there, staring at the blue door, not wanting to go back to the table. For some reason she didn't believe the story about the condo share meeting. What the waitress had said was still rebounding in her mind. She'd just say she got a call she had to return and cut things short.

But when she got back, Rebekkah beat her to it.

"I'm really sorry," she apologized. "My call has been moved up. I'll get this and we'll hang in a couple more days, ok?"

"Oh you don't have to," she said, shooing away her money.

"No, I insist. Next time."

"Ok," smiled Saara meekly. "Enjoy your cruise."

Watching her leave, she shot a glance at the lounge front desk, but the hostess was nowhere to be found.

Maybe she'd be back at breakfast.

Sliding the money towards their drinks, she gathered her things. The night was going to be busy as it was and now much more complicated too.

Outside the lounge, Saara hurried towards the elevator. The hall was quiet and she needed time alone to think. But when the elevator arrived, the hostess re-appeared, stepping inside with her.

"*You are in danger*," she said matter-of-factly, hands chopping the air like no uncertain terms. "The minute you left she was on her phone talking to someone, looking like something hadn't gone according to plan."

"Ok, now you are fucking freaking me out," cried Saara, backing towards the glass wall as they started to rise.

"Look, I am sorry to do this to you, but I have never felt so right about anything," said the woman, pressing a crumpled piece of paper in her hand. "If you need a place to stay, call me."

Ding! At the second floor the doors parted on an empty hall and she began to feel a little dizzy.

"I, I... may...," she found herself replying, wiping a sudden sweat from her forehead, her other hand shaking and trying to clench on to a railing. "But... butttt, I,, really have no idea about any of this. I mean, wh, whyyy..."

The small space was spinning now and she felt hot and foggy. Attempting to right herself, a wave of nausea crept up her throat, threatening to explode.

"I...., I, don't feel well," she screamed, as she began to fall forward into the astonished woman's arms.

"Something is happening," she choked, collapsing further into the woman's body. "I can't think..."

"Oh my god, what am I going to do with you," cried the woman.

And she fell, desperately groping at the uniform, as another floor passed and her core strength drained.

It was the last thing she saw before everything went black.

Chapter 20

They'd been in the same garden shed for five hours and Ethan believed the chance to leave had come.

For two days they'd evaded capture by taking over backyard shelters and sticking to the bush along the outskirts of town. He shifted his weight carefully on a half-filled air mattress lodged between a John Deere tractor and some empty gas canisters and tapped Francois.

The choppers had been buzzing their location, which was somewhere upriver off Florence Crescent. It was the second time in an hour they'd flown over and he hoped they hadn't left tracks.

Must be about 4:30am, he thought, watching through a slight crack between the shed doors as the search beams flitted nearby backyards. The last ground vehicle they'd seen was a white SUV and that was about eight hours earlier.

As the choppers headed westward, he motioned to the young man, signaling it was time to move. It was the first chance they'd had to leave the cover of a suburban backyard since they beat the river.

"This way" he whispered, crouching as they climbed through decaying corn stalks in a particularly muddy section of a garden. A quiet new street came into view, although they still didn't quite know where they were.

The soft street lamps cast a welcoming glow, and, reaching a row of parked cars, they crawled along them street side, peaking up through their windows back towards the homes.

From this slightly higher vantage point beyond the backyards they could see searchlights and vehicle movements further downstream. On a road in the valley a tiny police car sped towards a flashing commotion in the downtown.

Gaining some of his bearings, Francois suggested he knew a place about five minutes away where they might be able to find a more permanent shelter, at least temporarily. They were about to move when they heard some twigs snap up ahead.

It was a bear ambling out of the forest onto the roadway with her two cubs.

As the wildlife passed, the mother paused mid-street sniffing the air. A man who was up on his front porch kicked a metal garbage lid down a walkway, scattering them back to the woods, then slammed his door.

At the end of the block they turned left, crossing a newly paved parking lot next to a towering condo complex.

In the distance sirens screamed and after a seemingly never-ending jaunt through more lots and alleys, Francois started to slow. Raising his hand, he alerted to a causeway running through the centre of town.

The harbor master was just setting sail in a small tug out onto the lake. The morning watch had begun, and they slid behind a waist high concrete wall until he passed. The boardwalk would take them towards town from here to where they could slip between some row houses at the edge of the urban centre. Settling into a half sprint, Francois eyed home entrances as they passed. Each of the frontages faced a boulevard fronting the bay.

"Haven't been here for awhile," he panted, stopping behind a parked bus. "It's all good though."

In a moment he chose one with a shiny red door, and before Ethan had time to think, had gone up and knocked.

A light came on inside, then the door opened revealing an attractive middle-aged brunette wearing a floral patterned bathrobe. Lit cigarette in one hand, her other arm gripped the robe protectively, then relaxed as she saw who it was.

"Knew I'd see you again," she said, flicking some ash on the porch. "Let me guess, you need a place to crash?"

"Yes," replied the young man, without any hint of urgency.

You are smooth, thought Ethan. Just get us inside. Atta boy.

It wasn't until they were both standing in the stylish, Moroccan style landing that she noticed something was terribly amiss.

"What the hell have you guys been *doing?*" she asked, staring them up and down.

"Extremely long fucking story," said Francois. "Is anyone else here? We don't want to draw anyone else into this..."

Starting to look worried, she closed the door behind them, not taking her eyes off their mud bedraggled clothes. Carla Sue Redmond had no children and was a nurse at a local medical clinic - she'd seen much worse.

Crushing her cig in an ashtray whilst taking Ethan's jacket, she led them back to a den that had a couch, coffee table and two love seats.

A large window with a sprawling view of the bay revealed the tug way out on the water, just a point of light now against the fog enshrouded cliffs.

The hope he'd kept alive despite all that was happening was like that tug, a tiny beacon. Picking up a pack of cigarettes and lighter from the windowsill, Ethan unconsciously pulled one out, lit it and drew a great haul.

"Make yourself at home, darling," chuckled Carla, her raspy tone indicating that everything in life was up for grabs.

At his side, Francois looked like he was recounting the night's events to make sure he didn't leave anything out.

"Dare I ask that one of you start explaining?" she asked. "I don't see any blood, so that's a good thing - right?"

"We're running from people who seem like cops but who are even more dangerous," said Francois. "They want us for what we know."

"And what pray tell is that?" she asked, her interest piqued.

"This stuff, er, we better chill for a bit," he continued. "It's so fucked up I don't even know where to start."

"Weird shit," said Ethan. "Flying things, but I'm sure it's just their toys."

She paused and stared at them. Her face tensed and they wondered what was wrong.

"Ohhhh, fuuuuck," she said slowly, her eyes closing as she spoke.

"What - you're not surprised?" asked Francois.

"Wish I was," she said after another long pause. "No, no, not at all. I know people who've dealt with what I think you're describing and it's not pretty."

"But, who, how do you know..." he asked incredulously.

"My brother's family," she said. "Gone into witness protection. These people are not police. Police hate them. Even the CIA despise them. These are the meanest bunch of fuckers you'll ever encounter if it's the same people. I'll tell you what they did to my brother's wife. Oh wow. They'll find you if you don't get something going and fucken' fast. Fuck, figures you'd come here."

She got up from the seat and headed towards a hallway off the den.

"Follow me," she beckoned. "Let me show you what her family saw."

Climbing a spiral staircase to a loft, they crossed a small space to an inset bookshelf behind an old armchair. Pulling the shelf away, an entrance to a hidden cubby space was revealed.

"Had this built while Steve and I were still together," she said, glancing back at Francois. "You still remember *him* don't you?"

Inside were boxes of old family memorabilia, piles of clothing and rustic furniture.

Opening a large chest, she reached in, pulling out a brown paper envelope. Emptying it onto a small table, she sorted through several grainy Polaroid's, finally choosing one to show them.

"This is how it all started," she said. "My brother took this from his backyard porch."

The photo appeared to be of a cylindrical object hovering over a lawn at dusk.

Looking closer, they could see it had antennae coming out its sides and not in any particular order. The lighting was good and the object's smooth metallic looking edges were in sharp focus, unlike most photos circulating on the net.

"My brother died that night just after this photo was taken," she said matter-of-factly. "That thing ripped him to pieces."

Francois studied the picture. It looked like there were dried blood splotches on the back and a slight burn at one of its edges.

"It's from that night," she whispered, her hand betraying a slight tremor.

"A special coroner was called in. Ruled it a lawn tractor accident. No burial - there was nothing to bury. Family were given money - lots of it, in order not to talk. But it was too much for Shelley. She got messy, started talking. They finally got to her while she was institutionalized in Penetang."

Wiping a tear from her cheek, she said there was more.

Deep in the chest was a glass mason jar, which she raised cautiously to the light.

"When the thing left, there was a burned-out hole in the grass and this liquid was at the centre. Shelley gathered it up before anyone got there and gave it to us for safe keeping. The team members apparently knew this stuff should have been there. There were other cases where it was left behind and they wanted more samples to study. Shelley said fuck that. She wasn't letting anybody have it."

In the dim room the strange contents held an amber glow, not unlike maple syrup. Ethan had seen this before too, had washed it from his own back lawn several years back at the estate. Same surrounding circumstances too - circular mark and burnt grass. He'd thought it was kids having a late-night bonfire and had let it seep into the ground. In a few days it was gone.

"Does it have an odor," he asked. "We should have it tested."

"It does," she replied, loosening the lid. "Take a whiff. Sulphur."

The pungency was strong and she quickly tightened the lid.

"His kids saw the whole thing," she said, starting to sob. "Trevor, his eldest, shot himself a year ago and his sister Dianna is hooked on meth. They're all in witness protection now. My other brother's family hears from them like once a year."

"You said they got to her while she was inside," said Francois. "What did you mean by that?"

"They came to visit her at the hospital and after that she was never the same. I don't know if they hypnotized her or what, but she completely changed after that. She's helpless now, like a zombie. Stares into space, doesn't say much. Goes through the motions but that's it. She's been through so much."

Collecting herself, Carla put the jar away and sat on a stool. "What are your plans?" she asked. "You can stay here for as long as you want, but you won't be able to go anywhere. Soon there'll be some story put out to media. 'Two men missing' or wanted for something. 'Call police if you see them'. Shelley had grand plans of taking the kids east, buying a home and starting over. Such a horrible thing. And they still have no fucking clue what it was."

"If we can stay, can you check out the town and see if there's any gossip going around," asked Francois. "Like you say, we won't be able to go anywhere, but we need to know what's happening. Oh, we might as well tell you it's back too. Lots of sightings. Weird shit at Ethan's place."

"I'll check things out," she said."But they will be looking for you. You can't shop or phone anyone. They have live recognition tech now, pick you out of millions of calls. The public doesn't know how fucked they are. Could go your whole life staying out of trouble, but if this shit finds you, it claims you."

"We know," said Francois. "But something has to give. There isn't anyone else who had a handle on this stuff you know about who could say what is going on? All I see are books with big theories, but none of it rings true. It's like anyone who's ever really come close to it just wants to forget."

"I know Shelley wanted to find out more," said Carla. "It's not of this world. We just aren't told about it. You see the limits of our freedom and education systems pretty quickly when this touches your life. I'd always been told people that see this shit are cranks or delusional. Nothing would have prepared us for it. They tried to say it was dogs at first, but changed their story to the tractor when it was apparent it was done with blades. I never expected I'd be reliving this shit today and that you'd be involved."

"You never even hinted at this the whole while we were together," said Francois. "How long were we a thing? Eight months? I wouldn't have believed it back then. Ethan, I went out with Carla about ten years ago. Met while I was doing Internet installing. I wired this place. You never moved though? Thought you'd have settled down with Steve. Those were different times."

"There was one thing she found," she said. "One guy who seemed to know a bit more than the others, but he got creepy, was always showing up where she was, even months later. A short bald guy with a weird smile. Told her he was from the future and I guess she'd had enough. Went into protection after that. Think that stopped it."

Chapter 21

The wire Ronnie had rigged around the perimeter of the cottage had gone off again.

It was the second time that morning, but he`d slept peacefully otherwise, a feat given his arm. Once again, he sat upright and poked his nose through the moth-eaten curtains of the lower bunk where he'd set up camp.

The cottage was a few kilometers along the trail through Longford and he'd stayed there before as it was the easiest of three in the area to break in to with no alarms or owners.

An old beer can fell onto the back deck, revealing a raccoon.

At 7am he was able to scrounge some coffee that'd been left in the kitchen cabinets by the last squatter and there was enough water still in the lines to fill a canteen. Outside he brought it to a boil over the fire pit, enjoying a moment`s peace in the mountains. Autumn in Longford never changed, he thought, sitting on a log taking his first sips. It was clear again, with not a cloud in the sky, but it was colder as the temperature had dipped with an influx of crisp late fall westerlies.

He'd leave his things here, his bag of clothes and wallet. Come back for them in a few days.

At 8:45am he left with a significantly lighter duffel bag, just the gun and ammo, his money and a bit of food he'd found in the cupboards. At the dock he maneuvered an old canoe into the water and prepared for the trip across Bird to the portage at Saw.

After fastening a small motor he'd discovered in the shed, he hauled a huge canister out and poured some gas in with his one good hand. Then he dragged the canoe out further and poured in what was left. He was extremely relieved when it coughed then started up. On the trip across he counted two campfires along the south shore, but wasn't close enough to see who it was. Nobody would think anything was amiss. It wasn't unheard of for some cottagers to still be around.

At Pine Point, he lugged everything ashore, dragging the canoe up as far as he could across a small sandy beach then along a rugged trail that snaked through the woods for 10 yards.

Saw was the most remote lake in Longford with only one cabin on it, as he remembered.

The sun was getting higher and it was turning damn hot. So hot he decided to brave a sunburn, taking off his shirt in return for some soft wind on his overheated, pale and clammy white skin.

On Saw he faced the canoe north and pushed it off the beachhead near a no smoking sign that was riddled with bullets, then waded in after it. He had to kind of jump and roll into the back end, which inevitably pushed the canoe beneath the waterline, momentarily filling the end with stinky leech laden muck.

Bailing as much as he could, he sat quietly for a moment staring up into the clear blue sky and thought about just going home. *Do it now, you'll wish you had,* said that little voice which was usually right. But somewhere in one of the whispy clouds he saw her - Sam Blackwell - and he just couldn't.

With no real plan other than to check out the lake, he decided that if nothing was there, he`d pack it in and go home. *I'll go back to Jordanna,* he thought, *she still needs me.*

Again, the small motor leapt to life. The cabin he was looking for was on the north shore. He'd boated past it before, but never looked inside. Today the lake was calm, with geese flying south overhead and the odd loon calling. The hum of the motor and the idyllic, undisturbed fauna called to mind times he'd spent fishing there with Fred in his teens.

Soon he was passing the sister islands, which were little more than three small jetties that'd broken off from the mainland as the water rose at the height of each season.

Shifting in his seat, he cut the engine as he approached the north shore, guiding it in with one paddle. An old rickety dock pushed out from a rocky beach area, but it was so weather worn it was of no use.

Beyond it lay an overgrown lawn and a tiny dilapidated stone cottage. At knee depth he stepped out and dragged the canoe the rest of the way in, perching it securely between some beach rocks.

Then he made his way up through the tangled grass and brush.

Everything looked like it needed a fresh coat of paint. The stairs had collapsed, and the two front windows were thick with years of dark grey film. At the side entrance he turned the door handle, but the lock was jammed. He'd have to find another way in.

Around the back a rusty beige propane tank and derelict black BBQ stood on a sun worn porch that also had cracked, broken steps. The door at the top was locked tight, but the window beside it was slightly open. Prying it further with an old piece of lumber, he leveraged about two more feet of crawl space. Then, hoisting himself up and through the opening using what was left of his energy, he pushed himself through, landing sideways in a dusty, bug filled metal sink.

Whoever had owned the place had money at one time, he thought, as his eyes grew accustomed to the dinginess.

With a thud, he landed hard on the floor after twitching sideways to brush at a wasp that had come in with him. Now was not a good time to get stung out here with no epi-pen, he thought, rubbing the back of his aching, but un-stung head.

Crawling to the living room, he pulled himself up against an old wicker armchair and took everything in. The walls were hung with old paintings that seemed European - depictions of old mills and castles. No one had been there for years, and the dust was an inch-thick covering everything. Silk curtains, half eaten by moths hung like ghosts over the large front bay windows, and there was mouse shit everywhere.

Standing, he walked down the hall checking out the bedrooms. More dust and decay, some dead mice and the skeletal remains of a long dead squirrel lying face up on the bed like it was sun tanning in hell.

In the washroom, the toilet was filled with more mice while the sinks and overhead lamps were congested with dead bugs. Near the kitchen area there was a staircase leading down to the basement. It was pitch black going down, but things brightened at the bottom where he made out a den with some light pouring in through a pair of sliding glass doors, in from the wild back lawn.

Opening these, he spied a rusty swing set yawning in the late morning sun near a back fence where a thick-woods overtook the grass. Beside it another contraption creaked in the gentle wind. It was a blue rocket ship shaped iron jungle gym, the kind found in children play areas and public parks in the late 70's and early 80's. Odd. Those hadn't been privately available and especially not at remote lake access properties. But there it was, glistening with dew and a faux red planet at its rusted tip to boot.

Making his way through the waist high reeds, he could see as he drew closer, it was part of a larger playground.

Running his good hand along the aged chipped paint of an old see saw, he could hear laughter.

It was children, children running and dancing and laughing. Children dressed in white. and older people in dark suits.

The sun is so hot today, he could hear them saying. *What's there. She's over there. Don't look at it. Don't loo...*

Somehow they drifted away and the vision ended before he knew it had even happened.

He was shaking now and there was sweat pouring from his brow. He was on the ground and it was night too - *but how...?*

How did I get here?

Looking around, he feebishly wiped his sopping forehead.

The wild yard was empty and the moon shone in the reeds and tangles of the now glistening grass. He was alone. No swings, no fence, no rocket ship jungle gym.

Like a creeping nightmare, he knew what had occurred:

It was her.

Quickly, draw the mark. Ronnie, draw the mark.

Grabbing a stick, he furiously ripped at the grass with his hand, then the bare soil, stabbing the puny branch as deep as he could, etching a rough half circle and upside down cross. Jupiter. Jupiter had always worked.

He let the image sink deep, felt it burrow inside him mixing with his out of control heartbeats.

Let it do its work, it just needs time.

Laying back, he stared into the endless night and felt the cool air wash over his body as his good fingers crawled feverishly in the mud. Closing his eyes, he could feel it fading. He'd forgotten how disgusting and raw it was. His good fingers, still clutching at clumps of moist soil and twigs desperate in their attempts to claw back to a more stable reality, felt like they had lives of their own.

Memory is the key, Ronnie. Like a bread crumb trail, through the worlds. Focus Ronnie, what it's doing is not real.

He focused until it was all there was, there in his mind, Jupiter, magnificent, a savior, blotting out all other possibilities.

Between gasps, he cried, wondering how he'd walked into it without knowing?

He`d taken the pill. Had they lost their potency? Opening one eye, the limitless starry firmament shone with tiny fires, as they really were. The clay in his clutch, kneaded now hard and cold, crumbling and dry.

It was gone.

Had it known he was coming? If so, where was she? The effect could occur over miles or just a few feet away. Saw was a remote area of the District, the closest other water body was Lake of Bays, 5 kilometers West, through the forest.

"The subject exhibits a proclivity for naturally occurring water bodies, stated one of the old reports, *Available data shows naturally inclined habitation patterns, with the subject having migrated of its own free accord to such geographical features throughout the subject's life. The reason for this staying pattern is not currently understood."*

He'd been too young to understand that when he was 9, but Fred had made it crystal clear:

"Stay away from lakes and rivers, Ronnie."

Now the silver lit lonely ramshackle cottage stood barren, devoid of such stories and beyond it, the lake.

The forest path he'd have to take to Lake of Bays lay ahead, starting where the rocket jungle gym had landed.

The bright full moon would remain Jupiter until dawn.

Chapter 22

I

Ivan stood in the estate's front foyer watching shadows stretch in the garden as the silver moon passed overhead.

A door creaked open in the hall and Jack's tall looming figure emerged into the glow of the always flickering hall lamps.

"Come with me," he said, ushering Ivan towards the door with a welcoming, outstretched arm.

They passed through several winding corridors, then down a flight of stairs to the cellars, on the way through the room that was the men's den in his own time.

He marveled at how completely alien the estate was to its modern version, and, as they strode through its halls, the cumulative effect was that of a maze in an inner psychological register, not a real physical place, but one beyond the limits of perception alone.

They came to a wall at the end of one of the cellar halls. A teak mirror hung on it stretching from floor to ceiling, adorned with exquisite Vedic Indian carvings. Knowing his antiques, Ivan thought this piece dated from the late 17th century. Reaching out, he drew his fingers across its ornate detailing. Jack brought a lamp closer and gently pressed on its mirror face.

A click sounded and the wall moved, revealing the mirror to be a doorway. Ivan felt a slight annoyance at having to leave it as they passed through its threshold. The huge door/mirror closed behind them and they were now in a tight stone passage with granite block stairs leading down what appeared to be several flights in a spiral pattern. More lamps lit the space about every ten feet, but it was dim going.

Down they went circling the stone column wall, the lamplight flickering, casting maniacal, gloating shadows, distorting their own with the dancing black flames.

Peering down, Ivan could see the bottom slowly emerging. There were outlines of another large doorway. As they drew closer he could hear a murmur of voices through the wall.

Jack opened the door and he could make out five figures, clad in black from head to toe, some wearing hoods.

He was introduced to the group as 'our friend' and an immediate respect seemed obvious.

An older man with a shock of white hair handed them two black cloaks. After putting them on, Jack admonished the others to listen:

"Tonight we complete the rite," he said. "We know our parts, but should we have to separate before or after, we meet back here using the usual routes. Are there any questions? John, have you brought adequate protection?"

The burly man he'd seen in the room motioned to two other men who Ivan hadn't noticed at first, who were standing by another door. They were packing muskets and one had a crossbow slung over his shoulder.

"Well then, we all know our roles," continued Jack. "Follow my lead at all times. Not a word until the given signals."

Falling into line, the door opened and a blast of cool fall air rushed in. Leaves crunched beneath their feet as they made their way out across a small cobbled courtyard towards the thick, black woods.

An absurd tension stretched within him, speaking to somewhere between hopelessness and purpose. How could any actions, magickal or otherwise, possibly bring about change in his own time, he wondered. One look up into that thick, deep, wondrous black ink and everything was rendered temporary, insignificant sparks.

The path gave way to hilly terrain and they paused momentarily as Jack conferred with the man he'd called John. Just within earshot, Ivan could hear them talking:

"At the narrows we meet up with the Magistrate's men," said the man. "Burke will be there too with the orders of the Queen. But if we take the corduroy road we'll lose valuable time due to this past week's rain. We need to arrive at Mkjininnk before dawn, set up camp and a perimeter. Don't forget - we only have a few short hours from then to prepare before the invocation and it's still uncertain as to whether we'll run into trouble. I don't think we will, but we are dealing with an extremely mad shaman as you know."

Jack scuffed the ground with his boots. In a low tone he said the narrows would be best and that he had boats waiting at the mouth of the channel.

"We open ourselves to discovery if we take it, but for time's sake we really have no other choice," he said. "Let's hope the orders don't include surprises."

"I was told they wouldn't," said John. "They lost five men in the hills this past month, served up in the usual way."

Ivan stepped back behind a tree as the two men walked closer.

Mkjininnk - he couldn't even pronounce it.

The whole idea of places being magickal in a real sense was rekindling memories from his youth.

Magick had entered his life mysteriously when he was 14, while staying at his aunt's cottage on Lake Joseph in the district. Searching the grounds one day, he'd been in an old root cellar when he discovered a most strange book.

It was a copy of Israel Regardie's the Golden Dawn which he read over the course of his weeklong stay between campfires and boat rides.

Devouring it and anything else similar that summer, it was a love spell he first cast which had really got him hooked. The subject of the working had been a girl in his Grade 7 class Shary Turner. He'd willed to bring she and he together romantically and within a week he was sitting on a couch making out with her at her birthday party.

With Wham!'s Careless Whisper listing through the damp basement, he was on to something.
The working had really been about getting to sleep with her, but it had been a major victory sliding some tongue down her throat.

Soon he found he could predict other people's decisions and put into motion events simply through concentration. But one day something scared him off it.

It was August 1983 and he'd been sitting in his then home in Guildwood Scarborough when he'd had an upsetting experience. The night before he'd performed a ceremony calling on a spirit to clear his path of any obstacles which might hinder his prowess in skateboarding half-pipes. Standing in a circle he'd fashioned out of twigs in the forest, he read out a prepared statement over a doll he'd bought to represent him.

He'd wrapped it with sigils drawn on parchment paper with the intended outcome in mind, then poured gas on it and lit it, capturing the darkest smoke in a jar which contained another doll that represented him in a more animus/instinctual way.

It was rebirth and playing with essences basically - all so he could perform airs like Tony Hawk.

But while he watched TV in his home's front room the next evening, he'd heard a tap at the window and seen a pure white man with silver hair peering in holding a skateboard. It was the loudest white he'd ever seen and the figure disappeared in an instant. Running outside, he'd searched for any more signs of the strange man, but he'd disappeared.

Up the road he spied the mailman, which was odd as it was 6:45pm and getting dark enough that the street lamps were just turning on.

Back inside, the phone rang.

At first there was silence punctuated by an odd hissing crackle. Then a metallic voice faded in as if from another frequency like someone with a mouth full of TV noise. The words were robotic, but plainly understood.

"We are inside," it told him.

Hanging up in shock, he'd realized he was too old to tell his parents. This was the kind of nonsense they'd say wasn't really happening and besides, he already knew it was a direct result of his testing the rules of reality.

That was what had made him give it up. The fact that things *did* happen with magick, but at his own psychological expense.

Soon after he'd shut it all down, burning his I-Ching and Ouija boards. But you can't easily un-know something.

In the following weeks he'd suffered a bit of a breakdown, getting into fights at school and mischief with the kids from the townhouses. So he found himself relishing the simple things in order to cool off. Dinners out at restaurants with his parents, walking his Shetland sheepdog, playing Atari. Anything that could be used as an anchor for his own consciousness. He had the foresight to know there'd be triggers he couldn't control, like déjà vu and premonitions. If he needed to, he'd read he could get hypnotized in order to try and forget.

He thought about this on the long march to Tretheweys, where, two hours later Jack told the group to make camp.

They were by the waterfalls, its warm mists rising like rushing specters in the early chill morning.

Several in the party huddled over ground fires preparing small meals and tea.

Rummaging through his coat pocket, he found a lighter and before he could put it to use, was seen by an older woman in the group.

"What is *that*?" she asked incredulously.

They'd never seen one, so he flicked it again, producing a small flame.

"Where did you get that?" echoed an old grizzled man. "Jack, what do we have here?"

Noticing the commotion, the master peered closely at Ivan and his flame, which he was now waving in slow circles before the others.

"Ivan has travelled far to help us out tonight - Ivan, if you'd be so good as to put that away for the time being. I'm sure everyone would love to see all the inventions you have, but in due time, yes?"

"That's all for now, I guess," he agreed, flicking it off and nodding towards their leader.

In his tent he placed it back in his jacket amidst the other few belongings he'd had on him when he was taken. In a pocket, his hands brushed up against the feather.

Thank God it's still there.

But why would he say that? He still didn't even know where it had come from.

In his hands he inspected it more closely. Purple and black, it was as long as his right hand and still shiny, so it mustn't have been neglected long. Probably a crows or a ravens. Its bone spine was pure white from tip to end. In his day people knew not to go picking up feathers - filthy things that could spread viruses and disease. He wanted to throw it out in the woods, but something wouldn't let him and his thoughts again returned to its origin. Had he brought it with him or had he found it at the estate in this time? He'd brought the lighter, so it was possible, but he'd never owned it, he was sure of that. Maybe he'd grabbed it at Ethan's for some reason. No, that didn't feel right.

II

At 2am they were awoken by the sound of someone shouting. As the others roused from their sleep, he could see Jack through his tent flap, standing over a fire, above him a swirling black cloud changing shape in a vortex of static and smoke.

He was chanting magickal incantations, beside him the burly man lay at his feet.

"John!," shrieked an old woman from her tent, in shock at seeing the body.

The floating mass was changing as Jack chanted, assuming the form of a figure.

Whatever it was, it had black tendrils for arms that reached out in all directions.

The older magician ceased chanting and leaned upon a staff he used in rituals for support.

No one had mentioned any of this being planned, thought Ivan, and one look upon everyone else's faces confirmed this. Something must have happened while they'd slept, but what?

The inky swirls were receding, and the figure danced away, reduced to a small spot before disappearing completely.

Falling to his knees, the magician cradled his dead comrade's body, sobbing and staring up into the empty night. As the others emerged, he turned to them mumbling something unintelligible about pressing on.

Releasing the body, he then arose and stood beneath a nearby tree alone in silence as the others paid respects.

"Who was that," Ivan whispered to the silent leader.

But there was no reply.

The older magician was gazing east, where, at the far end of a hilly section of distant sparse pines, wispy plumes of white/grey smoke twisted skywards.

"The Ojibway shaman Musquedo and his menageries," he finally muttered. "And with such little time."

Chapter 23

I

For what had seemed like days Saara had drifted in a hollow haze, little more than a dried husk with crashing dreams that streaked their own edges.

It had been a full 24 hrs before she'd even been able to open her heavily crusted, mascara smeared eyelids. Rain whipped against the window and the harsh white of Thursday morning's barren sky burned her irises, so she tried again to sleep, praying she'd really wake up.

But there was real cold stone tile against her cheek when she shut her eyes. Something was very wrong.

She was in her hotel room, that much she knew. She could hear voices carrying through the walls and the muffled squeaks of passing room service trolleys.

Someone was with her in the room too, in the visitor's den and there was a horrid, putrid smell.

Vomit.

Lifting her face from the floor, sweaty strands of hair remained stuck in the stone. There was a pungent chemical odour in the wretch, which forced her to gag as a pair of nylon clad feet approached, first across the carpet, then the tile.

Following them up, they grew into legs until the blurred lines of the hostess sharpened into view.

Leaning over her, the woman placed something on the bedside table.

"You must have fallen again, I'm so sorry," she said reaching down. "Oh, you are such a mess. You poor thing."

Saara felt arms around her, then lifting and pulling and straightening.

A flight of sheets, then slow warmth flooding her legs and spine.

She was in bed with warm miraculous bed sheets, her eyes still fluttering like moths, mouth still drier than cotton.

"Water?" asked the woman.

"Yesss...," she barely croaked.

The woman brought a clear glass cup to her lips, tilting her head gently to allow a flow.

Her lips quivered as the first sips came in. It felt cold and violent, but she was alive - almost.

Another nondescript hour passed, and she was well enough to sit up.

The room had seemingly aged since she'd last been there. Now it was more like a college girl's dorm, messy with secrets. There'd be no explaining all the equipment - cameras, recording devices, notepads, which were in full view on the coffee table. She couldn't tell how much of her stuff had been noticed. Probably all of it.

But there was daylight. It was all that mattered. And soon she was alone again.

Dark stains in the carpet to the left of the bed signaled numerous bouts of vomiting that had already been cleaned. Her heart was beating slower now, something that had worried her since she'd awakened. Didn't feel like potatoes were being forced through its ventricles anymore though.

The frazzled thoughts were dissipating too, back beneath the subconscious TV chatter where they belonged.

Whatever had been put in her drink was powerful. She was meant to have been taken right out of the picture.

Forcing strength, she lurched up and forward, swiveling herself and stretching her legs until they reached cold terra-firma. Hands at her sides, she attempted to steady her body, but the slight give of the mattress didn't help, and she drew woozy breaths as another wave of dizziness forced her to pause.

Finally she stood, but not without severe pulsing pain throughout her upper body. Slowly, in uneasy steps, she made her way along the walls with her hands, gingerly stepping over the piles of scattered clothing and her purse, towards the washroom.

By the toilet there was a note:

"I've been checking in on you and have your spare room card. Be back at six tonight. You can always call me 705-395-6623."

A mania of hopelessness set in. Like she was under a microscope with everyone in the hotel knowing more about everything than her.

Sloppy.

The stinging humiliation was odd though, as she hadn't considered anyone she'd met there in much regard. It was directed straight in the mirror.

Methodically she tried washing it away with strokes of a damp cool cloth across her forehead, watching herself slowly return as beads trickled down to her chest.

An aching throb was still inflating her temples and she cursed aloud, remembering she hadn't brought any Tylenol.

Through the pounding some recollections started to return. Dinner. The elevator. Something going on. Something.... It was slow in coming, but.... nothing. Then the hostess moving about in the room.

Wet cloth clamped to her forehead, she returned to the bedroom and sat in a chair by the window.

There'd been plans to listen in on something. What were they? Yes - the man, the men on the dock.

She shook her head ruefully. Chances were slipping by.

Before she could settle her thoughts, a series of loud knocks suddenly crashed the silence.

Freezing, she felt her blood pressure rise in distinct increments. Another two loud, forceful knocks rang out and she prayed the lock switch was turned.

Whoever was on the other side of the door did try turning the handle, but the barrier stood firm. Relief, then more heightened worry coursed through her veins:

Whoever it was was still there.

Was there was some secret to being in situations like these that she should know? Of course there wasn't.

Chest heaving, she finally sank deeper into the chair as whoever it was moved away and off down the hall.

Then the tears came. In frantic, quiet sobs the shambles of their plan was quite evident.

Sneering at the empty room, at her own ineptness, she cursed the bland mocking day outside, which was busy casting leaves across the lawn like some immense stormy bird releasing its plumage.

"One.... fucking.... thing...," she sputtered. "Not one fucking thing right."

Kicking off her heels she sat back laughing, relieving some of the over the top tension.

After long wipes at her nose and cheeks, came another realization:

The hostess.

She could trust this woman - *she was safe* - that's what the locked door said - *trust her*.

Scanning the room for her phone, she found it on the floor beneath the bed, but the battery was dead. Plugging it into the wall, she sat back again, resigned to wait for those first few bars of light.

In 13 minutes a brief electronic crescendo signaled sufficient power. Madly she dialed the number, which rang three times before a generic greeting put her through to voicemail. She didn't want to leave a message - few trails were best when dealing with unknowns. She'd sip more of her water and wait.

Shortly after 6pm, but before she could react, the door cracked open and she heard the hostess walk in.

"You are up, that's sooo great, how are you?" asked the woman, setting down a hot, steamy meal tray on the TV bureau.

"We have to make a plan," she replied quickly, looking up at her savior.   "Have you found out anything, have you seen that woman?"

"I've seen her around the hotel today," said the hostess, a worried look entering her eyes. "I followed her - she seems to know our owner, his name is Mark Edmons.."

"Edmonstone. Yes, I know him," snapped Saara. "How does she know him?"

"Don't know, but I saw her in his office with him early this morning. I saw her again in the halls this afternoon. She was heading out on one of the cruises at the docks. I'm sure it was her who slipped you something at dinner. You probably should just leave."

"Look," said Saara, sitting up in the chair, "I'm not going to explain everything now, but I am here on an investigation into serious matters. There's no way I'm leaving without getting to the bottom of this. I've already wasted what, two fucking days, and still have to figure things out. If you don't want to be involved I understand. But believe me, I am so grateful for your help."

"That's not all, let me finish," said the woman. "I can't say for sure, but I think whatever is happening with you and them is connected with what's been going on with some of the girls here on the island."

"What girls?" replied Saara, interest piqued as she acted completely clueless.

"The parties - the hookers. Some of the staff know about it."

"It's hard not to see what's happening," she continued. "The owner is said to be involved. It's my third summer here, so I don't want anything coming back on me, but you might want to look into that side of things - but after you leave."

Saara looked directly in the industry woman's eyes, where an honesty was beaming back like the headlights of a trusty old ford.

It's never just about trust though, she thought, *wish it was that easy.*

Getting people involved meant you became responsible for them, but wasn't life also a flow of experiences? People do get themselves into things all on their own...

"Ok, I'll tell you more," said Saara.

"I'm aware of the ring, but I'm here investigating a murder case - you may have heard about them - two girls killed this past summer. They were part of the service - rumored to be anyway. They are thought to have worked here on the island. I'm gathering anything I can about suspects. My partner and I are investigative reporters. He's not here, but I need your help. Does anything I'm telling you ring any bells? Anything you remember about the summer stick out? I can find you photos of the two victims..."

"There are so many girls that come out here," replied the hostess. "But yes, some of the same ones return. Summer.....lots of things about the summer and spring come to mind....let's see..."

"Look, at this point we also need to get out of this room," said Saara. "I just, for the life of me can't figure out how they and she got onto me or even what the hell she's doing messed up in this. I met her by chance on the ferry and knew her as a kid. Unless she Googled me and put two and two together because I'm a reporter.."

"I remember there was a time, about mid-July, when it all seemed to stop for a few weeks," said the hostess. "The other staff were mentioning it - the house staff mainly because there wasn't as much work to do in the rooms at that time - cleaning-wise I mean."

"That would have been right around the time these girls first went missing," said Saara, rummaging through one of her suitcases. "I just wish I could find the photos I packed, they are here somewhere.."

"*That's right*," remembered the hostess, tapping the wall. "I remember now. It was when the strange men were here."

"What strange men?"

"It was odd come to think of it," she continued. "Just before it all stopped for a few days, there were two new men, I say strange, because they didn't suit the regular profile. They were seeing girls in their rooms, but you could tell they weren't ordinary johns. They knew Edmonstone and were somehow associates of his. Very stiff. Almost like scientists. Not attractive - serious. Like they weren't in it for the sex. But who knows what goes on behind closed doors..."

That was interesting, thought Saara. She'd suspected Edmonstone was involved in the ring as a side business, but were these men there for different reasons?

The light rain had become a full-fledged storm outside, replete with lightning and ominous, echoing thunder and Saara drew the curtains tighter.

Lifting the meal tray and setting it down across both knees, she raised the metal lid from the dish, allowing some steam to escape.

"The drivers who brought the girls here didn't like these men, I remember," added the hostess. "One of the staff overheard one of them mention something about pulling out for good if their behavior continued."

"What behavior?" asked Saara, between mouthfuls of chicken kiev.

"Just that they were weirdos, that's all I know. Just...not right. Didn't fit with the scene."

Spying a brown envelope on the dresser, Saara reached out for it and quickly emptied its contents.

Two large black and white photos, each of the young victims, stared up at them.

"Chloe Germaine and Carrie Watkinson," said Saara.

Staring, the hostess sat down on the bed's edge and looked up at the ceiling.

"I did know Chloe," she admitted, swallowing slowly.

"What do you mean??," asked Saara, "the way that you say it - it's a little unnerving."

"The murders - everyone knows," continued her savior. "It's obvious why you're here."

"She and I got to know each other, you could say," she continued, as Saara stared incredulously. "She was one of the regulars. I met her one night down by the pool at a party. We hit it off, formed a friendship. She'd...bring me drugs."

"Go on," said the reporter calmly, putting the food away and lifting the photo of Chloe. "What was she like? Did she say anything about the johns?"

"Yes. I just need time. It's.... painful."

"There were times," began the hostess. "Close to the last time I saw her when she was really fucked up about things, but I don't think any of it had to do with the work. She had a huge coke habit. I chalked it up to that. It was disturbing come to think of it - she told me she was going away to do a big job - about a month long, with one of the new johns - at his cottage. Usually she'd bring me my stash, but this time she needed me to pick some up for her. She hadn't been back to the city in a few weeks."

"Did you get it?"

"Yes."

"And this john, he was one of the weirdos?"

"No, he was a friend of the owner's though. That's right - he knew the other men, but they had stopped coming about a week before he arrived. Again, wouldn't peg him for a typical john. Wealthy and educated type, but a little sinister, I would say. You could tell she was worried about the trip. What's the word - apprehensive."

"Can you describe him to me?" asked Saara, already jotting notes.

"He was older - seemed a little older than Edmonstone. Grey beard and hair, slightly balding in the middle. Was almost like a general in an army - a no nonsense type. Stern. Was like he was always thinking about something else. I was only around them together as a server, but my impression was he was just killing time. Always looking at his phone. Not much of a tourist."

Saara could feel her color returning and hints of strength in her legs as she fidgeted in the chair listening.

"Ok, we need to figure shit out," she said. "Are you good for the day? Done work I mean? I need a shower and if you're free, we need to start coming up with options as soon as I am dressed."

The older woman gave a wary nod.

"So... I'll just stay here with you for now?"

"Yes. Don't answer the door & keep it locked."

II

The first rush of warm water felt glorious, but there was so much to think about.

The hotel room was a temporary holding cell. They were likely waiting for her to leave.

And who were these men she'd mentioned? She had to get her hands on another computer. Maybe they'd go to the hostess's house, use one there.

Leaning back against the marble wall, she allowed the water to fall down around her. Everything was out of control.

In the den she put on a pair of warm grey slacks, the ones she'd planned to wear on a cruise, then thick black socks and a Mohican red sweater she'd bought that fall. Wiping the top of the full-length mirror, she dried her hair, then pulled it back, styling it in a tight bun.

Brushing her teeth felt good, so did spitting out the last two days with mouthwash.

In the bedroom she gathered a few essentials into her purse as the hostess watched. Her cell phone - where was it now? On the TV.

Dropping it and the charger into the mix, she turned and asked the older woman her name.

"Helen Crawford," came the reply.

"Well, Helen, I'll need a computer," she said matter-of-factly, placing her reporter gear carefully into their case.

"I have one in my room that you can use," answered Helen.

"Hoooold it," said Saara. "*You're room*? You mean you stay here at the hotel?"

"Yes, but it's in a chalet at the far end of the grounds. I share it with another girl, but she's away for a month, which is good timing for you. We all stay here on the island - the full time ones anyway."

"How are we going to get there?!" she replied, her purple lipstick dangling precariously in her hand. "They'll be watching the cameras and the hallways. You have a wig I can use? No - I'm being serious - they probably have a camera on my room right now. I mean, I would."

"I'll check, but I think the only cameras we have are at the main entrances," said the hostess. "I'll grab an empty cleaners cart and get you out that way. We have to clean our chalets ourselves. It's part of the deal."

Saara just smiled.

This woman probably needed some adventure in her life. She'd have to stop trying to turn her off, but they had to be extra smart. She'd lucked out thus far and the only reason she wasn't dead was this 5 ft nine dirty blonde example of pure chance standing before her.

"Cool. I'll wait here. I'm basically ready if you are."

Siding up against the window she watched the storm through a crack in the drapes while Helen Crawford went to get a trolley.

Nothing was happening out there. No one in the tree lines, just a service worker and a few waitresses running for cover down one of the paths. To the east, as far as she could see the grounds were empty. The hotel was surrounded by clumps of forest on all sides, some sections thicker than others which gave it an isolated feeling.

Helen had had the presence of mind to take her bag when she left to make for more room in the cart. When she returned, Saara stuffed herself inside, pulled the cloth covering shut then stuck her thumb out signaling she was ready.

Now they were in motion and the cart jostled with a slight bump passing through the doorway onto the thick hallway carpeting. The click as the door closed behind them sounded final in a way she definitely didn't like.

Once on the carpet the jostling gave way to a smoother, calming roll.

At the elevator there was a bit of small talk as Helen chatted with another worker. In no time they were at ground level and on their way out the back side entrance. Soon she was bouncing along a cement walkway, presumably towards the chalets.

Almost there. Saara bit her lip and waited. There was still a chance they knew she was being helped by Helen, but so far, so good.

A ways down the path, the cart stopped suddenly and she heard a key turn in a lock.

"Don't move," whispered Helen. "I'm still checking things out."

The door hinge creaked, and the trolley tilted, hoisted by Helen over the chalet's front door step. Through the curtain she could see a light turn on. Then Helen said it was alright to come out.

The chalet was open concept with a high A-frame roof and loft area. Downstairs were two bedrooms, a washroom and kitchen.

She found herself standing on a gorgeous orange-green Adirondack rug.

The place smelled slightly musty, but it was pretty cozy.

"This is it," said Helen. "What do you think?"

"I love it," she replied, sitting down on a green afghan covered couch.

"It's home for now," sighed Helen. "We get free room and board and make our money on top of that. It's a pretty good gig. Been here three summers."

She brought over a cold glass of water, placing it on the coffee table in front of her new guest.

"Are you one of the longest remaining staff," asked Saara, watching as the older woman closed the blinds above the kitchen sink.

"You could say that," she laughed, pulling out a small plastic bag from one of the cupboards.

"You smoke?"

Sure she did.

"Yeah totally, I need to relax. I mean, I was almost killed."

"Yes, you were. Come on, I smoke upstairs."

In the loft, two chairs by a small window were gathered around an old stand up onyx-black marble ashtray.

From the window the hotel and its gardens could be seen through the trees surrounding the chalet.

Helen took a toke and passed it to Saara.

Inhaling in four long drawn out drags, she still wanted desperately to be anywhere but there. Hitting a first wave of euphoria, she stared through the sparse loft. Besides the chairs and ashtray, there was a makeshift rug made out of golf turf presumably abandoned by a former employee.

Helen was right. She'd have to leave somehow. As she pondered this, something startled her in one of the dark corners

"*What is that*," she asked, suddenly pointing.

The weed was hitting her harder now and Helen giggled, jumping up to go over and fetch the setup that had caught Saara's eye.

"This is my costume," she said, returning with a large black gown and Com dell Arte mask covered in sequins and ornate blue embroidery.

Holding it up like a prized possession with one hand, she ran her other one up and down the smooth fabric.

To Saara, it looked ghoulish, like something out of one of those new wave vampire flicks of the late 70's.

"It's what I'm wearing to the hotel's Autumn Ball Tuesday night," said Helen. "It's what I was given - we were all fitted for them last week."

Swaying with the gown like it was a mannequin, Helen danced light twirls across the loft area.

Both of them couldn't help but laugh and laugh.

Chapter 24

People were bundling up outside and the trees looked almost skeletal.

From the condo's living room window, Ethan could see ice forming in some puddles too, down where the spray of the bay was landing on the boards of the walkway.

Leashed dogs walked brisker too. Winter was coming.

Francois nodded to himself. He was thinking about heading over to Europe. He had family there - maybe he could change his name and live in the French countryside with his cousins?

They had a dairy farm, he remembered. He'd have to find a way over by ship though, it was the only transportation that didn't have tight security these days.

There had to be a way. He knew a guy who worked in the shipyards in Cape Breton. They could find passage from there. This is why people disappear, he told himself, there really are breaking points.

Carla's cigarette smoke billowed endlessly and they all sat blankly staring into it. She blew smoke rings and Francois told her she was talented.

"You guys need to get cleaned up," she told them. "Frank, you can show Ethan where everything is. There's extra towels in the upstairs cupboards."

With that she was off, housecoat swishing, leaving trails through the smoke.

Later that night, Ethan listened to Carla and Francois talk as a neon light from outside flashed silently through his room.

They were no further from where they started. Worse, even. A delirious decline.

Carla had brought back Chinese earlier, which they had eaten voraciously.

Soon he dreamt, finding himself back home wandering the halls of the estate where he couldn't find his way to the library. In the dark he could hear Saara calling his name and he awoke startled and sweating, pulse racing, just as the dream had shifted to the spot in the back lawn where he'd found the oily circle.

It was 2:30am and there were noises outside - people talking and laughing in the street below.

They were up smoking outside Larry's All Night Laundry. A woman with an orange rinse who looked to be about 80 stared up at Carla's townhouse while some teens wrestled on the ground. Pulling the blinds open further he could see way out along the harbor wall where a lonely hobo lay huddled on a bench wrapped in newspapers and filthy blankets. Each fall they'd come in off the highways - the Town tried its best to give most of them rooms, but some were incurable, or just loved the independence. It wasn't widely known, but hobo bodies were dredged from the harbor, victims of their own waywardness as they jockeyed for vent space at the bench stations in the frigid morning hours.

Everything was relatively quiet now though and there was nary a vehicle on the street.

The ordinariness calmed him.

Soon he drifted off again, finding himself by the harbor outside. The scene was rapidly changing though, like different realities toppling one another.

That's how existence worked, he dreamt, blue skies changing to red, then to black, then back again. How did *whole* realities change, he wondered in the dream - at what levels do the switches get turned? Could humans access the knowledge needed to do it in real time one day?

In the morning around 6:30am he wrote his ideas down on a brochure on the side table.

Outside he could hear the fall wind picking up as dry leaves skittered across the townhouse's pointed red brick facade. Sitting up, he rolled his legs out and planted his feet on the cold floor. Stretching, he stood and walked over to the window. Morning quiet and he could hear Carla and Francois snoring in their room.

In the dim fluorescent light of the small washroom, he turned on the cold tap and soaked a washcloth. He was coming down with something and he raised it to his forehead, the coolness soothing his nerves.

How much longer did they have, he wondered. Could they elude this?

Back in his room he returned to bed, pulling the warm, thick comforter over his head.

He slept that way until 8:30.

Over breakfast Carla told them she'd be out shopping for most of the morning and to stay away from the windows. He and Francois got down to some serious talk after she left.

"Last night I dreamt they were here storming the building," said the young man. "Didn't sleep much after that."

"Me neither," Ethan replied. "They say to keep moving any time you're being...hunted. So, soon we'll have to get going."

"But *where* is the question," he continued, swatting at a lazy fly. "Also, we risk losing sight of what's going on if we're always on defensive. This is where things are happening - the window of opportunity is here, right now. Before we knew about any of this stuff, we'd always wondered, but now that we know something, well, it would be a shame to lose this chance."

"What chance?!" snapped Francois. "The chance to get killed? This thing is too huge. Fuck, you heard Carla about her family. You don't want any more of it. There's always going to be shit like this. Forget it - it's the least of my worries. I jus' need to get somewhere and start fresh."

"Ok, let's take it one step at a time," said Ethan, attempting to soften things. "Let's move in that direction, yes, but with a solid plan. Where do you think we can do that - Have a fighting chance to start again? You have a country in mind? I'm all ears."

"France," said Francois. "In France, they have people working on this problem in the government and they'd love to know what we know. We may get asylum there. They don't get along with the US program, is what I've learned through the literature. Different approaches - the West is typically bombastic, the French insular, more cultured. 'Disciplined' is how I read it."

"You have no idea about how the allied governments work," replied Ethan. "The recent terror attacks there have brought the countries much closer. They aren't about to play sides and risk that relationship over something like this. They'd hand us over in a heartbeat. Get a better idea."

"No, no, it will be ok," said Francois. "If we can make it there I'm sure we could stay. It's done all the time. New identities in return for information. No questions asked. Trust me."

"You know that woman I work with, Saara," said Ethan, "she still has no idea what's happening or where I am. If none of this took place I would never have dreamt life could take such bizarre turns."

"*Look*," said Francois, peeling an orange. "I have relatives there who could take us in. We could sail from the east coast, make a few discreet contacts with the embassy and speak with national security. They'd know we were legit by what we describe. It's just a matter of getting there. We can stay here a few more days, Carla says it's cool, but it's only a matter of time before this place gets very fucking small. A part of me says wait it out, that the phenomenon will move on, but that's wishful thinking. These people don't leave loose ends."

"So find out what you need," said Ethan calmly. "We have our answer then. But we're in Muskoka, Ontario and the shipyard you have to get to is in somewhere like Halifax. I'll travel with you, but there will be risks. Get Carla to search ships that travel abroad. See if they take passengers, see what's offered through the black market. I'm sure it's done, but we have to be sure about things. I'm with you, but it's got to be done right, or as right as it can be. We can't leave any traces."

Shortly before noon Carla returned with groceries and to their surprise, whiskey and beer.

"Might as well live it up while you can," she said cheerily, clearing the kitchen counter. It wasn't long before the booze was flowing.

But Ethan took things slow. There still had to be a way to find out more. The case was off the rails and he wondered about Saara and a tinge of embarrassment came over him. Here he had led things, but had ended up totally abandoning them. Some reporter. He wanted to go back - to before everything had split apart - to the time of clear goals and the mechanisms to achieve them.

A crash in the living room and a burst of new laughter broke his concentration.

It had been awhile since any of them had day drank. He was pretty sure Francois had made a habit of it throughout most of his life though. He and Carla seemed to be growing closer again and he watched as they flirted by the sofa. Making another drink, he joined them.

Carla was laughing and teasing Francois about his screw-on haircut:

"You'd think being chased would have taught you to try and fit in more," she said, trying to part things along a natural hair line.

Tipping backwards, she fell on the sofa and looked up at both of them, obviously happy to have some new company.

Talk turned to social media and how most everyone were brain dead consumer zombies.

"Everyone is medicated too," said Carla. "It's a joke - everyone's a victim. Fucking pussies. When we were young it was embarrassing for your friends if they were put on meds. Now it's the first thing the weaklings reach for. What a joke. Grow some ballsss..."

They were all in agreement. Francois said it was Big Pharma's greed, whereas Ethan saw it as societal control.

"Likely a mix of both," concluded Carla. "Can't put it down to just one."

Society's problems were old, said Francois, the uber medication was just the latest symptom of a latent anxiety in the soul of man, he explained.

His speech was slurring, his whiskey hand moving freely to Depeche Mode's People are People. Then they played some acid jazz pulled from a dusty CD rack Carla had stored in a closet.

By four they were toasted but not enough to dare heading outside.

That night they dined on a pork loin roast Carla prepared and knocked off early - Ethan in one of the living room love chairs, Carla and Francois in her bedroom upstairs.

Following breakfast the next morning, Carla said she was meeting with a friend that day who might have knowledge about the shipping yards out east.

Before noon while awaiting her return, they became aware of a commotion going on in the townhouse next door. Pressing his ear to the wall, Francois said he could hear a woman's voice talking excitedly about something she was seeing out her window.

"Yes, it's exactly the same thing as yesterday, I am not hallucinating," she was saying, likely into a cell. "I'm watching them right now. They're crawling the walls."

Racing to the living room window to see what she was describing, they scanned down, up and sideways, until their gaze landed on the buildings across the street. They could just make out tiny movements on the exterior walls, like a small swarm of bugs were crawling towards the roofline.

In and out of crevices they dipped, sometimes stopping at once, then changing direction, swarming to different areas of the buildings.

They were nanotech, something governments had had for some time and used mainly in situations like hostage takings and hijackings. The 'bugs' were near invisible to eyesight, but as a swarm produced a fast, dark cloud while moving across terrains. They could easily separate and become completely undetectable within seconds.

They were evident on at least two buildings across the street. The search had never ended.

"No sudden movements," cautioned Ethan. "They pick up on everything - blood pressures, voice strain, sudden movements. We'll have to go completely silent. Follow me."

Jotting a note for Carla explaining the situation, they directed her to watch the doorways and windows when she got home.

In the secret loft room, they huddled amidst the clothes bundles, maintaining silence, whispering only when needed.

After several hours light footsteps approached the wall. It was Carla. "Nothing out there now," she whispered. "Would they stay in one area long?"

Ethan didn't know. He surmised there'd be several passes across different areas of town. He was sure they had no tracing detectors on their clothes, but said the clothes which he and Francois had arrived in should be destroyed as soon as possible.

'The bugs' had many purposes.

In the late 80's they'd been responsible for many a psy-op, entering through the nasal cavities of unsuspecting victims, causing hallucinations as directed by governments that had the technology.

In the early nineties, entire trenches of soldiers were dug up in Iraq following the gulf war battles after they'd been bulldozed in with sand following nano-scale attacks that made them go crazy.

Those in the mainstream press who addressed the finds thought chemical weapons had caused the soldiers insanity, but typical of mainstream news outlets, the reporting hadn't dug deep and it was quickly forgotten.

Francois had heard this too, but hadn't given it much credence.

"They pick up on body warmth and can differentiate between males and females," Ethan explained, adding that he only knew what had been reported in trade papers.

Who knows how advanced it was now, decades later.

"The technology was bought up by the military and research went deep black," Ethan whispered. "But they haven't found us yet and that gives me hope. A superior tech would have had no problem doing it by now. We can't underestimate them, but we can't think they are omniscient either."

Carla had spoken with her friend and had made plans to meet him again in two days.

"I'll be back in a minute," she whispered. "Just have to get something I want to show you, that I picked up for us today. I think you'll like it."

Falling silent, they listened as she returned the bookshelf to its position covering the door, then tiptoed down to the kitchen. Then there was a loud scream and the sound of chairs being flung across the floor.

They were inside the condo.

Ethan and Francois listened helplessly as Carla struggled downstairs with her attackers, but it was brief. A few seconds of muffled screams, then more voices and heavy footsteps spreading through the rooms.

The lights were out and there was no way casual observers could find the secret space immediately. In moments though, two men had reached the loft and could be heard speaking beyond the wall.

"Affirmative, nothing," said one.

"Secure the front area," commanded another voice. "She'll talk."

Carla was screaming again.

Clenching his teeth, Ethan grimaced at the sounds of slapping skin and more muffled cries.

If she could keep their secret, a truth serum would eventually work.

Chapter 25

I

Henrietta Chapter had busied herself that morning with her usual rounds. Feed the pigs, tend to the horses (there'd been dwindling hay supplies since the start of September, the result of the harsh dry summer months, that had ruined so many local crops). It was now 2:30pm Saturday and there was still much to do.

She'd have to think of something to reduce her workload, she thought, as she pulled up to the barn doors, dust settling outside her jeep.

She still wanted that vacation her husband Richard had promised her, but any hopes of kicking it in the Bahamas that fall was dwindling. Richard had broken his left knee in August while corralling the cows and the bulk of the farm work now rested on her shoulders. At age 53 a reticence was developing in her that she hadn't quite come to terms with.

In the barn, the horses murmured in their stables awaiting their feed. They were fed twice daily - she and Richard had used to share the duties, but here she was for the second time since 4am, trudging through manure in her big blue rubber boots, swatting at horseflies, watching the Bahamas recede into a precarious future.

It was still dark in there. It was kept that way for the horses due to the still stifling Indian Summer they'd been having. Old Charley stomped his front hoofs and snorted as she approached his stall. Strange, she thought, checking him up and down, wonder what's got him so excited?

Grabbing an old thorn brush from its hanger, she ran it slowly down the old Sable's mane. But he only whinnied more and she quickly put it away when she saw it had no effect.

Some of the others in the stalls were similarly agitated, which made her double check that the barn doors were secure and they were. She searched the floor for any sign of foxes, but there were none - no scrape marks or tracks.

They'd had a devil of a time the previous year with foxes and she was relieved to find no evidence.

In the final stall which was empty, she found the door unlatched. That Richard, she thought, always sloppy, didn't he know *all* the stalls had to be secure? Grabbing the door, something in the right back corner caught her eye. For a moment she didn't know what she was seeing and decided to switch on the lights to get a better look.

Her hands grasped the side railings tightly as a wave of shock rushed through her.

Sprawled out on the hay floor was the body of their pet cat Nancy. She had been disemboweled and splayed out with all fours facing upwards, stomach exposed and contents dripping out, her eyes vacant gazing into the dim heaven of a swinging lamp.

On the back wall a crude drawing was etched in the feline's blood, some sort of glyph or symbol.

Peering closer, she gagged and pinched her nose.

What was it? Looked astrological, but it was almost indiscernible, due to the dripping blood.

Reeling, she slammed the door shut, turned and wretched in a pile of dusty hay piled in the main hall.

Then, realizing someone had been there the night prior and might still be there for all she knew, she ran for the main doors, gasping as she burst into warm sunlight.

Richard, I have to tell Richard, she thought frantically, careening her way across the small lawn separating the barns and the farmhouse.

Inside she found her husband in the kitchen putting away dishes.

"*Nancy*" she screeched, "*Someone killed Nancy...*"

"Now hold on, hold on," said Richard, hands reaching out to still his severely shaking wife.

"Just sit down," he ordered. "Here, sit here."

Pulling up an old kitchen chair, he helped her down in, his hands gripping her shoulders, attempting to ease some of the fright from her shaky distraught frame.

In sobs, the image of Nancy's dismembered corpse poured out and her husband sat back, staring out the window, a look of aghast shock on his face.

"You know, I did see something peculiar yesterday near the barn and I just didn't think anything of it," he said slowly. "It was a young man limping through the far end of the field. Looked like he was worse for wear, but heading towards the lake, not the barn."

"You, you think he might have done it?" asked Henrietta, wiping her cheeks.

"Could be, could be," he said. "Now come here honey, I'm sorry this has happened to our Nancy. I'll call the police and put in a report. Main thing is you and I weren't harmed or any of the kids, thank God they're coming tomorrow. I'll take care of the rest of the chores today, you just sit yourself here and I'll get you some tea. My god, what on earth's happening when someone kills a defenseless cat. Land a' livin'."

"That's.. that's not all..." she said, raising her soaked eyes towards him.

"Oh?"

"There was some sort of thing - an image drawn on the wall in her blood, some kind of....some kind of symbol."

"My god."

"We have to call the police now," she said. "You can show them where this guy was walking. Maybe they can catch him."

II

During late fall, in the weeks following Thanksgiving, a large number of area contractors closed up shop and went on pogey. For many, the Muskoka winters were too harsh for outdoor work to continue and only the big outfits could afford to soldier on in construction, not halted by things like ice and snow due to their teams of horses which were used to bring equipment and lumber out to the islands across the frozen lakes.

Now, as Halloween approached, many were storing their boats for winter and tightening loose ends in anticipation of the season's first snowfall, which, from many of the reports of late, was expected to come early that year.

Atop a large granite outcropping far above the choppy Stephen"s Bay, Ronnie watched as the workers moved far below, dragging another boat trailer through the marina's storage facility gate.

Using his teeth, he'd wrapped the red scarf tighter around his blood covered left hand, while his other arm swung loosely at his side. The prior evening's sacrifice would buy some time, but a dead cat does not a guaranteed outcome make.

He hadn't sensed her since the cottage and his plan was to travel blind, without pills. There was no other way. Something in him said he could remain blind awhile longer, opening himself to it, but only for directions. That's how it worked, how Fred had taught him.

Below, a whistle blew and movements in the yard came to a grinding, hydraulic stop. They'd misjudged the size of the vessel and it now had to be lowered from the crane and moved to another set of larger stalls. Work like this would go on for another few weekends, he knew. It was Sunday morning and there must have been what, 30 men at work? And only another 40 or so boats to go.

The men were taking their first break and out behind the washroom building, an old timer went to fix one of the gas pumps. He took his breaks in private when he could, sick of listening to the young whippersnappers talking about who-knows-what-and-all every goddamn day. Today's problem was a rusty socket. Water gets them every time.

Reaching into his tool case for a wrench, he'd hardly had time to react to the shuffling figure who was down upon him in a flash.

A searing, stabbing pain stole the wind from his throat and he struggled forward, blood squirting like a garden hose.

Ronnie's knife went in just right of the heart and before the old one could let out a hoarse cough, his good hand was inside the stomach, pulling beneath the ribs.

An explosion of guts curdled up the old one's arm and the body staggered back, rolling its eyes and dropping, lungs flapping like ugly black wings, flailed out across the pump concrete.

He looked like a robot with its wires ripped out.

That's what we are, thought Ronnie, automatons.

Tossing the knife in his bag, he turned calmly towards the docks. Folding the body, he zipped the duffel closed and dragged it towards the water.

"I knew a cutter like you."

It had come from nowhere, but it was definitely her voice, somehow back inside his head.

One of his prior victims - she'd told him just before she died in 1988. He'd regretted doing her, but she was the only one with that privilege. The way she'd begged for her life in that cramped overheated trailer.

He could see her clearly now, rug burns for knees, puffy red cheeks and desperate thin hair with patches torn out from their fight. He'd been seeking blindness there too, regretful, because at the time he still couldn't discern who was friend or foe. Slit her throat and done the mark right there in the trailer's living room. And he hadn't needed too. That was what kept bringing her back, why she was still there.

Stepping over an old oar, he was at the docks, walking fast, trying to remain focused.

"*My father was one*," she'd pleaded, her sweating face half pressed into the linoleum by his then working, powerful right hand. He should have listened, should have thought things through. Now he'd wonder forever what she'd meant. He knew her name - Kathy Allsop.

Long afterwards he'd looked her family up on Facebook. The father had seemed normal enough. Businessman. In the shipping business. No, she was really in the wrong place at the wrong time, just like they say. It wasn't until it had worn off that he'd realized she was unnecessary. Rochdale and *it* wasn't there. His senses had been working overtime.

That's what he told her voice, which showed up every five or so years, but she never listened.

Lonely poor housewife. Could have sworn it was nearby that day.

For weeks after he'd had to restrain himself every time he thought he sensed the signal and for a long time his head wasn't his own.

In the yard's boathouse he hauled the heavy bag into the back of a medium sized pleasurecraft and stepped down in, crossing its wires at the wheel and the thing roared to life.

In minutes he was hurtling out across the waves, far from that awful bay.

"*Weeeeee, weeeeeeee,...*"

It was coming in from all angles now. The onsets. But these had a different, meaner edge than the ones before. These were real.

The cat had been wearing off since 8:30am. He needed to find another spot now. Somewhere private.

High in the sky the sun ignited the crimson shores revealing glorious, vivid reds and oranges that stretched into the mainland. He tried to think of Kathy Allsop, the way her desperate last glances spoke to a knowledge of something more about his world. Even as the blade slit clean through her jugular he'd watched as her eyes had welled up, exploding inside, taking with them any chance at learning more.

He'd almost released the knife at the last second too before his grip had tightened and the blood started to flow. No one comes back from a gash like that. Immediate shock to the brain and the heart. Life set free. She was free, but he and they, *it* were still there. And when he couldn't think of her, he focused on the clear spray violently misting his face as the boat bounced maniacally through the choppy waves.

"*Weeeeeeee*," they screeched, laughing at him now, rising like a choir in the unrepentant air.

"*We know her, ,,, weeeee knowwwww...*"

Their high shrill was like a multitude of lost hearts, oscillating between shimmering and screaming. Closing his eyes, he drove blind, throwing the throttle into high gear then opening them just in time to avoid hitting a small island.

And were the others after him now too? The cops - from some clue left behind in Barrie?

Near a cove, he let up on the throttle, coasting in until he was able to drop anchor amongst some large rocks. They were everywhere now, prodding, pulling and dancing, tearing at him in a space free of all the rules known to man.

His hands were shaking so badly, he could barely reach into the bag. Blood splashed down onto his shirt from where he was gnashing his own lips.

Yanking some stomach, he edged himself out forward onto the bow.

"*We are everywhere.....weeeeeeee,weeeeeeeee....*"

The bow groaned beneath the pressure as his hand made the mark across its sticky, hot vinyl like a squeegee of the damned

Over and under. A half loop. A dripping red cross.

Chapter 26

Saara knocked over a table lamp and they laughed some more.

Grabbing a dustpan and broom, Helen swept the glass, then said she was going to make dinner.

But before reaching the stairs, the sound of a door opening froze her in her tracks. Somebody was next door.

"Oh," she said, releasing a sigh, after a quick glance out the window, "it's just the cleaning lady."

Saara looked too, but couldn't see anyone at first.

"We call her 'the Baboushka'," laughed Helen. "She does the heavy cleaning when no one's around. Nobody's occupying that chalet."

She went downstairs, leaving Saara higher than a kite.

The current plan was to wait for the Halloween ball, then slip off the island during the festivities. Saara stared at a Marlon Brando poster on the loft's wall.

Better not let us down bogey, We need this.

Next door, the Baboushka certainly lived up to her name.

Through the chalet's windows she could now see the elderly woman moving amongst the rooms. Old and heavy, her thick swollen legs wrapped firmly in brown nylons and a tight dark green pencil skirt. She was lugging what looked like a set of ancient vacuuming equipment and Saara imagined the woman's thighs, thick and grey as hams, stretching to two sausage points in scuffed, wooden yellow clogs.

Her chest protruded like a bulging barrel through an old white work blouse that choked a thick, veiny neck head centered above it. A bulbous proboscis poked out from a worn red scarf that haloed her face, scarcely revealing two dark inset eyes.

Was it really Halloween in three days?

The exhausting, uncontrollable tumult of the last few now seemed totally in control and she it's prisoner.

Taking a last toke, Saara killed the roach in the ashtray, crushing its heater into dirty mini-embers.

Helen had left her costume hung over the railing and she reached out for its mask.

Turning it over in her hands, she ran her pale fingers along its fine embroidery, skirting its haunting eye sockets.

It was staring back at her like it was the only one who knew what to do.

Halloween would be her last night here, she repeated to herself pensively. *Just leave the whole fucking thing behind. In way over our heads.*

Downstairs the chalet door creaked open and she put down the mask as a gust of icy, late autumn air rose to the loft.

It was the Baboushka talking to Helen in a series of grunts and half spoken English:

"You need cleaning?"

"No, not today, thank you."

"No, you need it, they say."

"I do, but not tonight. It's fine. 'Busy.'"

"I come back in morning?"

"Maybe. I put sign on door to say."

"I leave Tuesday."

"Ok."

The door closed and the odor of Helen's warming casserole reclaimed the air.

Waiting a moment, Saara tiptoed to the stairs and leaned her head out over the railing.

"That computer you mentioned - is it up here?" she called softly.

"Come, we eat first," answered Helen, mocking the old woman's accent and motioning with her one free hand, a hot casserole dish in the other.

She looked like the Hindu god Kali as she kicked the oven door shut with an outstretched leg to boot.

Keeping the lights low, they ate in a back room that served as the dining area. It was one of the chalet's only cordoned off spaces made possible by a thin, plastic retractable wall. The chalet was warm now with oven heat and the propane fireplace and Saara must have been famished, as she ate about half the whole dish.

"We're on wi-fi here, but I don't trust it and I definitely don't trust it for anything now," said Helen. "We can go to this spot at the tip of the island where the cell signals are strongest. A few of us use it for private calls and Internet."

Saara nodded.

"I just have to do a couple searches and try my partner again," she said.

After clearing the table, Helen brought out a large black sweater for Saara to replace her red one with. They left by the back door, stepping down off the low deck onto a trail that ran through the woods towards the island's south end.

The moon shone brilliantly, and they could see it gliding through the trees, obscured only in spots where there were still thick leaves clung to branches.

In a small enclave by a pebbly shore, the vista opened wide on the lake, it's rolling waves casting sharp moon reflections for as far as their eyes could stretch.

Calling Ethan, Saara walked the shoreline holding the phone close to her cheek, hands buried deep in the new sweater's thick wool cuffs.

No answer. Was he mad about her bringing up Darby?

Something was really wrong. Ending the call, she sat on a rock and searched the web for more info about Edmonstone.

Focusing on his military past, she hit on some old news articles he was mentioned in.

A few screenshots later and she had her reading material for the night.

Passing her a joint, Helen sat down taking in the rolling waves.

"I really have to get out of here and I might take you up on anyone you know who can get me to the mainland before Tuesday," said Saara, watching the tide collide with the bricolage of shoreline rock, foam and sticks. "I'm not showing my face again while I'm here, that's for sure. And we have to find out who that bitch Rebekkah really is. What her fucking game is."

On their way back, Helen stopped short of the chalet lawn and raised her hand, motioning to take cover fast. Curiously, the Baboushka had returned and was just leaving the chalet, locking the front door.

They watched as the old woman shuffled off back towards the hotel.

"FUCK. They know I'm with you," whispered Saara.

"There goes everything," said Helen. "That hag is in the owner's family too - probably why she came."

"Now we have nowhere to go," said Saara dejectedly, heart sinking with each second.

At the back door, Helen unhooked the latch and told Saara to remain quiet.

"They may have the place bugged," she whispered.

Inside, they went upstairs, Saara watching the lower doors and windows from the top railing as Helen frantically tore through a suitcase, rummaging until she pulled out something shiny.

It was a silver handgun.

"Best defense is an offense," she smiled. Saara nodded approvingly.

Grabbing a string of bullets, she packed it all into a now bulging purse.

"She stays alone down in the old cookhouse," ventured Helen. "We'll go there, wait and hide. Find out what the fuck is going on."

Grabbing her costume and Saara's bag, they left by the back entrance.

Outside the air was getting colder as Helen led through a maze of paths stretching between several buildings and wooded areas. The cookhouse was in the island's west end. In the hotel's early days, it had housed kitchen staff who came from far and wide, most having attended the world's great culinary schools or worked in ritzy restaurants in the big cities.

The Baboushka had been there at least 45 years, said Helen. In the hotel's games room she could be seen in old black and white photos staring out from amidst the staff, her dark eyes brooding from beneath her scarf. No one could really say where she stood in the hotel family's pecking order - just that she'd always been a grunting fixture there - perennially old - the head of night housekeeping. Must have had some prominence though, said Helen, as she'd taken over the large cookhouse in the mid-sixties and remained there ever since.

The old building was certainly an intimidating structure. Clearly European in design and covered in ivy, there wasn't a light on in the place and when they arrived it was covered in shadows.

Helen had a key, made several years back when she'd been asked to water plants while the old crone was away.

Entering through a back door into a small room filled with crotons, Saara could see the kitchen lay beyond. It was as far as Helen had tread previously as the house and the old woman gave all the staff the creeps. Even in the dark Saara could tell the rest of the place was a mess with stuff piled everywhere - furniture, plants and stacks of old magazines.

The walls too were covered in yellowing photos and the odd taxidermied animal. The home of a cleaner.

In the kitchen they found a door to the basement and opened it. A blast of damp air escaped and they descended down a musty set of worn wooden steps into a sprawling subterranean space consisting of several rooms and furnace areas.

The home had three storey's. In the hotel's heyday it slept up to 12 cooks and still had space for special occasions and visiting musicians. Using their cell phone lights, they converged on what once must have been a leisure room at the end of the main basement hall.

There was a wet bar at one end, two couches by a central stone fireplace and leather armchairs dotting its perimeters. In the bar area, they hid beneath the long unused countertop, still littered with dusty bottles, many of a vintage circa the 2nd World War.

"We'll wait for her to return and leave in the morning," whispered Helen, taking the gun from her purse and placing it on one of the empty interior bar ledges. "Hopefully we'll hear when she returns."

Falling silent they sat in darkness for what seemed an hour before they heard anything.

"Listen," said Helen, suddenly nudging Saara's leg.

It was heavy tramping footsteps and they sounded close.

As they grew nearer, it was like they were coming from within the home's very walls and Saara and Helen were shocked to see a solid wall at the far end of the room open in a burst of muddy ochre light. Slowly, a slumping figure emerged from what must have been an underground tunnel.

The door closed behind her with a heavy clank and the old woman moved through the room, heading for the stairs.

"Holy shit!" whispered Saara, once they'd heard her climb to the main floor.

"Stay here," said Helen. "I'm going to try that door."

Tracing its edges with her cell light, she managed to find the mechanism - a simple push switch on the right that triggered the release.

"Come on," she motioned, beckoning to her terrified companion.

Must be about 30 feet underground, surmised Saara, her eyes darting above and to each side of the tunnel.

Wouldn't want to see that Baboushka down here, she thought, *get me outta here.*

The passage was long and in one stretch had no nooks or corners to take shelter behind. About 20 yards in they encountered the first turn. Presuming they were approaching the hotel's furthest kitchen, Helen sided up against the wall moving along it to the turn, cautiously glancing both ways as she went. Peering around it slowly, she gave the all clear.

This new tunnel section was shorter and they could just make out a set of descending staircases at its mouth.

Something about it was odd though, thought Helen. It should be taking them *up*, not down.

In front of them, a set of 12 steps led towards a lower, more dimly lit concave shaped area. From the top they could hear water lapping.

Gun at the ready, Helen ventured forward.

It was an underground cave that had been turned into a boat launch with five finger docks reaching out from side rock, each connected by concrete walkways at the cavern's edges, which met up at a main dock where another set of stairs led up to a metal door, presumably back into the hotel.

Four boats were docked there, including a shiny black wave liner and a gleaming light brown 1925 Baycrest.

The cave's entrance opened out into the dark lake and they could see it stretched a ways underground before reaching open air.

Climbing down onto the walkway they boarded the Baycrest.

In the bow, they found some pocket change and MayFOR code sheets. In the hull, a key still in the ignition, case of 12 beer and a pair of ripped rubber goulashes.

"I want to see where that door leads," said Helen. "If I'm right, it goes straight into laundry. There are rooms there nobody's ever used."

"It must be late by now," warned Saara, grabbing the hostess by the wrist. "It's probably close to midnight. Are we pressing our luck?"

Sighing, the older woman relented.

"You're right. Let's get back. We can check it out tomorrow."

On the return, the tunnel seemed shorter and soon they were back beneath the Baboushka's bar, sharing watch duties at three-hour intervals. It was 4am when Saara awoke for her first shift.

In the last hour, Helen had heard some movements up on the second floor, but it was just the old woman using the toilet.

Chapter 27

That morning was when they would go.

In another hour. It was what they'd decided after their long wait. The townhouse had been quiet for at least 16 hours and quick checks out the windows revealed clear empty streets.

How the team found the condo was a mystery, it could have been the swarms picking out their heat signatures, but Ethan suspected it was Carla's family's previous dealings.

They wouldn't have a vehicle and both he and Francois harbored serious doubts about getting far.

When they finally left the hidden room at 7am, they came to realize the full extent of what had occurred.

In the living room, tables and chairs were overturned and there were dark, thick blood stains on the carpet around the chair where Carla had sat. The sink, still full of dishes and water, also contained bits of smashed mirror. Shoes and jackets were strewn about too near where they'd been ripped from the closets.

They tried to piece it together, but it remained a blur as they hurried outside, heading east on the sidewalks past the harbor wall to where the downtown core started at the bay's edges.

The fresh morning air was welcome as they made their way through the bay park by the canal.

Students from some private school were up early, boarding a bus by the water while a few old bums cackled on the nearby benches, smoking with some pigeons.

By 7:30am they were close to the centre of town with no real destination in mind. In an alley between two old brownstones that housed a sub shop and Italian French restaurant, they paused.

"Do you have any idea of where we could go," Ethan asked, a serious concern swimming in his eyes. A narrow alley stretched back through a barrage of garbage bins, sagging clothes lines and petrified fire escapes towards a towering run-down apartment complex.

Nodding in that general direction, Francois took the lead without answering.

Near the passage's end they could hear accordion music drifting out through the restaurant's back window.

Rounding the corner, they almost collided with a young woman and a large pot of steam as she emptied the previous night's left-over spaghetti water into a gutter.

They were in the apartment complex's courtyard now, maneuvering around graffiti covered children's playthings that were planted every few feet across the cracked concrete.

A few gossiping mothers looked up from their kids long enough to watch them pass. Eventually the shouts of children playing faded as they ducked through a hole in a chain link fence to a dirt path near a 7-11.

It was here they heard the first siren burst on Main Street. Quickening their pace, they were just beyond the convenience store when the sirens screamed closer. Francois broke into a sprint and soon they were running full speed, hopping benches and dodging trees towards the distant waterline.

Ahead lay a field, then, more docks.

Cop cars could be heard in all directions and in the periphery, they could see reflections of the first lights hitting the trees around them. At the lake a speed boat operated by a middle aged blonde man was making its way slowly up the channel.

Ethan leapt, tackled him, then threw him over the side.

Landing behind him, Francois bashed his knee on the steering wheel in a spectacular, fumbling crash.

In seconds they were shooting across the lake at full throttle bouncing towards Gravenhurst.

Calculating in his head, Ethan gave them another 20 minutes before they'd have to deal with police boats and choppers.

"We'll ditch in this inlet I know in Gravenhurst," he shouted above the din. "Then aim her back out on the lake. They won't have a clue where we are."

At the jutting banks of Third Island where the water opened into Ardour's Bay, he carefully maneuvered between several smaller, nameless isles before coasting inland.

Coming to a stop, Francois immediately dove in, initiating desperate quick strokes towards the shore. Ethan turned the boat around, gave it some juice, then dove in too, sending the vessel off into the lake's centre.

On shore, they followed a dirt path up through a winding cliff, but no sooner had they started the ascent did they hear the telltale sound of rotor blades. Keeping low, they watched as three helicopters skimmed the shore. One hovered above the boat which was now doing circles beyond the inlet. The other two combed closer, inching towards their location.

Then there was something. At first a low moan, then a feeling of electricity in the air. A stabbing cold wave of shrill sound pierced things, causing both of them to double over.

Down they crashed through scrub brush and tree trunks, finally spilling out into plain view on the beach.

Above, a chopper descended.

- Barrie, Ontario -

In a rundown part of Barrie, an entrance off La Rue Street opened into an office supply store that was used as a front by local police to investigate petty crimes and to act as a drop in for officers on patrol.

A door at the side led to an entirely different section.

Built in the 90's with Improve Ontario! grants, this area was one of many way points throughout the city, connecting with a private tunnel system that met in a central underground hub.

Every major city in North America had one and it was here, in a non-descript concrete cell that Ethan awoke four hours later, with a serious splitting headache.

The cell was spare - just a toilet, sink, no windows and a bed of cement, on top of which lay a light blue rubber camping mattress.

Opening his eyes, a harsh light caused him to blink several times before he could prop himself up to take in the new surroundings.

The room was warm, but it's septic sterility conjured visions of anonymous prisoners stashed away never to be seen again. Part of one wall was chipping and there were numerous circular scrape marks etched into the floor beside the bed like sinister tree rings.

The space was completely silent and he sensed the walls were thick, judging by the size of the rusting bolt heads attached to a metal sink in the far wall.

There was no window, even on the only door in the room, but there were also no restraining devices. He wondered where Francois was being kept. The sound burst had knocked them out almost immediately and he still had a loud ringing in his right ear which was extremely painful.

He must have fallen back asleep as when he came to again about an hour later he was surprised to find a small black haired, well dressed man standing over him, addressing him by name.

The man wore a blue suit with a red and light-blue ascot. His small fat head fit snuggly into a crisp white dress shirt, a pair of tiny beady brown eyes squinting out from behind silver wired spectacles. It must still have been morning, as the strong scent of recently applied aftershave accompanied a semi-red rash at the man's neckline.

Seeing he was awake, the man hobbled over him. In the flickering light, Ethan could see that his eyes, although intelligent, contained hints of plain ruthlessness too.

Smiling up at him, the man didn't smile back.

"How would you like to stay alive?" announced the stranger bluntly, looking coldly down at him without any hint of sarcasm.

"This would be... good," Ethan replied.

Nodding, the man continued, typing something into a phablet.

"You will work for us over the next few weeks and if you like it you can remain working, You are fairly well educated, cunning and.... intelligent in your own way - this is not at all incompatible with our aims. You have a natural interest in this, otherwise you wouldn't have found yourself here."

Delivered with a cold, empty precision, the words hung in the air like they would in any good spy movie.

"You want to learn about your subject, which is fine, because that's what we want as well," continued his captor. "Oh, and....you're friend didn't make it. Sometimes the sound weapon causes cerebral hemorrhaging - which it did in his case."

Watching Ethan's eyes as he spoke, his words took on a decidedly more calculating tone.

"You are under our 'protection' and will continue to be until your time with us is through. Let's hope it's a long time."

"What do you mean by that," he asked.

"I mean exactly what I said - you must know you won't last long without our protection? *Ohhhh* - you are still under the impression we are the bad guys."

Sizing up Ethan's blushing complexion as a sign that somewhere a tinge of what he'd said had registered, he continued.

"Besides, that Russian sleeper of ours doesn't have a clue about what he's got himself into."

"Ivan? You've got to be kidding."

"You are kidding yourself. And you would have paid the price too had it not been for us."

With this, he straightened his ascot and left the room.

Two hours later lunch arrived, wheeled in by a male attendant on a food cart - steak, mashed potatoes, green beans, sauce and small carton of milk. A fresh cantilever of water. Slice of Black Forest cake too. Metal cutlery - he wasn't a suicide risk. This was slightly insulting.

But if Ivan were an unwitting spy, what was it that had led him to Francois, an otherwise ordinary guy in Canada? The sightings for sure, but hadn't he said they'd been friends for some time? The grey walls remained mute. They were just winding him up - feeding him lies so he'd give them whatever they wanted.

Fuck, he really wanted out. *And work with them?* What had been meant by that? He had to remember - they killed Francois and would probably have no qualms with doing him when he wasn't needed. He wondered about Saara - had she learned anything on the island? How had he let himself stray so far from their path? He wished he could call her, just ring her up, let her know everything was alright. Hell, he hoped *she* was alright. She would be - she was the level headed one. He wanted to tell her about the Darby picture breaking and everything that had happened.

- Sebright, Ontario -

Above ground about 15 and a half kilometers away, local Detective Constable with the Ontario Provincial Police Ted Mondieu turned on to Highway 11 North headed for the tiny hamlet of Sebright.

A call had come in about a body found in a field on a farm owned by a local magistrate's family.

Apparently, it was badly decomposed, likely dumped there a few weeks prior. A contractor who checks on the property for the family had discovered it. Said it smelt horrendous.

Forensics would be another two hours as the nearest officers had been called to another murder south of Vaughn. He'd be the first on scene.

Taking Concession #166, he munched on his blueberry muffin, wiping bits of crumbs from his lips which fell between his legs as he reached for his cell. It had been exactly seven minutes since he'd received the text, so he knew who was calling. It was one of *those* ones.

"Ted here," he answered.

"Yes, yes, I am aware," he continued. "I will send it the minute I arrive."

Ending the call, he placed the cell on the passenger seat and firmly gripped the wheel.

What do they do with this stuff, he wondered.

Dispatch said a symbol had been scrawled in the victim's blood on the back of a barn silo near the body. Spleen and liver were cut out, then used to make the symbol.

The last time one of these happened was about two years ago. He'd snap a photo and send it off fast - they rarely called back. He'd had four occasions in his 22-year career where his services had been needed. In another few weeks he'd get a fat little cheque in the mail.

It bothered him though, knowing that others were highly interested in these cases - the symbols most of all - while his own peers were ordered to chalk it up to lone nuts, conveniently leaving details about the markings out of media releases so as not to spread worry.

They never caught anyone, so no evidence was ever released. One time though - the second while he'd been involved - almost resulted in an arrest warrant being issued, but it had been revoked at the last moment on account of a late-night judge ruling not enough evidence.

There it was. Gateway Road. Farmhouse was the only address on it.

He was supposed to meet the hand there in another three minutes. Red pickup near the silo.

He'd park at the house, as he'd discovered the hard way that not all private farm roads are created equal. It was spring then and a tow had taken his sweet fuckin' time. He'd missed the start of the Jays season. Couldn't happen again.

Parking, he stepped out into the shitty smelling farm yard. It had one of those silver ones - the silo, it must have been about 100 feet high.

Down back he spied the pickup about 50 yards away. The hand waving him over.

"Morning" he replied curtly, as he approached.

Plugging his nose with one hand, the man pointed to the grass along one of the dried up irrigation ditches.

Fuck, that stench was some putrid shit. Thick-in-the-air shit.

Following his fingers, the officer's eyes settled on a patch of tall reeds and a thick swarm of flies.

Then he saw it. The corpse, so bloated it had popped the buttons off its own suit pants. Her face was like jelly, half the cheeks and forehead pecked off by gulls. Some of her blonde hair was still attached. Always good for identifiers.

"Alright, after I snap a few pics I'm going to have to clear the scene," he said. reaching into his pocket for his cell. "You get back in your truck and head on up to the house and wait. I'll get your statement there."

Nodding, the man scrambled back to his truck.

Snapping a few quick ones, he turned back towards the silo, fingers pinching each nostril. He gagged in the hot sun as the stench overwhelmed him. He could just make out a small red patch on the wall near ground level, about waist high.

Standing next to it, he could see it was a weird one this time. A circle with arrows sticking out from all sides.

Snapping a few more pictures, he drew some tape across the road tied it to a post and tree and walked back towards the farmhouse, hitting send to the number the people called from.

That's it for me today, he thought. *That's allll folks.*

Chapter 28

I

Around 8:30am Saara and Helen heard the familiar heavy thump of the old woman's feet descending amongst the floors above them.

This time they were followed by some general noises in the kitchen which lasted about half an hour.

At 9:15 the cellar door opened and she'd plodded back down through the room to the tunnel. Once she was well on her way, they headed upstairs.

The cookhouse was a sprawling, congested revelation in daylight, appearing to have been neglected for decades.

In the dining room, a table was covered in yellowed magazines, records and trinkets, some half wrapped in fading newspaper or packed in cardboard boxes.

It was the numerous framed black and white photos in the rooms that fascinated Saara.

The Edmonstone family sure were a strange bunch. The old cleaner was in many of the photos - a bulky out of place thing bundled in layers in stark contrast with the warm summer lawns and ballroom backgrounds.

In each photo her eyes remained impenetrable, either hidden at just the right angle by that infernal scarf or set back just so each time the camera clicked. Saara wanted to look straight into them unadorned in what she presumed would be a magnificent animal glory.

But the more she inspected, the more mysterious the pictures seemed. The family's hierarchy was easy to discern.

Grandpa Edmonstone was a sight - full white beard, gentleman's tweed hunting attire and stern wooden pipe. Grandma was another typical of her day - hunched and scowling from what must have been the overbearing patriarchal torture of a lifetime.

There appeared to be two sons, one blonde, the other dark haired, along with a winsome daughter and the Baboushka.

The quiet trance of the place was casting its spell.

Helen, at the dining room's other end rifled through a smattering of old letters and vintage silverware which looked in dire need of a good polishing.

"What's next, the upstairs?" she called out to Helen, hands clearing some dried leaves from a side table below a long dead aspergilla.

"Yes," replied the hostess grinning mischievously. "The lair."

"Wait - you go ahead," Helen added, pausing. "I'll wait down here by the door. I'll tap the railing if she comes."

Agreeing, Saara was off in an instant through the rest of the first floor rooms towards the front staircase.

Light was pouring in from the outside through the main entrance door windows as she reached the foyer - it looked like a perfect fall day out there.

The stairs were a maze of catalogues and discarded clothes, but she followed a trail up through the centre which had been worn into the tattered carpet through the years. Only thin frayed threads were left in places where the same heavy feet had trod for so long.

At the landing the trail veered right, towards a number of bedrooms.

The door to the first one was open and she peered in.

Her eyes met boxes piled floor to ceiling, hung with layers of old clothes amongst tilting paper stacks, faded annuals & books of all types.

In the room's centre was a queen-sized bed, its sheets appearing as if they hadn't been changed in a hundred years. Above it, a glass chandelier hung cocooned in cobwebs.

Off the main bedroom were two small outer rooms - one appeared to be a fitting area, complete with antique life size mirror. The other was a private washroom.

Sifting through some of the papers on the bed, mostly old articles written about the hotel, she noticed the clippings were newspaper stories printed prior to the 1960's.

On a dresser she found a medium sized wooden box containing family memorabilia.

This included more old photos and documents - Grandma Edmonstone's birth certificate and Grandpa's hunting license.

No makeup or jewelry. Lots of dishes though, scattered here and there with bits of half finished, moldy food.

The bed dipped in the centre where the sheets were slightly off color, a nasty yellow brown where the old one slept.

By the large front facing window, a taxidermied owl and lynx watched her every move as Saara made her way through the room. The lynx was poised on a faux log seemingly ready to pounce, but one of its paws had been ripped off and the log was broken too.

Nothing worse than damaged fakery, thought Saara, *it's the ultimate...*

Before finishing her thought, a loud tap sounded from downstairs and she stopped frozen, eyes darting for spaces to hide.

Diving in a closet, she'd barely had time to close its doors before she heard the telltale heavy trudges rising up the staircase.

It was dark in there, jammed with old dresses, long gowns and coats that fought her for space as she inched her way back, holding as many clothes hangers still as she could.

Through the spaces between the garments, she watched as the old woman entered the room bullying physical space with each step.

Even up close Saara couldn't make out the woman's eyes.

The old woman stopped suddenly, poised in the centre of the room, making odd guttural sounds and muttering gruff, half intelligible words, head pivoting, like she was searching the floor.

Then she started to disrobe. The heavy burlap sweater first, revealing a pit-stained white undershirt that outlined her upper body, a torso with solid thick breasts, almost indistinguishable from the whole of her bulky mass.

Saara watched as her fingers, thick like meat links, strained to unfasten a delicate silver belt clip which held the umbrella-like pencil skirt tightly.

A pair of white granny panties, sliding down graying, solid thighs grazed a pair of stump ended legs.

Saara gasped. The room had changed somehow - a noticeable energy - like the electrical feel of a calm before a storm had taken hold. The old figure twitched in place, a frenzy of movements as she hovered over an old pile of clothes.

The first yellow clog fell to the floor.

A wild fear exploded as Saara watched the woman, somehow arisen now in space, hovering in midair and twirling.

Repulsed, she closed her eyes tight, biting into a starchy gown to muffle a scream.

But she - *it?* was still there, above a wide armchair pulling on a new pair of stretched, stained panties.

Another struggle, grunts and barks as the pencil skirt fought the fingers, yanking futilely at the clasp in several passes before the costume was again complete.

Raising its arms high, the creature lowered itself slowly to the floor, turning on terra firma before heading back out of the room, taking the strange electrical charge with her.

Shaking uncontrollably, Saara fought to listen, the fluttering gowns an unwelcome buffer between she and the trudging steps as they faded, back into the normal world.

Sinking in piles of old shoes and belts which lay like snakes in careless leather heaps, she screamed inside, then sobbed in frantic, desperate bursts.

She lay in the piles, dazed and scattered as the room seeped in through the cracks, the image still racing in her head.

Eventually she arose and pushed the dresses apart and began pulling herself out, crawling at first and shaking as if to remove as much of the experience as she could.

Finally standing, she lingered where the creature had hovered, sunlight pouring down on her forehead as fine dust particles swirled around her.

At the main dresser she clawed open a drawer and with hands trembling, emptied its contents, unsure as to what she was even looking for.

Slamming her fist on the bed, she cursed ever having become involved with the case.

What was that - something.

Heart still racing, her attention shifted to the contents.

More folders containing more letters and forms.

Inside one, a letter with a photo attached - the old woman, as a little child.

"She is a very good little girl never cries unless tired or hungry"

It was foster home stationary. She wasn't from this family at all. "I dress her, then let her play on the floor till she gets cross around 10:30 (she does not like a play pen)."

Collecting the documents, she headed back down to Helen, who was beneath the bar, an anxious stare changing to visible relief.

"What is it now, 10am Monday?" she demanded, trying to see Helen's eyes in the damp semi-darkness.

"Whoah. What time is it?!? You were gone over an hour - I tapped the staircase when I heard the tunnel door. Thought she did you in - No, it's around eleven. What did you find?"

"There was no way I was gone that long," she stammered, edging away slightly so as not to reveal the bulk in her sweater.

She was confused. Had she been in the closet that long?

"Saara - you there?"

"Nothing... Nothing..," she mumbled. "Weird woman. Anyways - what are we doing, staying or getting the fuck out?"

"We should wait until tonight. We could go to..."

"Tonight!?" she demanded. "We should just steal a canoe and go now. Disguise ourselves. Once we're on the water, make it to the nearest point, get to a road...."

"I'm not comfortable with heading out in a canoe in the broad daylight," replied Helen. "My job is over here and I'm getting out of this place alive. If we go, we go at night."

Not for one more shitty second was she staying here, thought Saara. Not with that...thing coming back.

But Helen was right. In broad daylight someone would see them. For now, they were trapped in this dungeon of darkness, this...cookhouse.

"Alright, alright, we'll go tonight," she said, gulping air to keep up with her still speeding heart. "You said there was some dance tonight. Everyone will be busy with that."

"Hey, are you ok?" asked Helen. "Did something happen to you up there?"

II

Upstairs, brunch consisted of a couple of buns, slices of cold meat, pickles and some half-sour milk they were able to scrounge in the fridge.

In the basement their final vigil started at 1pm.

At 3:15pm, they heard her coming, watching this time as her shadow passed in a window well towards the steps of the back entrance. Then, upstairs, vague noises as it rummaged in a distant corner of the residence they hadn't yet seen.

Probably levitating, shuddered Saara. The thought made her want to scream, but she had to maintain calm if they were to get to the mainland alive. She could tell everything then, call some monster hunters.

At 6:50pm they heard a door open and shut. She had left by the front entrance. They could soon leave.

Upstairs, the front foyer was flooded with a mix of pulsing colored lights filtering in through windows from the grounds.

Peeking around the living room curtain, they could see the lawns had been done up in huge tents and band shells as costume clad servers readied tables and prepared makeshift bars. From their vantage point the beach area too was filled with activity, the Hawaiian drink huts transformed into Halloween spectacles complete with drifting, dry ice.

Two half costumed servers worked near the cookhouse by a picnic table setting up chairs in front of a small stage. Hung over the edge of a table bench lay a mask and jacket.

If they could just get to it without being seen.

"I'm going to grab it," said Saara. "Put yours on and get ready."

"Please be careful," said Helen.

Slipping outside, Saara moved to a stand of bushes near the two employees. She was only about two meters from the table now. When they moved away, she crawled to the bench and in seconds returned, costume parts in hand.

"I guess we're Boris Karloff and Phantom of the Opera tonight," said Saara, setting the bundle down on one of the couches for a closer look.

"They'll think it was guests," said Helen. "There are about 12 different Boris's tonight. He's popular this year."

Donning the outfits, they waited for more guests to arrive before exiting through the side entrance.

In the chill, clear night, they could hear the first lilts of woodwinds as a small orchestra warmed up in a band shell.

Many guests were also costumed in expensive tuxedos, masks and sequin gowns.

Some women wore 1920's headdresses to complete the classic Olde Muskoka look of familial wealth.

Creeping amongst the trees towards the back end of the island, they stopped in a small courtyard by the rear kitchen doors where staff were transferring goods from a supply boat.

"If we circle around we can get to the other side and the beach where the boats are," whispered Helen. "There's an old barge we could use. I know a cook here who sometimes sneaks it out to fish pickerel."

The last of the staff made their way inside and they broke from their cover, darting quickly past the main walkway.

"He gets the key over here in this shed," said Helen, moving towards a dilapidated structure that looked to be no more than an old outhouse.

"I'll grab it. It won't take a min.."

A commanding cough from the kitchen doorway sounded and they stared in its direction where a tall woman was just putting out a smoke and watching them.

"Oh, you've come for the canoe," she said. "Sechellion wants it down between the main stage and the huts."

"Do you need a hand" asked the woman, who appeared to be one of the evening's maître-D's.

"No, I have help," Saara responded, nodding towards Helen.

"You're a little late. It was supposed to have been stocked with ice and beer by now. They are waiting for you. Get a move on."

So much for Plan A, thought Saara, glaring at Helen's pudgy ass.

Without argument, they hoisted the empty canoe the woman was pointing at.

With one at each end, they held it over their heads, turned and headed back towards the front lawns.

Chapter 29

I

How strange. The lounge of the hotel bar was starting to fill with people wearing costumes.

Was it really Halloween already, wondered Ronnie, setting down his gin and tonic.

No, it was All Hallows Eve, said as much on one of the room's many wide screen TV's.

Looking down, he could see his right hand still firmly tucked in his jeans pocket. Thank god for this jacket, he thought, so lovingly donated by the old mechanic.

He'd arrived on the island earlier that afternoon, after discovering a deserted cabin on the south end where he could stay a few days. The boat would be fine, tucked in along an inland tributary where it wouldn't be discovered.

He'd order some food and a few more drinks before heading back - after he'd completed more recon.

In the packed bathroom he lifted a mask from a sink while its owner pissed drunkenly, rambling about who'd be heading to the Stanley Cup.

The news had carried the Stephens Bay murder since at least mid-afternoon the day prior. In the cabin he'd heard some people talking about it as they hiked the nearby shorelines. Police still hadn't tied it to any of the other deaths, or at least hadn't made it known they had. They must have though.

Beyond people like he, Fred and Sam, not many others would make the connections.

God, she was smart. In their time, she'd known so many things about their world which he'd had no clue of. It was scary - at times it was almost as if she was like him, but he was too young then to have been bothered by it.

No, he was just happy to have found her and her strength when the bad parts took over. Without it, he would never have survived. She alone had helped him see through it, she and Fred, both working with him to help retain control.

But now, fitting the pull-on alien mask to his face, he felt like he did back then. Adrift, alone.

The effects of the last one were just wearing off too. He'd hoped there wouldn't have to be another. But he knew *it* was here. Felt it even as he'd first neared the island - the pulses had grown stronger as he'd searched the hotel grounds.

The images and voices would soon come if nothing was done. Unless he was sleeping that was. But the thought of awakening to it all made him feel sick and the situation became clear:

Another sacrifice - but what/who would it be?

Outside the washroom he checked his appearance in a hall mirror and slid the mask up onto his forehead, pretending to read some travel pamphlets amongst the rush of partiers. The celebrations were being held on the front lawn between the hotel and the lake. The bar staff hadn't seen him in the mask yet, probably wouldn't make him out in a crowd.

He set the pamphlets down and headed out through the nearest door.

It was like noon at midnight with huge spotlights flooding the lawn as hundreds came from all directions, costume clad, ready to party.

Bands and fire jugglers performed as the wait staff hurried to and fro with drinks and hors d'oeuvres. He'd make a mark that'd be easy, follow and then do it quick, clean.

He could feel it even now, the first pulses growing more powerful. But he was still unprepared. He'd left the knife and gun at the cabin and had no real plan for escape. Barrie and Jordanna were a world away and he'd been sloppy the last few times. For all he knew, they'd made him and Jordanna was refusing to provide answers right now and calling a lawyer.

In the crowd he felt weak, nodding idiotically through the mask holes at the few faces who took him in. One of the pulses rang sharp as he passed an older wing of the building and his body braced against an old stone column for support. *It* was there, just inside, just beyond those walls. His hands grew clammy and one of the voices managed to break through:

"*Weeeeeee,*" it screamed in a shrill, high pitch, becoming plural as it faded, hissing off into empty astral space.

Two masked servers carrying a canoe walked by and he watched them, the taller one especially, as they stepped hurriedly down the cobbled lane, followed by a superior who was barking out something about their being an hour late.

The small entourage stopped at a cluster of tiki huts by the beach where a gang of young male servers had beer cases stacked high. Together they started filling the canoe with ice with beers and soon it sparkled like crystal.

"Here, make yourself useful," said another superior, handing the shorter canoe server a tray full of Halloween cocktails. "You take B section. Come see me when you're empty."

At the main bar, the older thin gentleman with pure white hair and a name tag that read Pierre Sechellion was overseeing the work, straightening ties and snapping suspenders while maintaining small talk with guests.

The shorter server paused facing her tall partner before moving off towards the far end of the section, offering drinks amidst the swelling throngs. The tall one was seconded to Section A where a wine soaked table cloth needed replacing.

Soon she was patting down the front of a woman's dress. He kept an eye on this female Phantom of the Opera. She was older, he could tell by the way she moved. Gangly too and awkward in the way she stepped, which was a kind of half stumble. There were other Phantoms. No one would miss this one.

But Sechellion hovered and interrupted the patting, giving bursts of new direction and sanctimonious smiles guest-ward.

She was being sent to the kitchen for new table cloths and before he knew it, was gone from sight, disappearing into the sea of bobbing costumes.

It was no good. The pulsations and voices were starting to break in everywhere. He needed to do it *now*.

They weren't usually this heavy at the onset, and he struggled, straining to concentrate. Something - some quality about it, was very different this time.

Setting his drink on the marble steps, he edged back into the shadows around a corner by the old wing. Here behind the trees no one would see what was happening and he fell to his knees, clutching his temple, cracking the alien mask in the process.

Desperately he attempted just willing them away, but it was like they were coming from two sources, the combination of which was leaving him in complete disarray. Something was beyond that wall, above him to the right, up through the window - there was a heavy light, filtering through diffuse soft curtains....

Rising, he strained to look in:

There were shapes. A tall man by a roaring fire. Two others by a door. The man speaking to someone, a woman, sitting calmly on a couch.

Then an all too familiar shape in the corner. *It was there*, standing behind the man slightly off to his left.

An icy pain shot through his mind and he started to fall, bitter, confused. The pulsations were coming from her *and* something else too. He'd never known others to have the gift, although there'd been rumors.

He rose again and peered in closer. The woman on the couch - could it really be her?

The shaking had overtook him. It was impossible now and his grip slipped, as he fell down into darkness.

But he knew those eyes. There was no mistaking them for anyone.

II

On the terrace, Saara set her tray of deserts on a marble stand and prepared to start serving, but before she lifted the first of the plates, she felt a fierce tug on her left sleeve.

She hoped it would be Helen telling her they needed to get the fuck out of there, off this godforsaken island before anyone made them.

"My dear, would you fetch me a handkerchief, I've apparently left mine in my room."

Fuck. It was another old babbling witch.

She swiped one quickly from another table, returned to the woman and tapped her gently on the shoulder:

"Oh thank you," said the old socialite. "My, what prompt service."

Some of the other servers carried large bus pans full of glasses and dishes up a set of stone steps towards the main kitchen. Waiting in line, she searched the crowds for Helen, who annoyingly remained AWOL.

Gathered a pan she ascended to a pair of glass doors which led to an empty dining room.

It was from this point that the servers accessed the pantry and kitchen areas for more ice, booze and linen.

A blast of warm dense air met her as she entered the dishwashing pit. A young Chinese boy motioned for her to dump her load, then watched curiously when this seemed to briefly confuse her.

A line of chefs moved behind a rack of hanging pots over their fiery grills, waiters collected dinners and shouted their latest orders, while hostesses cut bread and polished silver.

Setting the tub down, she ducked into a cramped hallway, squeezing between a wall phone and several servers clambering from the opposite direction.

In seconds she was in a terracotta tiled hall outside the main dining room, which was vacant save for a Maître D in one of the corners pouring over bills. She snuck by, headed down the hall trying to look busy with a new tray.

Around a corner she passed two banquet rooms, one on either side of the hall and proceeded towards another foyer where there was an elevator and doors leading out to the back lawns.

Intending to head back outside, she had to duck into a side room when the clear glass elevator doors started to open.

It was Rebekkah, Edmonstone and the old woman heading straight towards her.

Holding her breath, she watched as they passed just inches from her, through some doors leading down to the basement.

Beneath the mask, her temples pounded at the sight of the creature, its docile presence in the hall mocking all that was normal.

But it was a question mark, one she had to follow.

At the bottom of the stairs, cool basement air met her nostrils as she slowly pried the door open. She could now hear their voices, predominantly Edmonstone's, speaking loud and angry.

They were far ahead, almost silhouettes, low lit in the hall's lamplight.

"We'll do it now," Edmonstone was barking.

"Just like everything, no preparation," protested Rebekkah. "It's why this is has gone to shit and created this mess."

"Hold your tongue," snarled the hotelier, taking hold of one of the Baboushka's arms.

"You'll see," replied Rebekkah coldly. "People like you always do. *Can she* even call it at this point?"

At this, the creature raised its hands to its head, as if deep in concentration.

There was something then, the strange energy Saara had felt in the bedroom, electrical and pulsing.

Rebekkah felt it too and Saara watched as her old acquaintance gasped, covering her mouth as it started to grow stronger.

It was waves. In and outside their heads and Saara tried to pull the door shut in a futile attempt to block it. Pulsing flashes of images - childhoods? No, something murkier, darker. Movement outside space - hesitations, seasons, the turning of gears.

It was too strong. She screamed and saw the others turn back, watching her fall in agony.

Then more flashes, images of walking on wet grass. Female voices - the old woman - she was showing them this.

It was the two girls, Chloe and Carrie, beneath the stars. God, what is that?

Scratching, metallic scratching and whirring.

Then screams. One by one. They were screaming, like butterflies released, free to fly up, up into the night. God it was so biggg....

A warm trickle rushed down over her lips, spilling to the carpet as she twitched.

Their steps drew nearer.

Chapter 30

Helen carefully filled the man's highball just shy of the brim.

It was now 9:30pm and the house bands were jockeying with the swollen crowds to be heard.

Every five minutes or so, she'd watch for Saara, half hoping the next mask would be hers, she could tell her from beneath it somehow, she'd have to.

Stealing a few minutes for a smoke she'd lifted from a lonely champagne stained pack, she stood in the shadows of a private garden, enjoying the curls swirling in her chest.

Long, cool exhalations. But with each one, a sadness grew. She felt it. Saara was gone - there'd be no way to find her in that crowd.

But maybe she'd returned to the cookhouse? She could just see it from where she was, down through the woods, gloomy lines filtering through the canopy.

Would she be there waiting? It was possible.

Repositioning her mask, she made her way towards it, keeping close to walls as she moved between buildings.

It was now just 20 feet away and she dove behind a small hedge between its entrance walkway and living room windows, crouching to keep hidden from the lawns.

Making it around to the back door, she tried its handle, found it open and slipped inside.

Down by the bar she found the room empty.

Give her a couple of hours - she might still show up, she told herself. But for all she knew, Saara'd been caught and was already dead or about to be.

Just wait. People show up.

But after an hour, it seemed unlikely.

There was the door. She wondered if she should open it and head to the underground boat area.

But what if the old woman returned? She'd have to just try. She could at least steal a kayak, get out on the lake and tell somebody.

The tunnel was damp and her breath played in the soft mists rolling in from the lake.

Cautious on her approach, she imagined the old woman was following her, waiting ahead even, which helped keep her alert. The tunnel was still echoey and its final stretch carried voices and shouting.

Peering down the stairs into the cavern, she gasped.

It was Saara, laying at the feet of a group - Edmonstone, Rebekkah, two other men and the old woman.

Her chest and mouth were dark - was it blood? She wasn't moving. It looked like they were preparing to take her somewhere.

Reaching down, one of the men was lifting Saara by her armpits, while the other helped with her legs. They were transferring her to one of the boats.

Edmonstone turned and she saw there was another body on the dock too, lying just behind him. A man who looked dead.

Joining the guards, Rebekkah helped place his body into one of the Starcrafts.

She felt helpless, but she'd have to try and follow them.

They'd probably dump them in the lake. They'd probably never find them. Never believe her story either. She could just wait and run, far away and not look back...

One of the boat's engines started and lights filled the cavern.

"No, you follow us," shouted one of the men. "We'll meet you there."

The first boat was pulling out. Then a second engine sounded.

She could see it moving - Edmonstone and Rebekkah backing into the underground bay, following the first boat out towards the lake.

Waiting until they'd rounded the corner of the cave's mouth, she leapt down and jumped into the boat they'd searched the night before.

Easy, she thought, starting it up, but she'd have to give it time. There wouldn't be many boats out in the dark. She'd follow from a distance and hope they weren't tossed on the way.

There'd be no way of knowing without headlights, but she'd at least see where they went, be able to tell someone once it was over.

Shifting it into reverse, she pulled away from the decking, righting the vessel left towards the mouth and the open water.

Outside, she could hear their high pitched whines fading into the distance.

Far in the thick black, two tiny lights skipped across the water like sparks.

Increasing speed, she drove blind, feeling her way through the spray, every bump and jolt registering icy shocks through her tired body.

True to its reputation, the lake was a mix of open water and inlets. The island was its one great solitary land mass although there were others. So far the lights were maintaining a steady course, veering only slightly west.

They weren't heading for any public docks, that was for sure. She knew the lake. They were headed down past the craggy cliff face where she'd fished with employees in other years.

It wasn't long before she could see they were beginning to slow.

Gearing down to little more than a trawl, she cut the engine and watched.

One of the lights had now faded from view. Soon the second disappeared also.

A boathouse.

Aiming her craft towards the cliff face, she drifted in around its shoreline, dropping anchor about 20 yards from a small moonlit pebble beach.

The multi-colored stones gleamed brilliantly in the silver cascade. She'd swim to shore, then travel to the property up around the cliff's crest, down through the thick forest if she had too.

Plunging in, the stab of frigid water sliced her to the core. In long swift strokes she brought herself in through the rolling waves. Pulling herself up on some rocks, she fumbled amongst boulders and logs until she found slippery, but solid footing.

Her gun - it was still there, tucked in her gown's inside pocket.

And she was off. Her aching feet sinking in the dense pebbles with each leap.

On firm land she jogged up through the pines, following as close to the shoreline as she could beneath the cover of overhung twists and branches. At the outcrop, she gazed down on an inlet snuggled tightly into rocky, tree shrouded hills.

It was a brightly lit cottage property with people moving out across a back lawn.

They'd made the trip in one piece - she could see them transferring Saara and the man up some back stairs.

Checking the gun, she had six bullets. Down, she had to go down...

Dust and pebbles skittled as she started her descent. At ground level the voices became clearer, though they were still separated by a small bay.

"Bring her in here," she could hear Edmonstone saying. He was standing by a pair of back sliding glass doors

On a brick patio outside, the largest guard motioned them in to a sprawling, glass surrounded living room.

Delivering Saara and the other man to its centre, she watched as their bodies were laid out on the floor. Edmonstone dragged a chair in from outside, setting it close to their captives.

Helen had reached the edges of the back lawn and could hardly breathe, her hands clenching the gun in shaking, wet grips.

Rebekkah was helping gag them with cloths. Along the room's perimeter, the old woman moved like a cold, emotionless lizard.

I leave on Tuesday.

It was Monday. There still might be time.

III

Inside, for the first time since she'd blacked out, Saara stirred.

Staring up from a warm wooden floor, there were bright lights and she couldn't move her hands or feet. Slowly her situation hit her in throbbing, vivid awareness as her eyes took in the faces of her captors.

Her mouth was gagged and that hideous thing was staring right at her.

"Irina, see what you can learn from this one," Edmonstone was saying, beckoning for the old creature to move closer.

What she can learn? Oh no..

But it was already over her with that deep inset reptilian gaze. *Inside her,* no, it wasn't possible.

Looking away, she drew at every ounce of strength she had left, but the first wave seared like hot pokers and she screamed, the gag fluttering in her gaping mouth.

Probing. That fucking rubber monster. That cunt in myyy heaaaddd.....

Choking, she wanted to vomit as the attack came more forcefully.

Drifting, she moaned, flashes of the witch levitating near the ceiling fused with confusion.

Throwing her head back, she kicked at a chair, tipping it over, as new waves sent her sprawling across the floor, legs rigid, body writhing in heaving spasms, soaking the rag completely.

That fucking thing. What is it doing? But they were barely thoughts as she kicked aimlessly like a fish gasping for water.

IV

What the hell is that thing???

Brandishing the gun like a rosary, Helen kept her eyes on the strange spectacle unfolding inside, as she darted between picnic tables and chez lounges.

Just go in firing, take them all out, she thought, whispering a quick prayer in a final push for the doors.

Inside, what was left of Saara's mind was reeling. That thing knew exactly what it wanted. Ethan, the girls - it was finding it all.

A commotion. Men by the door turning, flashes of gunfire, a rock smashing through a window in the open concept kitchen.....

Saara watched the first man fall as all hell erupted, then the other one, sliding down a wall, gun half clutched, deep red spraying from his chest...

Edmonstone running to a hallway, Rebekkah pulling out her purse gun...

Rebekkah firing back at someone, someone shooting at her, two bullets in the wall missing her head by centimeters....

Now she could see who it was, Helen, through a mirror in a side room, by the back entrance.... firing at the bitch through the wall....

Screaming, Rebekkah fell, blood gushing from her stomach....

Raising her fingers to her lips, the hostess motioned to her as she rushed towards the fallen woman who was now writhing like a stuck pig in her own mess.

Down she brought the gun on her skull, finishing her, then prying the weapon from her hand.

It had stopped. The old creature was nowhere to be seen, but somewhere a gun was being loaded...

A door slamming. It was Edmonstone, backing out onto the lawn, shotgun in hand, Baboushka led by the other.

Rushing to the sliding glass doors, Helen fired once, striking the old woman in the back of a leg.

Howling, the creature let out a deep growl and stared Helen down.

God, she has no idea...

Edmonstone, still tugging, half dragging it backwards, firing back, shattering windows, towards the boathouse....

One bullet left.

Stepping over the men back into the room, Helen knelt at Saara's side, undoing the gag.

Gasping, the reporter thanked her in desperate, manic sobs.

"What was that thing doing?!" she screamed.

"A powerful psychic - in my mind," Saara shuddered, head still shaking, wiping crusts of blood on the carpet off her trembling lips.

"They're after specific information. Stuff only my partner and I know - about the killings. We have to get Ethan. He'll be able to... help us."

The old hostess worked at her hands and feet.

Half slumped against the wall, Rebekkah's body suddenly slipped further, startling the pair.

Finally able to stand, Saara walked over and emptied her old acquaintance's pockets.

Hotel room card, ID, cell phone.

A boat was starting up down at the lake. They were getting away.

"We need to get back to the island - can we make it?" she asked, stuffing the items back into the dead woman's blood-spattered purse.

But Helen didn't answer. She was searching the room for something.

"Where's the other guy?" she asked, flipping over a couch.

"What guy? Was there somebody else here?"

"Yes, a young man, tied up, just like you - only he really looked dead. Laying right over there."

"I have no idea. But we have to get out of here pronto. Look, I have her stuff. We can learn more from her computer, but we have to go back. That's where the rest of it is. We have to get to her room before anyone else. Look, her name isn't even Rebekkah. It says its Samantha Black. *That's right.* She was a Black back at school. I knew there was something weird going on. We have to get back to my room too."

At the pebble shore, they swam out in the now calm open air waves.

At full throttle they sped back, mooring off the kitchen side. Still soaked, they made their way in and through the halls to an elevator.

Room 224 was an easy find. Three rooms in to the left. The card clicked and they were inside.

Sitting for a few seconds, Saara laid out a plan in her head.

The next few hours would be crucial - everything that could be learned from the room would be invaluable in the coming days, maybe weeks ahead.

This bitch. Who was she really?

Start with the luggage.

Two black carry-alls stacked one atop the other on a fold-out stand in the corner.

The upper one packed with clothes and toiletries. The bottom one far more interesting.

Pulling out two shirts, Saara gingerly lifted a dark green binder from a bottom compartment. Its pages were well worn at the edges. A manual of some sort.

The cover simply read "Rural 12".

On the bed they found the documents Saara had grabbed from the old woman's bedroom. Helen gasped as she sifted their contents.

"I know, I know, I'll tell you later, there's no time now" said Saara, snatching the papers from her hands. Placing them in with the binder, she continued packing bags.

This woman is something special, totally involved in the case in some way, thought Saara. *Mixed up with the Edmonstone she had to be.*

"Where are we going?" blurted out Helen suddenly, with a wave of her gun.

"To get Ethan," she replied calmly, hauling the bags from the bed.

Chapter 31

They'd made the falls at the Moon River two hours earlier and the invocation had started without much fanfare.

Dawn was approaching, and Ivan, close to exhaustion, watched as the group uttered incantations over pockets of incense positioned at each of the cardinal points, around a large circle marked out on rock beside the rushing waters.

Jack, garbed in white ceremonial robes, stood at its centre, passing bowls of smoke to the others. He'd be summoned when his contribution was needed, he'd been told. All he could do now was sit and watch as the inexplicable process continued.

In general, it was to ward off the approach of the Ojibway, but in some way it had more to do with the future than the coming months, he'd learned. Ridiculous.

The nagging memory lapses he'd been suffering had been growing - it was all amounting to a bunch of weird abstract worry with no defined parts - a big bag of psychological shit, as far as he was concerned.

Hurry up people, I want to go home.

One of the women stepped in front of him, signaling that his time was approaching.

Kneeling before her, he allowed makeup to be applied to his forehead and cheeks, then he was fitted in a robe and led close to the circle through the smoke, until he stood before Jack.

Motioning for him to turn, the Master led him to the front of the circle, positioning him as he uttered a prayer:

"Take thee, who is offered and lead through his actions, thoughts and heart," he intoned.

It felt strange being talked about like that and he had to admit he'd begun to feel strangely sleepy, breathing in the god-knows-what they were burning.

It was an acrid, rich brown colour and it was thick - pungent like nothing he'd ever smelled before. Shaking slightly, he listened as Jack continued, now in softer tones, lowering his voice to almost that of a whisper:

"The vast eternities your blessing, choose oh night, this be your glory."

Now he was really feeling weird. The air seemed to be crackling too with sparks that were flying, then growing to flame balls the size of hands.

Something *was* happening. The magick was taking effect.

Uncontrollably he found himself tearing at his robe to reach inside his jacket. It was the feather. the one the man had given to him at the mall. The man? Now he remembered - he'd been waiting outside Toys R' Us for Francois. The day they'd first met - the man had just smiled, pulled it from his own waistcoat and presented it to him while speaking some words.

He felt fuzzy now, things were happening too fast.

Sweat poured from his face. Could they see he was changing? What *was* happening? The spark balls had formed a circle - a ring of pulsing fire directly over them. Some of the women danced, ecstatic looks on their faces, just like in the scary photo. He stared up. What was it up there? Darkness, darkness as he'd never seen.

Without thinking, he hurled the feather straight up into the gaping void. He had to feed it. It wanted it.... Would it be enough?

The whole circle was beginning to shake and the rock shuddered beneath them.

Something had happened. Something Jack didn't like. Turning, Ivan could see his captor screaming at him, face distraught in anguish, but he couldn't make out the words. A dreadful silence had drowned them and they were in some kind of a bubble.

Oh God, what have I done? What have I done?

Chapter 32

At the docks by the kitchen, Saara fidgeted nervously.

She'd watched as Helen brought the boat closer to shore, then waded ten or so feet through the water, grabbing the back end with one hand and pushing the luggage over the side before climbing in.

Under her direction they headed to Dorset - her car, still at the Baysville docks, was completely out of the question.

There they called a cab, asking to be taken to an address a few kilometers from the estate.

On arrival they paid the cabby and spent half an hour trudging through the now snowy backyards and fields to the outskirts of the old property.

Through the thick woods, they could see the estate's buildings dark and frozen in time. So much had happened in the past week that returning to it felt like an eternity had passed since she'd last stepped foot within its halls.

Looking back at Helen, she drew a deep breath.

Pausing, she flicked the latch on the old garden gate and both women entered, moving slowly through the maze of lattices and paths around to the front porch.

The door was locked, so Saara pulled the wooden table over to a post, hoisted herself up, and, with Helen's help, shimmied the wood to the second-floor veranda.

Helen listened as her companion jimmied an upstairs window, gaining access to the master bedroom.

In a few seconds she was back downstairs opening the front door.

"Something's gone on here," she said, a worried look in her eyes.

Inside, Helen could see she was right. Chairs were overturned as if there'd been a struggle. Drawers had been rifled and at the end of a main hall, red tape had been strung across as a barrier.

"This isn't police," whispered Saara, moving past the tape towards the library.

He'd followed that SUV from the auctioneer's.

The library seemed untouched, but by its door were a pair of leather boots which she knew weren't his. Had someone broken in and harmed or kidnapped him?

Moving to the kitchen, dishes were piled high in the sink and several wine glasses were on the counter still unwashed with some plates and leftovers from a steak dinner.

Three plates. Whose were they?

Everything pointed towards a hasty departure, she thought, emptying the food into the still full garbage, but why?

It was chilly inside and she wasn't surprised to find the side door had been left slightly ajar. Closing it, she motioned for Helen to follow and they retraced their steps to the foyer to climb the main staircase.

At the second-floor landing, there was more evidence something had gone horribly wrong. The attic hatch staircase was hung open and for a moment Saara thought she heard movement beyond it, but was relieved when a flying squirrel dove down past them, colliding with the walls on its way towards the main floor.

Hearts pounding, they checked each of the bedrooms, where they encountered more clutter, broken mirrors and overturned dressers.

She had to get in touch with William, see if he'd heard from Ethan or knew what the hell was going on.

It was now 3am and, leaving Helen with some hot coffee, she hiked the half mile to the nearest store where there was a pay phone. On her way, she picked up a few egg cartons that had blown up the driveway, the remnants of the previous evening's Devil's Night.

Ethan had always loved Halloween and each year took pains to decorate the estate in a suitably spooky manner for trick or treaters. No doubt many would arrive this year only to be disappointed.

For now the countryside was quiet save for some chattering squirrels.

The street lamp was still lit at the store. She wondered if William would even answer. He was a bachelor used to early mornings, hopefully he would.

After three rings a groggy voice crackled on the line.

"Hello?"

"William, it's Saara. I'm sorry for the early call, but are you alone - can we talk?"

Click.

The line went dead.

Hanging up, she shook with rage, melted frost dripping from the receiver.

She'd never fully trusted him anyway. Fucken' cops. Why had Ethan?

No one else knew they'd made it off the lake - but now he did. She had to get back to Helen, hopefully before the whole force arrived..

A soft drop touched her cheek. Then another. *Great. More snow.*

It came in single tiny flakes at first, then a gentle multitude of waves.

It was no more than a strong dusting, but it still seemed much too early for winter.

Pulling her jacket tighter, she hurried back.

By the time she'd reached the driveway, enough had fallen that she'd started to leave fresh tracks.

Been leaving tracks since this whole fucken' thing started. Such a total fuck up, she thought.

Reaching the veranda she stood looking back on the trail she'd made, watching as tiny squalls danced through the trees.

The seasons were changing and things were much worse now.

She spied a half smoked joint in the ashtray on the wooden table. Striking a match, she lit it, and, after several deep tokes, remembered Helen.

The white silence had lent the estate a feeling of being larger than usual and in the darkness she could hear its old walls creak as the frozen vines chattered.

She must be in one of the bedrooms, she thought, finding the kitchen empty.

Turning the light out, she turned to head back down the hall when she noticed light through the crack between the basement door and the floor.

That's odd.

In the man cave she found her friend knelt down, looking desperate over a man who was shaking uncontrollably in some coma or trance.

"He came out of that room," yelled Helen, pointing at an ajar door in the corner. "I've yelled, but I'm too afraid to shake him. Thank God you're back. I went upstairs, brought him some water. He's hitting his head on everything, like he can't wake up."

Crouching, Saara grabbed the figure by his shoulders, shaking him in an attempt to end the madness.

"Is this the one you saw on the island?" she asked, dodging gobs of spit shooting out through his clenched teeth.

"No, that one was younger, had different hair."

The shaking started to take effect and slowly the young man began to come round, eyes flitting rapidly at first, then remaining open, one by one.

"There," she smirked, stepping back, pleased with the results.

He lay in a half daze staring up at the ceiling and they watched as his eyes descended, taking them in with the rest of the room.

"Am I... safe?" he asked, looking startled, eyes bouncing from Saara to Helen.

"Yes, but are we?" shot back Saara caustically.

"Where.... where am I?" he asked, struggling to sit up.

"Take a look around - where do you think you are?" responded Saara, pressing her foot into his chest, thwarting his attempts at rising.

"At that guys mansion....?" he asked, eyes coursing along the walls.

"Yes, but the question is what the fuck are you doing here," she said, tugging on the freshly lit roach. "And why were you in that closet? Where the fuck's Ethan?"

Rubbing his temples with both hands, he shook his head like he didn't want to remember.

"I... I was here when they came, I....could hear them upstairs," he stammered, pulling at details.

"Who came?" blurted Saara.

He looked about 25. His clothes were ripped and he was thin. Looked like he hadn't eaten a real meal or had any real sleep in several days.

"The people studying this shit... the sightings," he replied.

"What sightings?"

"You don't know? How...how do I know you aren't with *them*."

Moving to get up, Saara quickly trained Helen's hands, which were still clenching the handgun, directly at him.

"Now, you are going to tell us everything that happened here or we're going to shoot you in the fucken' leg and you won't be going anywhere ever," she snapped. "Start by letting us know about Ethan. Do you know him? *How* do you know him?"

"I..., I..., I don't know him really," he sputtered. "We met him on a stakeout by the house they were at. Don't ask me who they are - a private corporation is all we know. They tracked us here. They are studying sightings in the area. Didn't he tell you?

He said he had to call you. I can't....remember your name, but he said he was calling you. They raided this place. What day is it? How...how long have I been out?"

"What was the last thing you remember?" Saara asked coolly. "What happened before you supposedly blacked out?"

"He was upstairs with Franck," he replied. "We were all going to bed and then the team came. I don't know what happened after that. I think they sprayed something to make us pass out. I got in the closet... The last thing I remember was some type of thick fog."

None of it made any sense. The team?

Shaking her head, she motioned to Helen to keep the gun trained as she took a glass of water from the bar handing it to him.

With huge gulps, he pulled himself back up against the wall, still shaking. With her other hand, Helen threw him a blanket.

Wrapping himself, he looked like he was about to speak, but stopped before any words escaped.

"No, no, go on," said Saara, calmly coaxing.

"It's just that..... more was going on here than just the team arriving," he said. "Are Ethan and Franck not here?"

"What did you mean 'more'?" asked Saara, but she could sense it. Something wasn't right. A man doesn't spend three days in a closet in a rambling incoherent coma for no reason.

"I..I...don't know how to explain it, but there is something here," he said. "In lots of places around here. It takes you somewhere. Almost like it's.."

"Haunted?" asked Saara, though she knew this wasn't the right word.

"In the same realm, but not quite," said Ivan.

"It's like reality here can be different. We'd heard similar descriptions over the scanner from people who were experiencing it. I wasn't just in that closet. I was here, but somewhere else too. Can't explain it. It was....another reality."

There was no point telling them about Jack, he reasoned. They were already giving him blank stares. *Just shut up. Be happy your alive.*

"It's probably just the drugs or whatever they sprayed wearing off," said Helen. "I notice a bit of an odour."

"No - I want to know more," said Saara, eyeing him up more intently.

They'd seen the old woman. Things were fucked up.

"What...was this 'reality' like?"

"The reason I think it's real, is because we all experienced it before the team came," he said.

"Who's 'we all'?"

"Ethan, Franck and I."

"None of this makes sense," said Saara. "So who is this team? We just came from an island where there's some fucking horrible shit going down. People out to kill us. Psychic shit."

"They probably have Ethan and Franck right now," he said. "They've been here in the area, renting a house in Muskoka Lakes where they've set up monitoring equipment."

"So *that's* where Ethan was going..." said Saara, stamping her feet angrily. "Why didn't he tell me?"

She felt stupid again - he always had that effect.

She hadn't considered any of this yet. And all those strange books he'd been leaving around the place. She should have paid more attention.

The night she saw the man in Noctivagus too - the procession along the river. But that had been just a dream....hadn't it?

"I don't know what else to tell you," continued Ivan, tracing his still seeping rash.

"We can't stay here," said Helen. "This'll be the first place everyone checks."

She was right, thought Saara. Very different worlds were moving towards their own conclusions - how had they ended up in so many?

She longed for a simple night's sleep, a simple morning's coffee and some simple love from a simple man. Where had her own world disappeared to?

But they were all staring at her, their de facto leader, pleading for direction.

Hiding the fact she didn't know where to begin, she nodded, burying the roach in a plant. Kneeling, she suggested they find some antiseptic and bandages.

"Let's head upstairs," she said, helping him to his feet. "And stay together."

Upstairs they found enough food in the fridge & pantry for one meal.

There were still cars in the garage too. They could get in one and head south, just leave, thought Saara, as the others munched on dry cereal. The cops might arrive at any second. They'd have to move fast.

"My parents have a cottage nearby....." Helen said suddenly. "I was thinking we could go there for a bit, they're down in Florida until mid-December. We could go there and just hide out for a few weeks, I just don't want to stay here much longer - like for another minute. They'll be here in no time you know."

"Don't worry - I don't want to die either," said Saara, nodding. "Where is it?"

"That's the thing. It's on Lake of Bays, but we could probably get to it without being noticed."

"Oh fuuck me," said Saara. "So risky."

"But we are sitting here waiting to die," argued Helen. "We have to get going. We have to be on the move. I'm going, like, right away, if you're not coming."

If you're not coming, thought Saara. *It sounded so threatening.* She wanted a warm bath is what she wanted.

Pulling away, Helen gathered her gun from the counter and started to move towards the back door.

Watching, Saara let her go, to see if she'd actually do it.

The door started to swing open.

"Ok, ok," she said, raising her hand.

"I'm not joking." said the hostess lingering at the threshold.

"I'll grab some things - you get ready too," Saara told Ivan. Helen stepped back inside.

But then she raised her hand sharply. There was a flash of light in the hall and the front door was being opened.

Without a word, Ivan grabbed the hand gun from Helen and left the room. A shot sounded, followed by gruff screams.

"This thing's empty and more are coming," yelled Ivan, storming back through the room, pulling a meat cleaver from the wall.

Squinting, Saara could see another vehicle approaching. They must have been nearby keeping the place under surveillance.

In the garage there were still two vehicles.

In the pickup, they braced as Saara gunned the motor, lurching the old rust bucket forwards.

"Get going," screamed Ivan.

Saara hit the gas.

Chapter 33

AAF Central Film Library
AAFCS No 348-1
Reel No 1
Footage Ground
CCU 9th/4
Date Photo'd 4-13-43
16 mm K and 35 mm
Title: Capture and Film of Subject: Irina Choloucheskou
Found wandering near Hoia Baciu Forest on April 12th, 1943. Estimated age: 5
yrs old. Reported to have moved among three orphanages during early years of war,
the last expelling her due to 'disturbances'. Fires, teleportation. Young girl at
orphanage burned alive. Provided the name Irena Choloucheskou by Echo Units.
No birth records.
Quality Good

I

The clink of a heavy latch echoed through the large greeting room Mark Edmonstone found himself in as a butler opened the wide doors to the inner chambers of Dagmar Mansion.

It was the second time he'd been there this month. He'd recently dreamt of that sound and the pair of accompanying white hands, gnarled like old trees, which pushed them all the way open.

The always starkly dressed 'Thompson' had steel blue eyes which he'd found increasingly difficult to tolerate. Today would be more trying than others.

"Back so soon?" the old servant asked with a cold gaze.

He didn't answer, choosing instead to brush past him into the main hall with a brusque inquiry as to where he could find his uncle.

He had to repeat himself as the butler had remained transfixed by the sight of his companion's own haunting stare projecting from the half opened window in the dark limousine idling outside.

"I'll be right with you," answered the old man, not relinquishing any authority which hadn't already been stolen by time.

Snapping his fingers impatiently, (the war between them would easily be over once his uncle passed) Edmonstone followed him into a dimly lit dining hall.

"Leave us be," said the hotelier, watching to ensure that the doors were tightly shut as Thompson left.

Now he could feel another set of eyes on him, but before he could speak, their voice broke the silence.

"Where is she?" it asked, in deep garrulous tones.

The words carved him and his blood coursed like heady wine. It showed in his face.

"Outside." he replied calmly.

A chair scraped worn wood flooring and his uncle was up, his thin wiry frame haloed by lamp light behind a large desk at the end of the chamber.

He watched as the elderly man stepped towards him until they were not two feet from each other, eye to knowing eye.

The soldier sighed.

"It wants to see the other one," he said. "I tried to explain what has occurred, but she doesn't understand."

"There's no question she would want to see it," said his uncle, stroking a silver goatee, and rubbing his coarse sandpaper temples thoughtfully.

"It's not got long to live and she senses it. That's all they do remember, sense things. It's just whether she will continue afterwards. Where is her injury?"

"The leg."

"Bring her in, we'll fix her up. I suppose we'll let them see each other, but it won't be good."

The men stared at each other. Time had slipped past and there were no other foreseeable avenues for the project. The last sighting had been more than a week ago. It was the endgame they'd feared for years and now it was here, proving more hollow than they ever could have imagined.

Valets were sent for and the old woman was brought in, making animal sounds plucked from the depths of mystery.

Each time Herr Vonn saw her, it ignited cooled embers in his charcoal heart.

Outside, the machines were creating brine, others snow, while still others padded it into the hills.

The Germania Ski Area would be open for the season this coming weekend.

The snow was falling heavier now and through the large windows, Edmonstone could see chalet staff moving like mice through the growing drifts in the ski village.

They were also using the tunnels beneath the shops and chalets close to Hills 1 & 2.

He dreaded those tunnels. As a boy he'd spent too long in them and had jumped at the opportunity the army had provided. It wasn't hard. His father and then his uncle, wavering now before him, had secured everything - his rise through the ranks and the numerous soft tours. They'd granted their boy the illusion of a life separate from the family, but had been in control every step of the way.

Their work depended upon it. And now he was back inside.

The old familiar underground must greeted them as they strode into the antechamber that led down to the underground.

Below, the valets had unlocked a door leading to a large mainly empty room with dark tinted viewing windows covering the far wall.

Beyond it was her sister.

Shuffling to the glass, hands tracing circles along the panes as if to erase the tint in order to see in further, a wild nervousness manifested in snorts and concerned growls. The handler opened the large iron gate door and was almost trampled as it rushed inside.

A terrible thick wail which both men had always hated erupted from within the chamber.

It was dying, there was no hiding that now.

Clenching his fists until his knuckles turned white, the hotelier tried to think of groups of happy skiers tracing the hills and families lined up for their boots and x-country shoes.

Then it came.

At first a barely noticeable chink in the side of a pane which spread to a line across the entire width of glass.

With a groan, the iron door to the chamber folded as the horrible sounds of twisting steel mixed with the sharp pangs sent flashing through their skulls.

Behind him, his uncle readied his weapon, but it flew from his hands before even locking in.

Metal scattered across concrete as the room filled with the powerful throws. The sounds of anger and helplessness.

Again she roared and more glass and wood fell.

Then, stepping from the chamber, her crumpled kin in her arms, she stared them down and continued moving, heading for the tunnels.

In the chaos he only saw the figure briefly.

Gangly and decrepit, the once six-foot tall creature now no more than thin clumps of flesh, bone and hair, one eye screaming about the room in panic.

They could escape.

Face down, the images crashed around Edmonstone as more waves were sent searing through his mind. They would make the tunnels but would have to be stopped. Something final - there was no way people could be stuck out there with them.

Stumbling, he dragged a table and chair to the wall, balanced the latter on the first and climbed up to pry away a vent gate. Clawing desperately at its edges, it finally gave way.

Inside he pulled himself towards the outside, kicking another gate free, out into the crisp early winter.

But it was too late.

He could see them already hurtling through the growing drifts towards Village 1.

Containment, he thought, *that's the stage they were in.*

Above, he saw his uncle in the tramway corridor that connected to the main chalet in the village. He was spiraling through it, workers cowering in fear of his machine gun which he was waving fanatically in all directions.

That's when the screaming started.

In the village courtyard by the hot tubs, two lift operators, teen girls, were being suspended in the air.

In furious turns it was shaking them, then hurtling each to the far corners of the square.

Two shots rang out from his uncle's gun.

No, not the guesthouse.

But he could see she was already looking in that direction.

Another howl spreading in an invisible wave buckled the overhead tram walk, causing it to fall to the ground in a smoking crumpled tangle.

Employees scattered from buildings, fleeing for the parking lots, vehicles roared from the property.

In the guesthouse, excited voices from the bar area. Many of these employees had arrived on site earlier than usual this year, called in due to the fortunate weather. Their moans now followed by other horrible sounds as the beast went room to room.

For a moment silence held sway, save for the faint shuffling of wooden clogs on the highly polished floors.

Stepping inside, the full horror of what was occurring hit him full on and his knees buckled when he saw it. Limbs everywhere like ripped doll appendages. Melted faces and eyes.

One bullet... in the head, he vowed, clacking his fallen uncle's gun into position.

The lifts could be accessed from the bar's upper deck and he could already hear her heavy feet up through the ceiling.

Another scream and the sound of clanging metal, the mountain lift had switched into gear.

Raising the weapon, he climbed until he could see her cradling its sister in one of the chairs as the thing started to rise.

Overhead a sign read 'Mountain Two - Wolf Run'

She'd be an easy target now. *One clear shot...*

II

"Shots have been fired at Germania Ski Area and police have cordoned off the roads leading to the facility. Reports of three people dead are now coming in. Witnesses say there are at least two shooters."

Saara turned up the volume to hear more.

"That's the ski area Edmonstone's family owns," blurted Helen from the backseat. "It's probably them."

They were now on County Road 113 near Town line 4 and daylight was finally starting to break. Their getaway had worked so far. Nobody behind or in front.

Ivan punched the name Germania into the GPS. It was roughly four miles away.

"You'll want to take the next left," he shouted watching Saara skillfully pass several pickups which had stopped almost in the middle of a back road for some reason.

"The family have owned it for years," shouted Helen. "But we shouldn't go there. Let's just get the fuck out of here. Out to the cottage."

Saara turned left.

"You are fucking crazy, just let me out," Helen screamed. "I'm done. Let me out. Give me the gun!"

"Shut the fuck up," yelled Ivan, "Or I'll fucking clock you…"

The land raced by. They were deep in the hills now, careening with the force of a small tornado.

"Local police have called in the army in what is now being described as a chaotic scene unfolding at Germania Ski Area," interrupted the radio. *"We have just received word all traffic on Highway 11 near the resort is being rerouted three miles south of the area and all roads leading in are blocked."*

"Is there another way in?" screamed Saara, adjusting the rear view.

Silent, Helen stared into the dark hills.

"Is there another fucking way in?!?" she screamed again, hitting the brake, briefly jolting Ivan and Helen forward.

"We're so going to get killed," sputtered Helen, grabbing her neck. "So fucked…"

"Never mind, we'll find our own way bitch," replied Saara, hitting the gas.

Rounding a curve, they raced through more rolling farmland.

Two miles in the distance they could see helicopters circling, dipping low through plumes of thick black smoke, making passes and hovering.

Chapter 34

I

Ronnie awoke in darkness with mist on his face and there was movement.

What was it? Boots sloshing puddle spray as the floor beneath him bounced and thudded. His legs and arms were bound and there was a soaking rag in his mouth. He could hardly breathe.

Was he on a boat? The last thing he remembered was the window.

Straining, he pulled his chin up onto the floor, leveled it between two cracks and stared straight up.

A tall man with a long leather overcoat stood behind the wheel yelling to someone else. *They must be going at least 100 km an hr.* The back of his head throbbed and he felt like throwing up.

Just give up, he thought. He was as good as dead anyway. *Snuff it.*

But trying to expel the air he had left in his own sunken chest only elicited coughs. His shoulder was in spasms so he just closed his eyes.

Let it be quick.

"*Oh, old friend, we have a lot to learn from you before that.*"

It was *her.* The *new her.* The *old her. In his head.* His eyes searched left and right.

"*Still cry yourself to sleep at night?*"

Betrayal. But he'd already steeled himself. He'd feel nothing. At least they couldn't have that.

"*Oh now, don't try and hide, you know that won't work.*"

Burying his chin deeper in the wet wood, the pain in his arm was unbearable and he thought about making a move up and out of the boat.

Roll to the driver's chair, edge yourself up and with one push be gone forever. Then open your mouth. Let it all in.

A boot heel settled firmly into the base of his spine making it impossible to move.

"*Go ahead, try now,*"

"*You... you were my friend,*" he pleaded. almost mockingly, embarrassed he couldn't hide his true thoughts. "*We..we.. tried to save you.*"

"There were lots of little boys like you,"

Her voice was smoother now and somehow....younger.

"Don't worry Ronnie, they can't hurt you, not while we're together"

He shuddered. The words that had been their pact, which he had trusted so implicitly during his darkest hours.

The boat dipped as it turned, and, for a split second, he thought he saw *the one*, silhouetted against brilliant yellow-grey flashing clouds.

Another flash. *She was there*, staring from another boat racing alongside he and Sam's.

With the change in Sam's tone came new flashes, pictures of a man he didn't know. Middle aged, responsible looking. A writer?

Why was she showing him this?

Never seen him before.

"Oh really?"

There was no way she couldn't sense his honesty, but more came like a demonic sped up carousel.

Hundreds of them, flashing fast. Some of the man and a police woman and the man at a desk. Then with a horse, then a car.

I really don't have any clue...

"You should have been in Croatia with us, said Sam. Mr. E secured lots of children with your same talents. She was magnificent there and flourished. We learned so much..."

The leather boot loosened and the boat started to slow.

And she was gone - lifted away. But to where?

II

Then in the cottage it had happened again, just before the gunfire.

Images of the man and Jordanna this time, in a car - then others of two girls laughing in a backseat. What could it mean?

She'd just stared from the corner this time - a slight smirk on her older face.

"You don't even know"

He was on his back then, scraping rope against a carpet staple when all hell broke loose. In the midst of it, he had freed himself.

He'd barely made it out of the living room and down some steps.

She'd been testing him to see how he'd react - but why?

III

After several hours, he'd crawled back up the stairs and re-entered the room.

She now lay alone in the corner by the hallway, a crumpled mess in dark clotting pools.

Had she known he was coming? It had never occurred that she'd had the gift.

How had they hidden this?

Kneeling gingerly, he righted her head until her dead blue eyes met his in a cold locked stare.

For most of his life he'd wondered what had become of this, his one true friend.

"Who are you?" he asked, wiping a tangle of wet hair from a cheek.

Shifting his footing, he felt something beneath his right shoe, and, bending to further inspect, saw what looked to be a palm sized crystal perfume holder.

"A parting memento?" he asked, reaching down to pick it up.

In his hand, he could see it wasn't perfume, but a translucent crystal, obelisk shaped with a pointed tip and red button at the base.

Turning it over, he clicked it a few times, half expecting a TV to turn on.

But nothing happened and with a slight huff of resignation, he lay her head back, closed her eyes and slipped the device into his pants pocket.

Exhausted, he plopped himself down in one of the couches and stared at the walls.

The first stirrings of 'the troubles' had already been returning. He'd have to find a squirrel or a bird.

Boy it's setting in fast...

This time it felt different. It had the last time too, but now it was lacking a certain shade and something else was not quite right.

A light was appearing over Sam's body and in seconds it engulfed the entire corner where she lay. Astonished, he watched as the torso sat up, readied herself and stepped out of a mysterious beyond towards him.

Pulse kicking into overdrive, he dove towards the open screen door by the kitchen, presuming she'd give chase. But she was still, turning ever so slightly to follow him with her gaze, remaining silent, a wide grin breaking out across the face.

"*Where are you going, we have so much to discuss,*" she hissed. "*There are so many things you still want to knowww...*"

Grabbing a metal fire poker, he flung it with all his strength. To his amazement, it passed right through, sticking into the drywall.

Laughing, the figure raised one arm towards him, a long pale finger twitching in circles.

"Come here my Ronnie, you haven't even given me a hug...."

Moving in awkward, broken steps, she lurched forward as he backed out onto the patio, fumbling through lawn chairs, relieved she didn't emerge.

Through a window he could see her moving aimlessly in the kitchen, smiling and peering around to see where he was.

But she was soon forgotten, as the very space around him was now filling with triangles and other shapes and shadows. His forehead and arms broke out in cold sweat as he flew blindly across the lawn, cupping his hands over his eyes.

There were others out there now, moving too. The dead bodyguards and frightening, flapping veils.

Oh god Jordanna.

Falling, he lay shaking in the frosty grass, rolling helplessly as it all came down, in and through him.

IV

He awoke to the sound of passing helicopter blades as several of the machines swooped low along the shore by the boathouse, just over the treetops heading west.

Groggily, his eyes fluttered, and, lifting a wet cheek from the snow laden grass, saw he was still on the lawn outside the cottage. Below he looked down upon the sparkling lake, the cottage dock and walkway. It was a mess and there was one body near the main dock, but thankfully it wasn't moving.

On the horizon, he watched as the line of choppers dipped and swayed over an area about three kilometers away where smoke was curling up from the forest. Wiping the dirty snow from his shirt, he felt another swoop low overhead, screaming in fury on its way to join the others.

They were circling now above the one specific area where dark billowing smoke rose in four or five tendrils, undulating to the squeal of distant sirens.

By his foot lay the crystal device, half covered in muck. It must have fallen out when he fell.

Checking himself, he was ok, minus the arm. What the hell had happened?

Picking it up, he clicked the button again. Slowly he began to see diffuse shapes forming in the air around him - at first triangles, squares and circles, then half formed faces, some turning into fantastical creatures which set down and lifted off from the lawn silently. Others who started to walk. Some of these seemed familiar - were they from his past?

"Hello there," said one as it passed hovering just two feet in front of him - a girl he'd known in grade school.

It was his own subconscious - the device had somehow brought their images to life.

Standing, he walked back to the cottage through the phantoms clutching the crystal tightly in case they were real in some way.

Inside he found Sam sitting on the couch watching TV.

"Quite the morning we're having isn't it?" she hissed without looking up.

A reporter was going live near the scene of a mass shooting. There were helicopters. It was close by at a ski hill:

"We're hearing of mass casualties," said the journalist, a desperate sound to his voice. *"And some of what we are being told is odd. One survivor says a woman is levitating near the main ski hill. Officials tell us to discount this as part of the mass hysteria now engulfing Dagmar. Many of the employees we're told, had only returned to work this week in anticipation of the early ski season. We can tell you that police have cordoned off a five-km radius around the property. They are helping evacuate people trying to flee the scene. There's currently no footage from what's happening inside except, as we saw earlier, the cell phone footage from a woman that was posted to Facebook. It seems to show an elderly woman being chased into one of the ski village's chalets. That footage now being analysed as it seems to show her lifting huge tables and flinging them at several gunmen who are chasing her through the compound. One of the last witness reports had the woman on one of the lifts attempting to climb the mountain."*

Smiling, Sam seemed to stare harder at the screen.

"You know who that is, don't you?" he asked.

Silence. Then, clicking the button, she vanished.

Stepping outside, he stared off into the still developing madness.

He'd have to hoof it if he was to finish things off. The real feelings were still returning, building up preparing to break through.

Slipping the object back in his pocket, he turned towards the road leading up into the hills towards Dagmar.

It would take about an hour to get there and there was no time to lose.

Chapter 35

I

The ground drew closer and the black forests spiraled in.

The buzz of radio chatter mixed with the thump of blades as the machine rocked and coaxed itself down towards the rock below.

Stepping out, the pilot opened the passenger compartment door. A blast of cold air and flurries blew in and he stepped down onto the ground, his leather boots crunching in the now inch deep snow.

Atop Wolf's Run he glanced back at Ethan through the window, wind whipping the icy sleet between them so he couldn't tell what look he had on his face.

Down the mountain, the winding ski trails were dark. Not at all like the brightly-lit, hot chocolate fuelled times he remembered as a child. To his right a lift line hummed as he stood waiting. Even as the chopper lifted away ascending back into the murky clouds, he knew it wouldn't be long.

He would wait. He'd waited for this chance now for half a decade.

II

Far below the grounds were consumed in chaos. From the window Ethan watched as another helicopter folded in half in midair, careening into a tree line in an explosion of flames and smoke.

Whatever was happening it was crumpling steel objects like they were toys. By the chalets, police moved like ants, guns drawn, in flanks, spreading out through buildings.

Something was keeping them there stuck at the bottom, but what was it?

Above, the clouds arched in red and green hues between thick dark sky cover rolling in from the east.

He could hear Winters now speaking with the pilot.

Mr. Winters. He'd learnt that much during their trip, but it was all he knew. They were going to have to put down at the back of the mountain now, wait there until the all clear.

The trip in had been fairly calm. His blindfold had finally slipped when the door opened.

The look in Winters eyes told him he may never see him again and that he had no faith in the pilot.

Staring at his cuffed hands, his true chances began to sink in.

The machine lurched, and they touched down behind the Wolf Run chalet. It was near white outs now as the wind howled menacingly, blocking even the slightest hints of midday sun.

Then he noticed it. The silver briefcase was missing. The one Winters had carried with him and had seemed so concerned about.

He strained to see if he could spot him, but he couldn't.

III

Another explosion sent new smoke trails curling towards the apex.

Near the top of Wolf Run, the large huddled figure emerged from the squalls on the ski lift.

She had company.

The old man listened as the lift lines creaked, their metal churn barely audible above the roaring winds.

In the hills, treetops swayed furiously. It was completely dark now and the lift was only illuminated by the flashing of searchlights. Shots were still being fired and in the midst of the volleys, the whole valley illuminated suddenly as the hills lighting system switched on.

"Can you see me?" he called out telepathically, kneeling to open the briefcase

He could see her now, protecting her brood as more helicopters darted menacingly.

Slowly the pair of haunted deep set eyes manifested through the blowing snow, gazing up towards the summit.

Below, soldiers rushed from the forest, guns raised towards the chair. The first of them made it less than a few brave feet, before dropping, hands clinging to their heads in agony.

She was now less than 50 yards from the apex, but at the base he could see they were organizing on sleds. Soon there'd be too many for her to handle. Closing his eyes in deep concentration, the effects were immediate. A great confusion erupted and the sledders fell from their machines stumbling blindly.

Some drove back into the woods. Others turned their weapons on each other or themselves.

Her eyes locked with his as he emerged from the trance.

What manner of beast was this, he thought, gazing into her cavernous sockets.

He'd only heard of this creature, never actually been in its presence. There were rumors about the powerful psychic at the academy, here she seemed feral, almost as a wild beast.

In calm assurance, almost defiance, his eyes met hers as she moved from the lift still hugging her thin mass closely.

They stood opposite each other. It took all he had to not show intimidation. Slowly he raised his right arm, gesturing towards the thumping helicopter behind the chalet.

Another chopper was circling up from the bottom. Turning, she stared and howled. In seconds it began spinning, wobbling uncontrollably before crashing in a tremendous explosion near the moguls.

IV

Saara stepped on the gas. A new explosion had just rocked the countryside adding to the mix of orange and red flames already searing the horizon.

They were nearing the 10th line and the truck was weaving, uncontrollably at times, especially around bends, making Helen think they were even more doomed. Ivan shouted for her to slow down, but she wasn't listening.

Have to get through, her thoughts screamed, blocking out any communication from the others.

Down 10th she could see the flashing lights of cruisers, ambulances, army vehicles and god knows who else they'd called in.

On the GPS they were honing right in.

Rounding another bend, she had to slam on the breaks. A train was stopped at the crossing blocking the road.

"Fuck," she and Ivan exclaimed at the same time.

Helen looked pleased.

"*Fuck, fuck, fuck!*" screamed Saara, slamming her forehead into the wheel.

Switching the engine off, she threw the keys in her pocket and looked at the others.

"Ok, we have to move."

Reaching behind her seat, she grabbed the bag she'd left in the right back passenger well.

"C'mon. We're going."

Glancing at Helen, Ivan opened his side door. Groaning, she opened hers.

In 15 minutes they'd crossed a corn field heading towards the smoke which continued to rise steadily.

At a hill, which they climbed quickly, they waited a few moments monitoring the still distant resort.

Police and army personnel had each exit blocked, but Saara could see movement to the east near the forest halfway up the main run.

Two figures were moving there amongst the trees near a forest access road. They were on foot, carrying guns.

Jogging now, the figures were headed up the mountain away from the base, following a winding road which led higher towards the apex.

Sprinting, Saara, Helen and Ivan moved fast beneath the cover of trees along the roadway.

It was a ways to get to where the figures had first emerged and Saara was worried they'd soon lose them.

"Just keep moving," she huffed. "We can't let them go."

About 40 yards from where they first saw them, they paused to catch their breath. The figures, now just two tiny dots far above, had disappeared back into the woods.

"They're heading in," panted Ivan."Where are they going?"

Smoke drifted hazily along the road mixing with fog and gloomy darkness in the now thick falling snow. Below they could hear sirens and yelling. It had turned into a rescue operation, thought Saara, winded from the climb.

"We have to follow," she said, arching her back and stretching her arms in preparation for the next ascent. "Nobody else sees them, but we do. They could lead us to what this is all about."

In her head she knew it was grasping. She'd probably never hear the end of it later - if there was a later.

After 12 minutes of steady climbing, Helen saw movement about 50 yards above them through the trees.

It was a man, looked to be in his late 60's, talking with a younger man. Both had semi-automatics. It appeared they were searching for paths that could take them higher.

The older one had a shock of white hair which hung down past the collar of an aviator jacket. The younger one was blonde, following the older man's lead.

Helen gasped upon seeing the older man more clearly.

"That's the one from the island I told you about who had shown the interest in the girls," she whispered to Saara.

"What girls?" asked Ivan.

"The girls who were murdered - what started this whole thing," said Helen. "We'll fill you in later. Don't let them out of your sight."

The men were moving again, trudging back through knee deep snow, before turning by some rocks to ascend higher.

Saara was the first to follow. Waited until they were a good distance ahead, it was freezing and they had to keep moving.

In 20 minutes they'd reached the summit and Saara cautioned them to pause. The men were creeping along the tree line, weapons drawn as if half expecting company.

There was a machine somewhere nearby making noise - a helicopter, they could hear the thumping of blades.

The men had taken up position along the front of a chalet and were moving around the building towards its rear.

Through the storm, they drew closer. Snow kicked up from behind the chalet as the rotors continued their powerful turns.

The man with white hair reset his weapon and ducked beneath a pair of windows

Bright lights flicked on as the whirrs sped more rapidly to a full pitch. The chopper was starting to lift away.

Behind them, the sounds of snow machines snarled in the darkness. They were climbing, getting closer by the minute.

Police no doubt, thought Saara, *they'll probably ruin everything.*

Rapid machine gun fire pierced the air, erupting in bursts, first two, then three more.

The younger man had reached the chopper. The older one jumped out from behind the chalet and opened fire as the helicopter hovered just above ground.

In jolts, it began swinging in lazy, half swooping movements. A violent scream was heard, quickly quelled by high winds as a downward swipe of the blades took the young man's upper torso clean off.

The older one continued pumping round after round into its bobbing black frame.

Horrified, Saara had unconsciously stepped out in the open, mesmerized by the unfolding spectacle. Pulling her back, Ivan held her tight, but she struggled free, spotting something as the careening machine spun madly above the chalet.

Ethan - What is he doing here?

The chopper lurched maniacally, its pilot frantically trying to right it, but a rotor caught the edge of the roof sending it fast into the ground, parts ricocheting across the summit.

Racing to the fiery hulk, which was now perched atop a cliff in sections of charred ground, they could hear moans coming from the interior.

Hung upside down in handcuffs and bleeding from deep gashes across his chest and arms, Ethan swayed flimsily. Beneath him, the bulky old woman muttered away, semi conscious, but with no real signs of trauma.

Pulling them free, the group dragged them out into the freezing drifts. The old woman started to stir violently and without warning, sat up, staring wildly.

"There's no time for this," Ivan began to caution her.

"No! Ivan..." Saara screamed, but it was too late.

An ear-piercing howl erupted, knocking them both against an exposed outcropping of rock.

"What the fuckkkk..." exclaimed Ivan, shaking his head trying to gain his bearings.

Now she was on both feet pacing rapidly, screaming into the smoldering wreck.

Nearby a snowmobile approached the summit. Leaping, Ivan took a branch from the ground, and braced himself as it crested the hilltop.

Whacking the driver, he hopped the sled, bringing it back around towards the wreck. Lifting the soldier's weapon, he motioned for Saara and the others to get on.

They were tranquilizer guns. *They must want this chick pretty bad,* he thought.

Firing into the old woman's shoulder blades, he watched her stagger before slumping to the ground in strange moans.

What was that thing doing with Ethan, wondered Saara, as more explosions rocked the cliff's edifice.

Chapter 36

I

Laying the soldier's body back in the soft snow, Ronnie pondered his next move.

Already the squalls were covering the sign he'd made on the birch tree, but he'd shut them out, closing his eyes, allowing the symbol to take full precedence.

He hadn't expected it to be so easy - the young man had been staggering about, mumbling about not getting to work on time near his still running sled when he'd found him.

It must have been the device. He'd been toying with it on his hike towards Dagmar, noticing how squirrels and birds reacted to their own hallucinatory visions along the way. But he'd had it clicked off the better part of the last hour. He'd just arrived though, it could have been something else...

The mountaintop looked relatively quiet save for the faint revving of snow machines and the crackle of a fire where a helicopter had gone down.

Peering through his own breath he listened to the creaking branches and lonely winds as they travelled through the forest.

He'd take the soldier's snow machine up there soon himself.

Who knows what he'd find.

II

Hopping one of the other chalet sleds, Ivan pinched Ethan, flicked the switch and hit the gas, leading the others towards the mountain's back trails.

To the east, one met more concession roads and then farmland. The snow in most places wasn't as deep as the summit, just in patches with areas of exposed soil which choked the machines, making for a sloppy course through the still raging squalls.

Helen drove the second sled with the bulky woman strapped between she and Saara.

The machines were damn noisy and they'd have to ditch them soon, she thought, watching as Ivan plowed sloppily into a particularly thick bank, blowing snow back in her eyes blinding them.

Halting the sled, she jumped off after he and Ethan were sent sprawling, the machine flipped on its side down an embankment.

"You're going way too fucking fast," she yelled, stopping, then reaching to help right the machine.

They were by a lake and a faint early day sun shone brightly from behind the thick rolling black clouds.

To the west they could see the smoke trails rising from the mountain and watched as more helicopters and snow machines arrived at the summit.

They'd be on to them in minutes, thought Saara, jumping off the sled, sending the sleeping old woman slumping to the icy floor.

Running over to Ivan, she helped move the heavy machine back onto the trail.

Ethan moaned on the ground, pulling at his chest in agony.

Yanking his frozen hands away, she pulled his jacket up to see the wounds more clearly. They were deep, but they hadn't penetrated his chest cavity.

Ripping off her jacket, she took off her sweater and wrapped it tightly around his chest to restrict the bleeding.

Flipping open a GPS, she saw they were on Concession 14. On the map it lead another 2 km to Forrester Trail. If it wasn't blocked they could take it to Helen's parents cottage down on the lake. Could be there in five minutes.

Above on the ridge the sleds were starting their descent. They'd have to leave now.

Motioning to Ivan, they hoisted Ethan back on the snowmobile, securing him as best as they could, wrapping his arms around Ivan's waist then tying them with the loose arms of his torn windbreaker.

At Forrester Trail, they emerged from the woods and turned left, shooting down the centre of what was essentially a common residential roadway during the rest of the year.

Fucking snow, thought Saara, gripping the Baboushka tightly as the machine shifted over the icy, white laden road, *our tracks are going to lead them straight to us.*

The decision to take the old woman had been made quickly. She was theirs now, but Saara couldn't see how it would help.

Helen gunned the machine and they sped forward.

The others followed, swooping down off the main road at an intersection into the dark of a high school football field.

Where's the fucking cottage, yelled Saara, wind tears freezing on her cheeks.

She could feel the old woman's hands tighten around her own. It was stirring and they did not want to be in the middle of nowhere if she awoke.

A slightly bent, half covered street post came into view. Ashburn Street. *Sweet.*

Veering onto a narrow cul-de-sac, they were back amongst trees following shoreline by the shimmering water, separated from it only by a row stand of tall spindly pines.

Here there was little snow. They were reaching the end of the line.

Parking near shore, they dragged the sleds behind some bushes and headed down to the shore, pulling their still groggy, wounded charges.

It was a family owned cottage rental community and up against an old paddle shack there was a pair of red canoes yet to be stored for winter.

Hoisting one from its rack, Saara and Helen plunged it into the icy black water.

From the bow, Helen pointed the way. Just after rounding the jetty where the lake opened, they heard the first sleds arriving at the field.

Paddling close to the rocky shore, Helen scanned the row of cottages. She hadn't seen her parents in years and for a moment thought they were gliding too fast and might miss it.

It was three or four in from the point, she'd remembered.

Another 10 metres and they found it. A modest bungalow with a basement, overlooking an old weather-beaten dock.

"Pull up along here," she said, in a mixture of relief and overtiredness.

Splashing ashore, they hauled the canoe up a set of old stairs.

Climbing a stone walkway, Ethan and the old woman staggering in tow, they crossed the lawn and reached the side door quickly.

Stepping back, Saara aimed a solid kick and it broke open, snapping the frame from its bolt lock in the process.

"Glad there's no alarm," said Helen drily.

The wide canoe barely made it through the back sliding glass doors.

Laying Ethan and the old woman down in bedrooms, Helen took up position in the hallway while Saara and Ivan kept watch from the living room.

Within 20 minutes they heard the first sounds of search parties - a mix of paddlers and sleds.

A canoe with three soldiers passed along the shore, while a machine combed the woods near the forest access roads.

Safe for now, they couldn't possibly all sleep at the same time. They'd take turns staying up.

At midnight Ivan tugged Saara's sleeve to report a noise, but it turned out to be twigs rattling against a window.

Falling quickly back into a deep sleep on the couch in the living room, she re-awoke at four am to relieve him.

"We can stay here another day if they don't come," she whispered, as he curled beneath a blanket in a large armchair. "Helen says they may think we made it to the public boat launch up a ways and out to the main roads from there. If we keep the lights off we can wait and see."

Half nodding, he was already on his way to dreamland. She checked the others before settling in the kitchen.

The hum of the fridge was annoying and she wanted to pull its plug, but after looking in the freezer decided otherwise.

They must be coming back over the winter, she thought, eyeing a pack of frozen steaks and three TV dinners. There'd be enough for everybody for at least two days.

Sitting, she lifted a newspaper from the kitchen table and did the crossword, her thoughts drifting back to when she was a child, to summer parties and waterskiing on some lake. She and her mother had stayed at cottages like these, taking long walks on the beach, building sand castles and having picnics.

Her mother was beautiful then, wearing a satin beach dress on a few of the trips, her red hair waving in the sunshine as she laughed and dressed her sons in their frogmen flippers.

But something was wrong. Was it the exhaustion?

Saara had no brothers and her mother had black hair. Groggily she looked down - she'd been drawing circles overtop of the crossword.

A complex of emotions engulfed her, and she stared at her scribble and the black and white squares. She'd spelt the word 'iron' before drifting off.

Snapping out of it, she couldn't remember all of the scene now, but knew it hadn't been from her own life.

Gotta get some sleep, she thought, still puzzled.

In the living room she lay down in front of a couch beside Ivan.

III

"Hey, wine over here," Saara laughed, the dark liquid sloshing in the decanter as Ivan basically shoved it across the table still half involved in a conversation with Ethan.

They were eating steak, caramelized onions, potatoes and carrots. Right there - in the cottage.

Helen asked if there was any more sauce.

Nodding, she reached behind her to the side table to grab it.

She'd been keeping a semi-nervous eye on the old woman who sat at the end of the table staring and growling at her plate.

Ethan was telling Ivan about his time working for a paper in the Yukon early in his career.

"Oh yeah, it was an insipid nest of gossips, I had like three months left to go and it was the worst."

They'd had a few. Found some two-fours of Canadian in the basement.

The gash in Ethan's chest had dried nicely - they'd stitched him together with a sanitized darning thread and some dental floss in the bathroom. The dining room was low lit with candles.

Ivan, who'd begun telling his own story about growing up in Croatia, suddenly looked pale, dropping his fork, sending a slab of sauce laden beef splattering across the table cloth.

Shooting the old woman a fierce stare he screamed 'STOP!'

"What's going on," shouted Ethan, shoving his chair back in astonishment.

A half grin had spread across the old woman's face. Hands raised and folded together, her eyes focused beyond the tips of her fingers meeting Ivan's angry stare.

"She's in me too!" screamed Helen, falling back along the dining room's wall.

The energy from the bedroom was back - how had they been so blind? Had she even told Helen about her? So much had occurred, there'd been no time...

She watched them all helplessly, unable to move. It was like the hag was skimming all their heads at once.

She'd been in the kitchen, the sounds of carrots being cut, wafts of simmering gravy...

Staring at Saara, Helen's eyes were exploding.

The mind waves grew stronger - it was checking in on them through the kitchen wall.

The oven door swinging open - how was she seeing this?? A heavy casserole dish. There's no way it will fit....

Something brushed her cheek. Something touching her...

With a jolt she awoke, shocked to find herself in the dining room at the table with the others.

They were all staring at a large white candle. *Where was it?*

Rummaging around, opening and closing cupboards, in the other room, gathering utensils...

Out of the corner of her eye, Saara could see its backside moving in the pantry pulling pots from an overhanging rack, rinsing a large bowl.

Then something else, moving along the floor. Like a bug, reflecting the candle light....

Stopping, it turned and raced up the wall into some cracks between the joist and ceiling. Ethan saw it too - he was squirming, becoming half-free...

A terrific crash and then a faint odor, each of them sinking down in their seats, one by one...

Chapter 37

AAF Central Film Library
AAFCS No 348-1
Reel No 4
Footage Ground
CCU 11th/5
Date Photo'd 5-23-43
16 mm K and 35 mm
Title: Progress of Irina Choloucheskou
Subject Irina C. showing no acclimatization to new surroundings at Reading Unit in Oxford University, England. Spends time pacing in room. Attendants report hallucinations, nightmares in presence. Many won't stay. Subject enjoys spaces around water on the grounds. Signs of language impairment. Non-responsive to lingual stimulation. Disturbed sleep pattern, instead 'zones out' for times - 2-3 hrs in length. Emotion display minimal. Studies continue as to reported electromagnetic effects.
The End
Quality Good

I

Ivan was first to awake.

It was a white room, sparsely furnished with black furniture. A window onto a dim grey lakeside. Snow patches dotting the landscape. *Likely still Ontario.*

He tried to make his arousal unnoticeable. He was lying on his back on what appeared to be a day sofa, his hands and feet cuffed so if he rolled, he'd end up on the floor.

The room was done in clean, lightly varnished pine. There was a table at one end with two chairs. The heat verged on stifling, despite the cold winter outside. Through the window he watched the white haired man Helen had recognized standing below on a stone patio at the top of a steep granite staircase leading down to a dock.

He was speaking with another younger man in private.

The older man smoked a pipe in slow methodical inhalations, his graying beard lending a solemnity to the already stark surroundings. Dressed in dark clothing, they appeared to be planning something - it was one of his strengths, reading body language and he watched as their hands dipped and posed in the air.

These must be the two head honchos, he thought, turning away back to the room.

The in-ceiling lights hurt his eyes and he felt lingering grogginess from whatever had been used on them. He hoped the others were alright. *There must be a reason I'm still here*, he reasoned, before wondering if this was also true for Saara and Helen.

Perhaps he was the only one left. He listened for noises, but like most well built modern constructions the interior was near silent save for the low hum of electricity and wind against the windows.

There was nothing he could offer them. He just wanted whatever was going to happen to happen fast.

Then, and it only lasted a moment, he felt his mind being entered by the old woman. It wasn't as intense as the last times and it ended quickly, but it was palpable - like a flash going off in a photocopier.

He imagined her scanning the building, registering who was still there.

II

In the living room, Saara lay against Helen's chest on a warm wood floor.

Her first sight upon awakening was a spray of blood on one of the far walls. This and the lighting let her know exactly where she was: Edmonstone's cottage.

Helen's shallow breathing and faint heart beats worried her. She was still under and her own head was pounding.

A pair of men stood at the kitchen island drinking coffee. One of them saw her move, then put his cup down and walked outside.

The white-haired man and another middle eastern man came back in with him. The middle eastern man hung back while the old one walked right over, knelt and stared her directly in the face.

"You and your friend are going to help us my dear," he said coldly.

At this, Helen started to stir, her eyes opening wide in shock at the realization they were captives once again.

"Get the other one from upstairs," he ordered, motioning to the guard.

A moment later Ivan was brought downstairs and forced at gunpoint to stand facing them.

Tears streamed his cheeks and he said goodbye with his eyes as the middle eastern man pulled the trigger.

Both women screamed as his body dropped, bits of skull blown across the low ceiling above where he'd stood.

The pools inched across the floor towards them. It's syrupy warmth meeting Saara's bare feet and she flinched, smearing it in sloppy despair filled screams.

That was it. Another glimmer of hope snuffed in a single shot. Helen shook uncontrollably.

"Bring them outside," commanded the leader. "I'll get her from the basement."

Words were just sounds now, and Saara felt like she was ricocheting meaninglessly in a hall of funhouse mirrors. Both she and Helen remained silent as they were brought to their feet.

The hot white smoke from the gun still lingered as they were marched outside and down the stone staircase to a second back lawn.

She was confused. They were paused on a landing in the middle of the garden and the middle eastern man was blindfolding Helen.

Then they were assembled in the midst of an abandoned lawn bowling game, Helen was shoved into a chair and bound tightly with rope.

The old woman, arriving behind them, stood quiet, glaring into space. Saara shuddered at the sight of it and turned away to her own patch of empty, light grey sky.

A guard produced a metal container the size of a small kitchen garbage can. Wearing black gloves and what appeared to be a gas mask, he placed it down behind Helen, opened its lid and dipped a paintbrush inside, swishing it in circular motions.

When he pulled it out, she could see it dripped with an orangey-beige liquid. He started applying it to Helen's legs - long elegant strokes from her ankles to her thighs across the surface of her gown.

"What the fuck are you doing?" screamed the hostess. "What's happening!??"

The white haired man had pulled a chunk of metal slag from a satchel and placed it at the centre of a concrete birdbath. He led the old woman to it, helping her into a chair in front of the others.

Helen struggled fiercely, and the middle eastern man gave her a swift punch in the face. The other man resumed his work. Soon she was covered head to foot in the slick, strangely glowing substance.

"Now we wait," said the leader, dragging the tip of his gun down Saara's right breast, whispering mockingly: "She is not going to like this."

Another man bound her feet and wrists with more twine securing her to a seat

But she was already far away, determined to be free in their final moments.

Somewhere a line had been crossed in the days prior and it was only just catching up.

Closing her eyes, she dreamt of all the good years before this. Strong, vibrant years full of love and family. The tears fell as she went back, deep in her memories reliving simple things like running in a field with her mom and learning to drive as a teenager.

She'd met Ethan on a summers day in 1999, fresh out of college at her first job as a reporter.

Those first few years with him had been some of their best.

Her thoughts turned to other loves when she was younger, the lilt in her heart encountering new warmth and the strangeness of being a woman.

It was the little things that flooded back now. Craggy dark bluffs beneath full moons, lights left on above the pool by her childhood home way after dark. Everywhere was her spirit.

Even as he pressed the gun deeper into her ribs, she felt a kind of freedom.

She'd never open her eyes again. Not for them.

III

The young man trudging through the snow in front of him looked to be in total pain. He was mainly silent now - they both were - save for a few involuntary grunts whenever they stepped the wrong way into a hole or tripped on a rock.

Ethan watched as the soldier walked on despite a growing loss of blood which was left in splotches on the white ground behind him, one of his arms dangling aimlessly at his side.

Ethan thought it was only fitting to give him a chance, but if challenged further he'd meet his end pretty swiftly.

He was losing blood too, but Helen's make do stitch job seemed to be holding. *Can't think of the pain,* he reminded himself, instead focusing on the tip of his machine gun and the young man's head like a quiet, repeated mantra.

They were following tracks left by the snow machines that had stolen the rest of them away in the early dawn raid. It was snowing harder than ever and even in the trees the sting of the dry, cold wind was biting them raw.

They'd been marching now for three hours and despite the drudgery, Ethan was making it a point not to lose sight of the lake as they made their way through rocky passes and steep inclines - a tip he'd learned in Boy Scouts should one ever get lost in the woods.

But inside he was lost and just wanted to go home.

The soldier's leg where he'd been shot was getting weaker, slowing their pace noticeably. Soon a decision would have to be made.

In the fight that morning the young man had tried to kill him with his rifle and would have easily had he been any weaker.

The only reason he was still involved was to find Saara, and now, with the snow starting to cover the tracks in places, that chance was slipping further from his hands, disappearing with every step.

There was no point, he thought, watching the young man stumble as what appeared to be delirium brought on by exhaustion set in.

In the confusion of the raid he'd made it to an outside shed and waited as the others were rounded up. It wasn't the cops either - more of the same types who'd taken he and Francois, but not them - others.

Reaching into his pocket, he retrieved the strange object he'd taken from the soldier.

It was odd - a pure kind of crystal with a button on one end. Clicking it, he looked for a burst of light and listened for sound.

Nothing.

Useless, he thought, *probably out of batteries.* He slid it away, training his eyes anew on the soldier's bobbing, snow covered head.

The tracks were completely missing for long stretches now where the machines had skimmed icy earth, resurfacing for short intervals every 30 feet or so in places where there was a creek or a dip in terrain. It was no good. It must be about 3pm now, he thought, though one wouldn't know it with all the clouds and sleet.

It was coming down in big shiny clumps now and dazzling blurry circles. Sticking his tongue out he tasted them as he'd done as a child.

In front of him, the soldier paused, short of breath, but started up again with a quick prod from the muzzle.

Give him another 20 minutes max, he thought, watching as he stumbled into a muddy puddle, gained his balance, paused, then pressed on.

The puddle looked deeper than it was. *That's strange.* In fact, the entire woods were taking on a new sense, Ethan thought. *Wait a minute, the trees are different...*

Did the soldier notice it too? Shapes in the branches starting to change. The snow too in the wind - seemed to have.....patterns.

Shaking his head, he blinked his eyes repeatedly, rubbing them with the rough hide of his glove.

Hold on a goddamn minute. That looked like...

Rachel? And her mom?

His young lover was holding a candle out in the woods looking down at the ground. *That is her.* Standing back, behind the trees. Her mother - knelt down, staring at the same patch of earth.

He looked at the soldier. Nothing.

The young man kept marching without any notice despite the fact he must also now have *heard them talking.*

"Momma, you were always my best friend..." Rachel was saying, wiping a tear from her eye, candle quivering as her cold hands shook.

Staring at the soldier and to the women and back, Ethan coughed out an as-rigid-as-he-could "hold up, stop".

Appearing almost bored, the young man turned around, with a 'what now?' look on his face.

"Those girls over there," he stammered. "Do you not see them?"

"No, what of it?"

"How can it be - *I know them*," he said, shocked at the kid's surprising, dry response.

"I'd assume you would," replied the soldier, his lips curling into a smirk.

In the air between them now something was fluttering, almost mist like and a peculiar sense of dread was coming over him, enveloping him just as it had in his own warm study that day.

The amorphous shapes dipped and bobbed in the thick snowfall. Rachel and her mom still carrying out their inane discussion in low, emotional voices.

He must have had an incredulous look on his face because the soldier simply leaned against a tree watching him in abject amusement.

The whole space around them was filled now with voices and strange figures, each battling furiously for his attention.

The rifle dropped, and, reaching quickly to grab it, he was too late in his stupor.

In the soldier's hand now, it looked black and sinister, but it wasn't pointing at him.

"You really have no clue about what you've got yourself messed up in," laughed the boy.

Staring back bewildered, his tears were freezing before they even reached the tip of his nose.

Pleadingly he mouthed a faint 'help' as the figures overcame him, drowning him in their own peculiar version of the woods.

"The object you took from me - where is it?" demanded the boy. But it was no good. Whoever he was had fallen and was crawling around like a baby on all fours.

Patting the older man's jacket down, he felt slightly irked he had to reach into his pants to find the stupid thing.

Then, clicking it, he watched as the mirages vanished, enjoying the sweet satisfaction of observing even more confusion set in on his former captor.

"You can stop screaming anytime," he said nonchalantly as Ethan scuttled, hands still shielding his eyes.

Choking back his shock, Ethan rolled on his back, staring up, flailing like an epileptic snow angel.

"What happened?" he screamed, gasping. "Tell me. Those things.... they were people I know..."

Glancing over in the direction of where Rachel and her mother had stood, the spot was now empty save for the lush falling snow.

"It's a device they've made that exteriorizes our unconscious, that's about as much as I know," the soldier replied. "Now get up. there's quite the hike before we get close to where they're headed. At least another 10 minutes. And you'll need this - my one arm is fucked. Won't be much use with me."

Tossing him the rifle, the older man looked even more surprised.

Brushing himself off, Ethan took the young man's outstretched hand and pulled himself up.

"The thing's shelf life is pretty limited in the scare department when you've been through it a few times," said the young man. "Still, it's pretty fucked up what's in our heads. I just walk straight through it now, ignore it for the most part. Don't get caught in it emotionally if it happens again."

"I had no idea they had these things," Ethan said, wheels spinning in his head, harkening back to his first encounter with the figure in his study.

"I didn't either 'til a few days ago," Ronnie replied, wincing as he shoved his bad arm hand into his coat.

"Then you're really not with them?" Ethan asked, watching as the young man knelt to tighten his boot.

"Nope," he answered, half out of breath. "A pretty long fucking way from that."

Studying him for a moment, it did look like he'd been through hell and his arm *was* severely damaged.

"What part in all this are you playing then," Ethan began cautiously.

"I have to get one main thing done, let's just leave it at that. What I have to do is pretty much what you have to do, so if you follow, we need to get moving."

"But, wait - who are these people then," Ethan asked. "And you haven't even told me your name."

Turning, he held out his good hand and said: "I'm Ronnie - it's all you need to know."

"I figure you just got mixed up in all this like everyone who does - by accident," added the young man, eying up his new companion.

"You could say that I guess," said Ethan. "Wish I hadn't. I'm looking for my partner, then getting the hell out of here."

"Won't do much if she's still around."

"Who's 'she'?"

"The one this whole thing is about. Forget it. Come with me if you want, get lost if you aren't."

Turning he started to march through the thick snow.

"Wait, wait up," said Ethan. "Just tell me what is going on - at least if you can."

Still not turning, Ronnie looked skywards and let out a loud sigh.

"It's old. All it knows is what's in others' heads. Can't speak, not really anyway - can't communicate. They've been trying to learn its secrets, but they still can't figure it out. That device is probably as good as it gets."

"What's it got to do with you? Why are you so hell bent on destroying her?"

Stopping, Ronnie turned around in full glare.

Ethan could see the young man had had some brush with this creature, something personal, so he tried a different tact.

"You suggested to me back there that we were like her in some way, what did you mean by that?" he said.

"Did I tell you by speaking or did you just sense I did?"

"Well, I, I suppose you told me... in my head.." said Ethan.

"We're like that, like her, but not as powerful. It can sense people like us too, so I'd be careful," responded Ronnie.

The words dredged up feelings and he felt powerless, watching as they manifested. Darby. It was Darby who had the real talent. Was why she'd been enrolled in that special school - it's what she'd told him....

Why was he remembering this now? He hadn't thought of their games for so long. When they were left with a babysitter she would come to him, only not physically but from another room - mostly her room. Asking him to play, like she was talking through the walls directly into his head, only there was no sound, no real words even - just like the soldier. In time, he was able to answer, and she could hear him too. She'd taught him so much. In time, they were able to speak with each other from virtually anywhere.

Oh my god.

He'd spoken with her while she was being taken that day. Heard her screaming for him for about an hour before her cries had become whimpers and then finally, silence. He'd told his parents but they'd grown angry, livid he was trying to say that it was true.

The hopelessness surged up from the deep, causing him to stumble and Ronnie peered back at the sound of his unsteady steps.

He couldn't speak and just nodded as the soldier quietly continued.

"We're getting close to her now and when we do, I may get sick and I might need you to see this through. You might not like what you'll have to do, but it will be either it or us and I've come too far for that."

Chapter 38

I

Saara watched as the guard prepared another concoction of the fluid he'd smeared all over Helen.

It felt cold and smelt pungent to her friend, the sickly odour of new vinyl.

It was over-powering and she'd vomited twice, once from sheer terror, the second from the horror of being used and watched like an animal.

Turning towards Saara, her mouth opened wide, but she could only mouth a faint 'help me'.

The man was applying a second coat now, this time smearing her face as she struggled.

Her eyes stung and she gagged as the mixture seeped in through her nostrils and the corners of her mouth.

They're gonna' light me, she thought. *That's what's coming. They're gonna' burn me right here on the goddamn lawn.*

She could see the hotelier coaxing the old woman who's deep-set lizard eyes were already centered squarely on her own.

Shutting down, Helen prayed that whatever was to occur would happen fast. If the pain was enough, she'd give in to it, hasten it through her system - will a heart attack - whatever it took.

Happen NOW, she pleaded to herself, fingers clenched livid white.

What was happening? The old hag had closed its eyes now and was rocking back and forth, face raised to the sky.

They were waiting. Waiting for *something* and she was its target.

Edmonstone glared from behind a rock wall separating the lawn from the upper parts of the property, bristling his grey whiskers in the squalls which were again picking up.

One of the men began edging away, staring at her and then at the sky in wonder.

Her pulse was ratcheting up. Something was happening, she could feel it. A change in the weather - a palpable sense - a kind of electricity.

The air had changed like it had become charged and Saara sensed it too. Tasted it in her mouth.

She looked towards Helen. There was movement in the sky above. A translucent phosphor enveloping the local environment.

Above by the cottage two figures were descending. Saara saw them coming from the forest to the east, making their way towards the front driveway before getting lost from view.

The glowing phosphor had changed suddenly into a large black cloud which hovered in the squalls directly over the group.

Helen moaned, staring into the pulsating maw as it sent rays into the ground. The hired guns were fleeing across the lawn down towards the lake. Closing her eyes, Saara focused in on herself. Nothing was going to save Helen, not now.

II

Rounding a corner, Ronnie paused, pointing to a large man in a dark suit who'd just emerged from a side entrance, his handgun drawn.

He was gasping for air, like he was escaping something. Interesting, Ronnie thought, they hadn't heard any commotion...

"Jump him," whispered Ethan. "You could use his gun."
"No," said the gamer. "I have a better idea. But this is where it's going to get a little fucking wild."

Pulling the object from his jacket, he pressed the red button.

In seconds shapes formed in the air around them, becoming people and strange objects.

"*Why did you do that?*" spat Ethan. "*We were doing so good....*"

"You just have to remember it's not real," said Ronnie. "But they won't know that - or at least some of them wont."

The air was full of the things now. Edging through it, they watched as the suit began firing in all directions, screaming louder when the shots had no effect.

Ronnie leapt and tackled him, relieving him of the gun in a kick to his lower back.

Through the swirling figures, Ethan watched as the young man then knelt and snapped the guard's neck, dropping him to the ground in a heap of powdery snow.

"*What are you doing?!?*" he screamed, watching as his new friend held his hands to his head moaning in pain.

Finding strength, Ronnie, put the gun to the man's temple and pulled the trigger spraying the nearby walls and snow banks.

Speechless, Ethan watched as he gathered clumps of bloody snow and began etching something on the ground - a symbol of some type, which he couldn't see clearly for all the shapes in the air.

Stepping towards him, Ethan could see it was an astrological symbol of some kind.

"Don't ask, ju, jusst do what I sayyy," stuttered the young man. holding his good hand aloft. "There'll be others soon - they will all be affected."

The gamer was shaking uncontrollably now, emitting deep sobs, like he was having some kind of attack.

Down beyond the cottage there were faint noises, though it was hard to discern the real from all the howling in the air.

This guy has no idea, thought Ronnie, as the old one's effects kept building. She was close, the blasts were particularly strong, but there was something new again too - a fleeting sense of vulnerability, a slight relinquishing - again, different from what happened last time.

He looked up at his shocked companion as the figures danced around them, their screams reaching surreal crescendos, splitting and tearing apart the air.

"There's no time to think. We have to move," he yelled.

III

Saara choked back more tears. Through the figures she could see the cloud was pulsing stronger and had totally swallowed the space where Helen had sat.

Her final scream had died in the tumult of old friends and shapes swarmed thick around them. Was it LSD? Had they been given something, maybe while they'd slept?

Floating and swooping, the figures cavorted, spirits of the air, some just slippery arms and legs high in the sky cackling and descending close around the black mass in unison.

Fidgeting madly in her chair, she watched it all - undulating, mixed with shouting voices and sporadic gunfire - a bullet whizzed just past her head.

Convulsing, she clenched her bound fists, trying to translate her gasps back into normal deep breaths, but the pace of her thoughts wouldn't slow. Her heart was pounding so hard, so fast, she thought it would give out.

In that brief instant she watched awful faces hovering close to the black smoky object - others at the strange rite just hollow mannequins now, shouting and falling in and out of the flashing visions.

New rounds of gunfire accompanied an acrid yellow smoke which had started to surround it all too and she stopped trying to breathe.

Throwing herself back, she crashed to the icy dirt and with desperate kicks, pushed, dragging herself by her heels towards the water. Someone tripped over her as they ran in the smoke blindly, firing their weapons.

Opening her eyes, she could see she was about six feet from the granite staircase leading down to the dock.

Struggling across the threshold, she reached the steps, her left hand braising a sharp point in the rock and she felt a warm trickle smear her wrist as she rolled to the second slab.

Rubbing the twine furiously on the point, she prayed for more time.

The first clasp broke free and she rubbed even faster until her hands were untied.

Stretching her swollen, worn fingers to her ankles she tried untying the knots that fastened her legs. In seconds she was free.

Twisting onto her back, she screamed at the crowded sky. Colours swirled, weaving like dragons as the strange phantoms swooped everywhere.

There were new voices, some barking orders, others crying out. Others still cut short after bursts of gunfire exploding in the boathouse. She wanted to go with them, but could only move slowly, blindly, almost melting down the cold stone steps.

A deep metallic groan erupted and the ground shook as an apparatus they'd erected swayed ominously like a bird cage above the trees.

Drown it out, almost there, she pleaded.

Whatever they are doing, it will fail, she thought, as hand over shaking hand, she clawed desperately down towards the water.

A boat engine - she could hear it now and other movement ahead, a furious running - two, maybe three people?

The mass was now high above the buildings, turning in on itself in a swirling soup with flashes of light stretching from the ground to sky.

The boat - it was pulling away with two guards at the wheel.

Against the boathouse wall, Edmonstone stared blankly, gun in his lap, blood rushing from his forehead.

The mass grew smaller then, to a tiny point before blinking out, but the figures still swooped in a catechism of whispers and screams.

Drifting, she fell down through their layers drained, her last vestige of will a sacrifice to the howling sky.

Chapter 39

AAF Central Film Library
AAFCS No 348-1
Reel No 7
Footage Ground
CCU 12th/7
Date Photo'd 6-11-43
16 mm K and 35 mm
Title: Subject Irina Choloucheskou and Water
*Interesting note about subject's proclivity for areas surrounding water. As seen in
footage, young Irina C appears to enjoy water bodies, establishing contact with them
in elaborate, instinctual and ritualistic 'dances'.
Studies recently concluded at Stanford University claim to show water's conductivity
for mental thought. It is posited by M. Dunsworth et al; that in earth's earliest
stages, gravity was much denser and hence water thicker. A denser gravity would
have resulted in closer packed neurons in human subjects. In instances where a
predominance of densely clumped neurons have been discovered in those
demonstrating 'psychic' talents, studies have shown these subjects to be more
conductive and 'fresher' to their talents in areas surrounding water. Test results are
preliminary, but the team at Stanford believe psi may have been a predominant
feature of Neanderthals due to this early geo-climate situation. Those working with
Irina, (Ikeman, Huston et al) postulate she is an instance of a recurring ancient
gene who instinctively travels to points of fresh water due to this factor. More tests
are to follow next month. Of growing interest is subject's ability to call/interact with
apport phenomenon. Vallee et al.
The End

I

Tracing his fingers through Helen's remains, which were now mixed
with the scorched, ashen earth, Ethan looked out through the
screaming shapes across the shambled lawn towards the lake.

The woman's skull had been seared in half, most of her limbs little
more than dust, parts already blowing away into the forest.

Pulling his windbreaker hood tighter, he clenched his jaw chewing on what he did know. *A group of men. A woman. A...fire? Torture? Why?*

At the forest's edge Ronnie was making for a trail leading up through the trees into the cliffs.

Wiping away at the phantoms, Ethan placed the device on a dry birdbath, clicked the button and watched it all disappear.

II

Remember this, never forget this.

He was standing in the tunnels again and could see old Fred stooped and forlorn, mop in hand, speaking in his head from the doorway.

It can't destroy you, not as long as you do what I say. It's like birds, they fly in and fly out....

But my god, I'm too weak now.

She was using all her strength and it wouldn't be easy.

In the scrub brush, he knew each step could be the one that decided things.

Every few feet there were still tracks, but between where they stopped and took up again there was only blood.

She is hovering, he thought, glancing frantically up through the branches towards the ceiling.

She was there. Close. Waiting.

Some of it had dissipated. That guy must have shut the fucken' thing off.

Follow the drops.

They were heavy, thick blood spurts and there was more at each patch. He could sense it - She was *hurting.*

The wind blew him back and he scraped frozen mist from his cheek. Even here in the forest, the snow was dense and deep. At points it was hard to discern the trail. Time was running out.

Clenching the gun in his good hand, he paused beneath an overhang along the base of the cliff wall and looked out on the lake. Waves high and choppy, clouds black as night, but there was a calm there too. Was it already gone?

No, there it was, subtle and barely sensed, a faint thought heartbeat pumping in slow trenchant flashes.

Above him the path wound up the wall in tight arches and turns, twisting through more thick wooded plateaus until it broke free high in the empty sky.

She was up there, she could feel him as he felt her.

There. There was the pulse. Weak, but like the others when she first came to him. Fuck, he thought, *only a few bullets.*

What the fuck was he doing?

His bad arm drifted against the rock uselessly, striking the edge in tiny futility exclamation points.

His footing slipped, forcing him to lunge on to higher ground, stabbing the revolver's handle into the ice to maintain balance. The thoughts were starting again too. Soon they'd have full reign.

The trail was narrow, just underbrush in places, stone and slushy snow. *Slippery wet stone* and he fumbled as he went, up through the light and shadows bleeding in through the treetops.

'Weeeeee...'

It was the foster parents he'd had after escaping the cells, their voices disappearing into a high shimmering laughter and he watched the shapes begin to form around him.

Further up he climbed through former classmates, loves and turmoil's, each whispering their own deadly songs.

Like a wave, they mixed with his thoughts until he couldn't tell which were his own.

They are hers.

It was Fred again, screaming deep inside as the tears streamed warm like blood.

She was on the outcrop, he could see her now looming broad and solitary - a dark mass floating above the cliff.

Through the wind he could hear her moans, deep urgent cries mixed with the voices of her attacks.

They came in bursts, different in makeup every time. She was growing weaker, but....he didn't trust it.

Something's not right, she's not moving, he thought, maneuvering into the final approach towards the scrub strewn opening.

The sight of it.

Its eyes, cold and magnificent, unflinching even as new motifs, undoubtedly taxing for her, continued to attack his mind.

But she hovered still, staring solid through her relentless psychic throws.

Do it, do it NOW.

Raising the gun, his arm shook wildly and he centered it square on her.

Bringing his eye to the point, he bit away at the pain.

No, what are you DOING!!?

He'd paused because it was all wrong.

Throwing his head back he cried up into the early evening, even as new attacks penetrated deeper.

No, this can't be right. It wants this...it wants this....

A crunch of steps behind him and he turned, still perplexed.

Kerrang!

It was the writer, gun smoking and she….on solid ground.

Screaming, he turned back, watching it raise its eyes once more to the sky, reaching out for one last sniff of existence. And then…..nothing.

Lunging towards the precipice, strong arms catching him, dragging him back, throwing him to the cold, frozen earth.

Enough boy. It's been enough.

Chapter 40

A low hum and white walls.

Heart thumping. Painfully loud. The noise of it.

For hours he'd drifted, seemingly against his own will, as the space around him travelled in and out of focus. The sensation was accompanied by calm reveries which had slowly become heavier, allowing his senses to coalesce back into main experience.

The far wall with the large window covered now by heavy curtains was sharp and he watched as attendants gathered around his bed, unhooking attachments from his head, neck and chest.

After several more minutes of this the doctor returned, calmly to his side, a beige folder tucked in pale blue lab coat arms.

"You did it," he said coolly, patting his right arm with confidence.

It felt great and Ethan rushed inside, relief swooping through him like rivers of joy.

"Don't try to speak - not just yet," said the doctor. "There's lots to talk about later. That was quite a show."

After another hour he was able to move. An attendant said the effects of the drug commonly take a full 24 hours before wearing off, but he was happy to move across the cold white tile to sit by the window watching New York bustle with activity.

It was 10:35am on a cold November day and just knowing as much was the most beautiful thing in the world.

In the streets far below Noctivagus Corp's towering headquarters an early snow had fallen. Christmas shopping had begun and the storefronts sparkled with tiny red and white lights.

"Dr. Collins will be here at 11," an attendant named Judy told him after his second blood pressure check.

Sipping coffee, his thoughts drifted to Saara who was somewhere, perhaps at home, likely waiting for his call. She'd been mad the day he left for the trip. She'd finally confronted the two girls from Morton who had ruined a section of the garden that summer. With shears in hand, she'd jokingly threatened to kill them if they did it again.

At 11 Dr. Jack Collins appeared, ever present smile in place as he pulled up a chair by the window.

MATTHEW SITLER

Behind him, two other men and a woman entered the room, one pushing a large TV screen that was on rollers. Gathering chairs, they each sat silently waiting for the Dr. to speak.

"Jim, would you mind?" asked Collins, motioning towards the large screen.

The man stood up, walked over and turned on a machine, then returned and took his seat.

The screen flickered, slightly hazy at first with some numbers in the top left corner and a date stamp. Then the images grew clearer, settling into high definition.

It was his estate. From his own perspective. He was moving through the halls down towards the library.

In moments, he was with another man - the doctor? - as figures and colors swirled around them in the small circular room.

Remembering this experience startled him, like it was from another life he'd lived, but as if through beveled glass.

The doctor nodded and the man hit pause on a remote.

"This is it," said Collins. "Everything we have worked towards these past 5 years. We're the first to do it and we owe it all to you."

"You have it all?" asked Ethan. "It was like a week's worth. And you - you were there too?"

"There are parts that you 'provided' in the footage which are of full cloth," said Collins. "When you watch it, think of it as 'narrative comment' meaning we couldn't exclude any imagery created by you on the fly. But as for the main experience, it's all there. Now we can move forward and train our agents."

"In this world, where we are now, how will this help you?" asked Ethan."Won't you have to wait until it happens again? Won't you always be playing catch-up?"

"Ahhh," said Collins. "Sharp as always. In a word, yes, but having these images we can see for the first time their movements and actions, how they inter relate. Also, our AI has already identified several trace markers in the footage, identifying where their world starts and ends during the windows. This will allow us to complete tests in those exact times - your estate being one of the locations in this case. It will allow us to identify such locations and to act on them and enter them as they occur in real time in the future."

"Dr. Dan, tell him about how long he was out," the doctor continued, turning towards the woman, a middle aged Asian with long black hair.

"Twelve hours and 15 minutes," she said. "But the footage we captured covers the whole week. The drug was successful in bringing out the memories and maintaining them."

"Nice touch though, making me a ghost," laughed Collins. "I've been accused of worse."

"I'll be able to watch the whole thing - maybe later today?" Ethan asked.

"Yes, but under Dr. Dan's supervision - some of the moments are scary. Your heart rate recalling them was through the roof. Thought we'd have to abort the whole thing at several points. Don't need you going through that a third time."

"But where...where did it all go?" asked the journalist. "I mean in this reality, here and now? What was its purpose - I have so many questions, I mean..."

"All great questions," replied Collins. "But sadly we have no answers yet other than this historically significant first step at capturing it on video. There were two people at the resort who got footage of the woman, which we've since... acquired. Other footage of similar incidents are on You Tube but it's usually blurry, easy to debunk. This, on the other hand establishes a timeline of real time images via direct consciousness, which, until now was an impossibility. The footage we got from the two kids cell phones was just typical amorphous shapes of 'a woman figure'. Typical shit. Publicly, our technology won't be developed to capture these worlds within worlds. Besides, only sensitives like you can really 'see' them anyway - or people in the right place at the exact right times. You're 'seeing' has made history."

"But Saara - surely she saw it all too..." he protested, "She was there. She was the one..."

"No," assured Collins. "You'll see - it was all you - from her perspective. It was you at the island, the resort etc. Likely disassociated into her for you to be able to handle it. We can show you. It was only you and...them. Oh, and Ronnie - there was no childhood, no institution, although your trauma is likely real, probably stemming from a real event when you were young. Darby - your sister? Perhaps it was related to her disappearance? No, we are many, many people unconsciously. Now, as planned, you will need a few weeks of recovery at any location that you prefer. After that, we help you finish your book."

"Wouldn't this have made a lovely one," he answered, already wishing he hadn't signed anything.

"Yes, it would have," answered Collins. "But I'm sure this general one on the first dreams and unconscious experiences ever to be recorded in their entirety in high def digital imaging will be earth shattering enough."

Rising, the doctor gathered his folder and nodded to the others before returning to the gaze of his patient.

"No need to scare the shit out of people any more than necessary," he said sternly. "But we've discussed all this. For us - the first soldiers in this frightening new world - you've basically written the textbook, brought back first-hand images of what had always only been rumor. Now the task is to discover what they truly are, beyond how our primitive visual interface masks them. Remember, it's because of this - our perceptions - that the real often appears unreal."

And with that they left the room, leaving Ethan to sleep.

MATTHEW SITLER

ABOUT THE AUTHOR

Author Matthew Sitler is an award winning Canadian journalist whose talents also include oil portraiture and directing music videos. A former lead reporter with the Bracebridge Examiner and Cottage Country News Director with Moose FM, he's also appeared on CTV's W5 and City TV. This is his first novel. Follow him at @MatthewSitler on Twitter.

MATTHEW SITLER

Stoneaway Publishing Ltd.

Canadian imprint Stoneaway Publishing Ltd. is a publisher of fine novels and curiosities, specializing in tales of the fantastical, psychological thrillers and supernatural mystery.

MATTHEW SITLER

Coming Soon

A world obscured by the normal - the battleground of the mind!

Jekel - the upcoming novel by author Matthew Sitler.

Arriving Fall 2019.

Made in the USA
San Bernardino, CA
08 October 2018